"We have contact . . ."

There was a burst of static, then Sautran's voice came back.

"It's ascending. Eight thousand feet below and rising rapidly. Very big. We're trying to make contact with sonar."

A few moments of silence, then Sautran's voice, still calm, "No reply."

Dane could only imagine what was going through the navy lieutenant's mind as something huge and unknown came up at them from the deepest part of the Atlantic.

Dane said, "Is it mechanical or living?"

"Hard to tell . . . It's moving straight up . . . All I've got is radar and sonar. But there's nothing on the planet that big and alive. Hell, there's nothing been built that big. I . . ." There was a burst of static.

Dane tensed.

The static broke. "Five thousand feet and rising real fast straight at us! Whatever it is, it's not ours . . ." Another burst of static.

Then Sautran's voice wasn't calm anymore. "Get the hell out of here! Everyone to the escape pod, everyone to the—" A harsh burst of static cut him off.

Then, dead silence.

Berkley Books
by Greg Donegan

ATLANTIS
ATLANTIS: BERMUDA TRIANGLE

ATLANTIS:

Bermuda Triangle

Greg Donegan

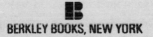

BERKLEY BOOKS, NEW YORK

ATLANTIS: BERMUDA TRIANGLE

A Berkley Book / published by arrangement with
the author

PRINTING HISTORY
Berkley edition / May 2000

The Penguin Putnam Inc. World Wide Web site address is
http://www.penguinputnam.com

ISBN: 0-425-17429-8

BERKLEY®
Berkley Books are published by The Berkley Publishing Group,
a division of Penguin Putnam Inc.,
375 Hudson Street, New York, New York 10014.
BERKLEY and the "B" logo are trademarks
belonging to Penguin Putnam Inc.

PRINTED IN THE UNITED STATES OF AMERICA

10 9 8 7 6 5 4 3 2 1

Prelude

10000 B.C.

Like a thousand-mile-long crimson snake winding its way across the middle of the ocean floor, a line of magma boiled up from the inner earth, met the cool water and, in that fiery intersection, built a ridge higher and higher.

In a contradictory way, the mid-Atlantic Ridge grew because the tectonic plates that intersected beneath it were pulling away from each other. Like blood from a wound in the very planet, molten rock boiled forth the wider the planet-long split between the North/South American Plates and the Eurasian/African plates grew. This process had been going on for millions of years, since Pangaea had split into the separate continents.

In the center of the Atlantic, about twenty degrees north latitude, the split was even more pronounced because there was an intersection of four plates pulling away from each other, both east/west and north/south. This widening process—no more than a couple of inches a year, but multiplied over millennia—had pushed so much magma through that the hardening lava had actually risen above the surface of the water, producing a cross-shaped string of islands, which over more time rose high enough to connect to each other and produce a landmass almost worthy of being a continent itself.

But it was a continent built over a crack in the Earth's crust with no firm attachment to the planet other than the line of magma that still boiled through many miles under the surface. This made it very different from the other six continents that were anchored on top of one hundred kilometers of cold rock that made up the tectonic plates.

Between the extremely fertile volcanic soil that covered the landmass and the bountiful ocean that surrounded it, the pieces were in place for species that could reap the food supplied by both sources and develop quickly. On that central Atlantic landmass, the first civilization of mankind arose. From packs of hunter-gatherers and fishers to villages to cities, generations of humans slowly gained dominance over their land.

But after civilization was well established, a strange darkness appeared in the ocean to the west, devouring any ships that sailed into it.

Other gates opened around the planet, bringing their own patches of darkness, but the main thrust was through the gate in the western Atlantic. It soon became clear that there was something in the darkness, a Shadow, that sought to expand and conquer.

A war was fought that the ancient ones of mankind didn't understand against an enemy no one survived seeing. The enemy came in the darkness, through the sky, from the water and under the earth.

Others came out of the gates to help the ancient ones defend themselves against the Shadow. These others called themselves the Ones Before. They gave the people weapons to fight the Shadow with.

The ancient ones of mankind fought a war that spread around the globe until the very existence of life was threatened. And in the climactic battle, the ancient ones and the

Ones Before stopped the Shadow, but the price was high.

The continent in the middle of the Atlantic was destroyed in a cataclysm of fire and earthquakes. The resulting tsunamis from that destruction touched every shore on the planet with such devastation that the legend of the Great Flood was written in both the Tibetan Book of the Dead and the Old Testament of the Jewish people on the other side of the world.

The survivors of the ancient ones, in a handful of ships, scattered to the four winds and planted the seeds for future civilizations to arise thousands of years later.

The Shadow that came out of the gates was stopped.

For the time being.

One

THE PRESENT

The missile broke surface undetected in the middle of the Bermuda Triangle gate. It was a Trident II, a three-stage, solid-propellant, inertially guided ballistic missile with a range of more than 4,600 statute miles developed by Lockheed Martin for the United States Navy. The Trident II was a more sophisticated version of the Trident I, upgraded mostly in terms of having a significantly greater payload capability. Forty-four feet long at launch, it was 6.9 feet in diameter, weighed 130,000 pounds at launch, and cost the taxpayer over forty million dollars each; which didn't add in the price of the nuclear warheads in the nose cone.

As it punched into the air, an aerospike telescoped out of the front of the missile, reducing frontal drag by 50 percent. The first stage, made of a very strong, very light material called graphite epoxy, released and fell back into the ocean.

The navigational system of the missile was designed to link with global positioning satellites to confirm location and direction, but this Trident didn't do that. Its course had been determined before launch.

Six thousand feet up, the Trident came out of the gate into clear air, just as the second stage fell and the third-stage motor kicked in. It was already traveling in excess of 20,000 feet per second.

The third stage burned for forty seconds and then released. The missile still had to reach its apogee and start coming down, but it was already 400 miles from its launch point.

The first detection of the missile was made by a satellite linked to the U.S. Space Command deep under Cheyenne Mountain outside of Colorado Springs, but it was already far too late as the information was processed and forwarded to the War Room at the Pentagon.

Just after kicking over and beginning its descent, the nose cone of the Trident exploded open, and the eight nuclear warheads encased inside separated in their own MK5 reentry vehicles, in a linear spread pattern.

The warheads splashed down into the Atlantic along a 300-mile-long line.

With no detonation.

The warheads drifted down into the relatively shallow water of the Mid-Atlantic Ridge until they touched bottom.

Then they exploded.

"The last time we met, you were pointing a gun at me," Foreman said.

Dane stared at the old man on the other side of the conference table, noting the changes the years had etched. Foreman had aged well except that his once-thick snow-white hair was thinner than Dane remembered. Foreman's face was narrow, hatchetlike, with clear eyes. His body was slim, the suit he wore well-tailored. If anything, the old man looked too thin, almost sickly.

"You were lying to me then," Dane said, reaching down to his left and rubbing Chelsea's ear. The golden retriever cocked her head and pressed against his hand.

Eric Dane was of average height and had thick black hair with a sprinkling of gray along the sides. He wore glasses with thin metal frames, his face angular and attractive. Just over fifty years old, he was as lean as he had been in his twenties when he had last met Foreman at a CIA forward staging base in Laos prior to going on a cross-border mission where Dane's entire team had disappeared.

"Withholding information," Foreman clarified. "Lying is too strong a word to be used for the situation."

They were seated in a conference room inside CIA headquarters at Langley, Virginia. Sin Fen sat next to Foreman. She was an exotic-looking Eurasian woman, whose past Dane knew little about except that somehow she had gotten hooked up with the CIA man and his obsession with the gates. That she had some sort of strange mental abilities, Dane was certain, just as he knew he had some. But the extent of hers was as unclear to him as his own.

Foreman would be leaving shortly for a high-level meeting in Washington with the president and the National Security Council to discuss what had just occurred in the Angkor gate in Cambodia and the other gates. The invasion of Earth from the "other side" through the gates at Angkor Kol Ker, the Bermuda Triangle, the Devil's Sea off the coast of Japan, and other locations around the world had been stopped by Dane with the destruction of the main propagating beam of radiation and electromagnetic interference in Cambodia. Beyond that, they knew little more than they had before the bizarre invasion started. Who the invaders were, other than the term *the Shadow*, why they were invading, where they were coming from; what they wanted; there were many questions that had not been answered yet.

The shocking reappearance of the submarine *Scorpion*— listed as lost in U.S. Navy logs in 1968—was being kept under wraps, but Dane knew it could not last much longer. They could not explain the fact that not a man in the crew seemed to have aged a day in over thirty years. Nor could the crew explain it. As far as they were concerned, just minutes had passed between the time they last radioed Foreman in 1968 that the reactor was going off-line as they entered the Bermuda Triangle to the moment Dane appeared on the ship two days ago, transported somehow from the middle of the Angkor gate to the submarine.

"Why do you still need me?" Dane asked.

"Because that mission you began thirty years ago never ended," Foreman said. "Because you stopped the invasion through the Angkor gate."

"For the moment," Sin Fen added.

Dane glanced at Sin Fen. Her mind was a black wall to him. Then back at Foreman. There, he could tell more, but not as much as he would have liked. He knew the old man was telling the truth, but he also sensed there was so much Foreman didn't know or was holding back. Based on his experiences with the CIA operative, Dane knew it was likely a combination of both.

"I put everything in my report," Dane said.

"Also," Foreman continued as if he had not heard, "we lost the *Wyoming* inside the Bermuda Triangle gate."

"Other submarines have been lost in the gates," Dane said.

Foreman steepled his fingers. "Not one with twenty-four Trident II ICBMs on board. With each missile carrying eight MK5 nuclear warheads rated at a hundred kilotons each. That's 192 nuclear warheads. And our friends on the other side, whoever or whatever they are—the Shadow, as your man Flaherty called them—seem to have a penchant for radioactive things. We defeated *their* weapons in this first assault, but we might not do so well against *our* weapons that they've captured."

"Great," Dane said. "We get the *Scorpion* back, the Shadow gets the *Wyoming* and its nukes."

"We have you," Foreman said. "You have some sort of

power, some sort of attachment to these gates. You made
it in the Angkor gate and out again. Two times. That's once
more than anyone else has ever done."

Dane simply stared at Foreman without comment. He
felt as if he were in a whirlpool, being sucked against his
will into a dark and dangerous center. And to be honest,
he wasn't sure how hard he should swim against the power
drawing him in or if he was even capable of resisting.

Foreman slid several photos across the table. "The top
one is the Angkor Kol Ker gate. Then the Bermuda Triangle and other gates around the world."

Dane looked at the first photo. It was a satellite image
of Cambodia. There was a solid black triangle in the center,
about six miles long on each side. It was located in the
north-central part of the country, in deep, nearly impene-
trable jungle.

"Each gate is now shaped the same and stable at that
size," Foreman said. "That solid black is something new,
and we don't know what it means. It's never been reported
as long as we have recorded history. No form of imaging
can penetrate it. Ground surveillance from those visually
watching the gates say the fog has coalesced into solid
black. Sensors sent on remotely piloted vehicles, whether
going via ground, air or sea, simply disappear into the black
and cease transmitting. And they never come back out, even
if they are programmed to return.

"The Russians—and this is classified, as is everything
else we discuss—sent a team into one of the gates on their
territory near Tunguska two days ago. The team hasn't
come back and is presumed dead. The Japanese are still
missing one of their destroyers that went into the Devil's
Sea gate.

"I'm afraid that, although we stopped the propagation,
it went on long enough to allow this thing to gain a solid
foothold on our planet at each of the gate sites. That's
something that never happened before."

"That we know of," Sin Fen added.

"It means they're waiting," Dane said.

"They?" Foreman asked.

"The Shadow."

"For what?" Foreman asked.

"To attack again," Dane said. "They've got their beach-head. Maybe that's all this last series of events was about." He turned to Sin Fen. "Do you agree?"

She nodded. "That is the sense I have."

Foreman tapped a finger on the top of the conference table. "I've been thinking about that. The 'again' part," Foreman clarified. "As Sin Fen noted, there is much about the past we don't know. That abandoned city you found in the center of the Angkor gate—Angkor Kol Ker—it must have been attacked a long time ago. And we have a long history of ships and planes disappearing into the Bermuda Triangle and Devil's Sea. No one knows how long these gates have been active, but a lot of evidence points back to at least as long as ten thousand years ago, when Atlantis was destroyed."

"You really believe that?" Dane asked.

"About Atlantis? Don't you now?" Foreman threw back. "After all you've seen and heard?"

Dane reluctantly nodded. He remembered Flaherty telling him the same thing—that the Shadow and the Ones Before were waging a war and it spilled over onto Earth every so often. That during one of those battles, Atlantis had been wiped off the face of the earth. There were also the markings on the side of the watchtower that Beasley, the Cambodian expert who had traveled with Dane into the gate, had deciphered. They indicated that the people who founded Angkor Kol Ker had traveled from somewhere in the Atlantic Ocean in order to escape the Shadow.

"It looks likely," Dane agreed.

"The key," Foreman continued, "is that we have to assume that this has happened before: the gates opening, the

Shadow trying to come into our world and take it over. And it's always been defeated. Even though Atlantis was destroyed so utterly it is just a legend, the rest of the planet survived. And it appears that there were survivors from Atlantis—the people who started civilization at Angkor Kol Ker, in Egypt, China, Central America, and other places."

"So?" Dane said.

"We stopped it this time, but we didn't defeat it. What we stopped was just the first assault, and another one is coming."

"You sound as if a new attack has already started," Dane said.

Foreman nodded. "It has." He pulled more imagery out of the top secret file. It showed a Mercator projection map of the entire world. Dane studied it. There were lines drawn through all the oceans.

"What am I looking at?" Dane asked.

"Lines of activity propagated by the gates in bursts," Foreman said.

"Radioactive?" Dane asked.

"No," Foreman said. "Low-level electromagnetic spectrum activity, barely enough to register. We think the Shadow is doing its own kind of imagery."

"Looking for what?"

Sin Fen leaned across the table and placed a long, thin finger on the map, tracing the lines. "The Mid-Atlantic Ridge." The finger jumped North America. "The Pacific Rim along our West Coast all the way around to the coast of Japan and down to Australia. The Mediterranean, bifurcating through both the Red Sea and Persian Gulf. The Antarctic Plate all the way around the bottom of the world. The Himalayas where the Eurasian Plate meets the Indian Plate. Those are just the major lines. As you can see, there are several smaller ones, here in the Caribbean, the Philippines. The Shadow is checking all the lines where tectonic plates meet," Sin Fen concluded.

"And this, I assume, is a bad thing," Dane said.

"We have to believe it is." Foreman ignored the sarcasm. "We have no idea what's going on inside those gates or what is on the other side or what they are up to.

"We need to look to our history and try to discover how our predecessors dealt with this," Foreman continued. "We believe people in the past faced the same problem we're facing, and they succeeded in stopping the Shadow."

"The people at Angkor Kol Ker didn't succeed very well," Dane noted. "Nor did the people of Atlantis."

"But the Earth wasn't overrun or destroyed," Foreman noted. "The Shadow tried to make its big push out of Kol Ker this time, but maybe the last time this happened, they tried their main effort somewhere else, and it was defeated. Or there is a pattern to their assault, and we've only met the first wave."

"But do you have any idea where this happened? Or who fought this battle?" Dane asked.

"The *Scorpion* didn't come back by accident," Foreman said. "There's something or someone on the other side of the gate that's trying to help us. The Ones Before. The same force that sent your teammate Flaherty to you at Angkor Kol Ker. It sent the *Scorpion* back to us with a message."

This was news to Dane. "What message?"

Foreman pulled a photo out of the file folder and pushed it across to Dane. It was an image of the sail of the *Scorpion*, the tower that held the periscopes and small bridge used when the sub was on the surface. Foreman slid a second picture, a close-up of the side of the sail. Something was etched in the metal, strange lines that Dane didn't recognize. He had gotten off the submarine in the dark, cross-loading directly to a Navy helicopter to be flown here. The etching must have been discovered the following morning. Below those lines was a drawing that Dane looked at for a while before he recognized that it was a map.

"What is this?"

"On top, runic writing," Foreman said. "It took us a little while before Sin Fen saw it and was able to recognize the language and decode it. On the bottom, a map. It also took some time to determine exactly what the map was of, because the scale and details are not exactly correct—or what I should say is—correct today."

Dane found the writing interesting and almost familiar. In between two horizontal lines, were a series of vertical and curved slashes. "What language is this?" he asked Sin Fen.

"Norse," she answered. "The language of the Vikings."

After all the strange things he had experienced in the past month, Dane didn't even ask how Viking runes ended up scratched into the metal on the side of a nuclear submarine that had disappeared for over thirty years. "What does it say?"

"This is the literal translation." Sin Fen handed Dane a piece of paper:

Here find the shield
to defeat the Valkyries
and those who follow the dark ones
I have done my duty
It stops the forge of Vulcan
Revenge me

"Vulcan's forge?" Dane asked.

"The power of the gods breaking through the crust of the Earth," Sin Fen said. "The Shadow might have used the instability of the Earth's surface along the juncture of the tectonic plates to destroy Atlantis."

"Who wrote this? Who has done his duty?" Dane asked.

"Your guess is as good as mine, but the important point is the Shield stops the power of the Shadow."

"There's not much information about this Shield," Dane noted.

"The Valkyries," Sin Fen said, "are part of Norse mythology. They were the handmaidens of the gods and were reported to devour the flesh of the dead on the battlefield."

"Monsters of legend," Dane said out loud.

Sin Fen nodded. "You ran into the seven-headed Naga of Khmer legend in the Angkor gate. And other strange creatures. It appears there is more truth to the Valkyries than simply legend."

Dane looked at the sheet. " 'And those who follow the dark ones'? Does that mean those who follow the Valkyries? Or humans who worship them?"

"That's not clear," Sin Fen said. "There are only sixteen characters in the runic alphabet. And it was not used very extensively, so there isn't a great body of work to draw upon to even be sure the translation is correct."

"Great," Dane said.

"According to legend," Sin Fen added, "the runic alphabet was given to the Vikings by the god Odin. The word *run* means mystery, so even the Vikings might not have been too sure about their own written language. Modern scholars aren't certain where or how it originated, but they have noted some similarities between Viking runes and the runes used by other ancient cultures."

Dane put two and two together. "So the runic language might have come from Atlantis?"

"That is possible," Sin Fen said. "Of course, by the time of the Vikings, the original writing was probably greatly corrupted and simplified. The height of the Viking expansion was about eleven thousand years after the great dispersion from Atlantis. That's a long time for a language to survive, even in a bastardized form."

"Where is the 'here' the message refers to?" Dane asked.

"That's the other strange thing," Foreman said. "Someone went to a great deal of trouble to etch that map into the metal. God knows how long it took, but it appears to have been done by hand with an edged tool."

"Where was the crew of the *Scorpion* while this was being done to their ship?" Dane asked.

Foreman shrugged. "Where was the crew of the *Scorpion* for the past thirty-one years? To them, no time passed between going into the Bermuda Triangle and coming out."

"Maybe they weren't on board the ship," Dane wondered out loud.

"I don't think we'll ever know exactly what happened," Foreman said. "What is important right now is that they came back with this map."

"Are you sure that's all they came back with?" Dane asked.

"The ship's in quarantine at the Groton sub pens, being gone through with a fine-tooth comb to try to figure out what happened to it," Foreman said. He tapped the photo, bringing attention back to the map. "It isn't exact, at least according to what we know now, but it's rather remarkable if it's the work of someone who only could write in runes, which means the message is probably over a thousand years old. But the ship is only thirty."

To Dane's eyes there was something wrong about the map, though. The proportions were off, and he couldn't get oriented on the continents.

Foreman reached into the file and pulled out another sheet of paper. "This is called Piri Reis's map. It dates back to the sixteenth century. Compare the two."

Dane slid the paper next to the photograph. "They're almost identical."

"Yes," Sin Fen said. "Which raises another problem. The Piri Reis map was drawn at Constantinople in 1513 by an admiral in the Turkish Navy. It emphasizes the west coast of Africa, the east coast of South America ending in the Caribbean, and the northern coast of Antarctica. Which is intriguing, given that Antarctica wasn't discovered until 1818. Not only that, but the Piri Reis map and the map drawn on the *Scorpion* both show an Antarctica *without* ice covering it. The last time that Antarctica wasn't covered by ice, as near as scientists can tell, is, at the latest, 4000 B.C., and most likely much earlier than that."

Dane leaned back in his seat and looked down at Chelsea. She pushed her head against his thigh, her golden eyes regarding him calmly in return. He envied the dog her ignorance and the innocence that stemmed from that. "How can that be?" he asked Sin Fen.

"Piri Reis, in his notes, readily admits that he didn't survey the map himself but rather copied it from other maps. It appears that the ancient seafarers had a much more extensive knowledge of the world than we have ever suspected. At least some of them did. Much of that knowledge was lost when the great library at Alexandria was burned and sacked.

"What is also strange," Sin Fen continued, "is that the map shows the use of longitudinal coordinates, something that wasn't invented—at least we thought wasn't invented—until the eighteenth century."

"Why Antarctica?" Dane asked. "Why would a map be centered around that continent?"

"Perhaps because that is where Atlantis was," Sin Fen said. Before Dane could say another word, she continued. "Albert Einstein had a theory about this. I know, you've never heard of it, but trust me, it is true. He believed that Antarctica was ice-free about twelve thousand years ago because it wasn't centered on the south pole as it is now. Rather, it was farther north in the center of the Atlantic."

"You're joking, right?" Dane asked. "How the hell did it move to its present location?"

"I'm not saying this is fact," Sin Fen said. "But who am I to argue with a theory of Albert Einstein's? He called the process by which it moved 'earth-crust-displacement,' and scientists we have consulted say there is something to his concept. It also ties in with the theory of plate tectonics—which is accepted by scientists as fact today—and that ties together with the Shadow scanning the lines of tectonic faults.

"If Atlantis was originally located in the Atlantic, it was over the juncture of four major tectonic plates. That meant it wasn't solidly anchored to the planet beneath it. It would have taken a tremendous amount of energy, but it is possible that the land was ripped free, maybe even completely submerged, before drifting—and drifting is a rather weak word for what happened as we're not talking about drifting on water, but rather on the magma of the planet below—to its current location at the south pole.

"Antarctica, the land itself, is now actually below sea level. Most of it is covered by a layer of ice several miles thick. It's only recently that we've mapped what the land underneath the ice looked like and it looks a hell of a lot like what's shown on this map."

"Is this Shield in Antarctica?" Dane asked.

"No," Foreman said. "Note the rune marking on the map right here. It is the Viking symbol for weapon." He reached across the table and tapped the photograph. "We correlated that with the Piri Reis Map and with current maps. That spot is right on the edge of the Bermuda Triangle gate. Just north of the western tip of Puerto Rico."

"Then what is the connection between that site and Atlantis?" Dane asked.

"We don't know that yet," Foreman said. "Although it's possible this site was *between* Atlantis and the Bermuda Triangle gate, which would be the logical location for a Shield."

"This site is in the water?" Dane asked.

"It appears so," Sin Fen said.

"And?" Dane said.

"We think that spot is very important," Foreman said. "It is along the line where the Caribbean tectonic plate intersects with the North American plate and close to the Mid-Atlantic Ridge, which is formed by the North

American Plate meeting the Eurasian and African Plates."

"Have you checked it out?" Dane asked.

"We've done satellite imagery of it," Foreman said. "Just ocean on the surface. Nothing there. What we're looking for must be below the surface. I'm having some other special checks run that might tell us something more, but there's nothing like having someone put a set of eyeballs on it."

"I ran a reconnaissance for you once before," Dane said, "and everyone who went with me died or disappeared."

"We have a better idea what we're dealing with now," Foreman said.

"Do we?" Dane retorted.

There was the buzz of a cellular phone. Foreman pulled one out of his pocket and flipped it open. "Foreman."

Dane studied the map, wondering who would have taken the time and the energy to scratch it into the metal on the submarine.

After a terse acknowledgment, Foreman flipped the phone shut. "I have to go to the War Room immediately." Foreman stood, abruptly ending the meeting. "Sin Fen will accompany you."

Chelsea had gotten to her feet, her head pressed against Dane's side. Dane ran a hand through her golden hair. "Accompany me where?"

Foreman was gathering up his files, stuffing them in the briefcase. "To the indicated spot, of course. To find this Shield."

"But—" Dane began, but Foreman cut him off with a wave of the cell phone.

"That was the chairman of the Joint Chiefs of Staff, General Tilson. A Trident II missile, obviously from the *Wyoming*, was fired out of the Bermuda Triangle gate twenty minutes ago. The warheads impacted in the center of the Atlantic Ocean along the North Atlantic Ridge, where the tectonic plates meet. All eight warheads detonated. We're still assessing what effect they had."

"Is the Shadow attacking?" Dane asked.

Foreman shook his head. "We think it was a test." He headed for the door. "Remember, they have twenty-three more Tridents with one hundred and eighty-four nukes left to carry out an all-out assault."

Two

The World Approaching the First Millennium

998 A.D.

A city that had taken an entire race of people five hundred years to build had been overrun in one night two centuries ago. Located in the northern highlands of Cambodia, Angkor Kol Ker had been the center of a magnificent kingdom extending south to abut the Srivijayan Empire of Sumatra and the Shailandra Empire of Java. To the northeast, the Tang Dynasty of China had ruled, while to the west, in the Middle East, the tide of Islam had begun to rise.

The capital city of Angkor Kol Ker, the heart of the Khmer Empire, had held architecture the likes of which Europe would not see for half a century. In the center of the city, a massive temple had been built stone by stone, with a central tower over five hundred feet high. Around it, homes and businesses were constructed, all secure inside a fourteen-foot-high wall surrounding the entire complex, over eight miles long by four miles wide. Outside of the wall, a moat over four hundred yards wide added protection. But those noble efforts of man had not been enough to stop the enemy that came.

A Shadow had invaded through a strange gate in the

very fabric of the planet. A dense fog covered the city and the surrounding terrain. No man had set foot inside that fog in almost two hundred years, and those who had remained to defend the city against the Shadow had never been seen again by those who fled.

The survivors of the Khmer kingdom had reestablished to the south at Angkor Thom and tried to regain some of their former glory by building the great temple of Angkor Wat, but the reestablished kingdom was a remnant of its former self, already on the road to decay.

The ancestors of the Khmer people had once traveled halfway around the globe to avoid the Shadow, and for many generations they had seemingly foiled the force that had destroyed their original homeland, until the new gate opened upon their city. Their home before Cambodia had been the legacy of the ancient ones; the ones who knew the secrets of the Shadow and the Ones Before. Secrets that their descendants had forgotten or remembered only as myth.

On the edge of the Shadow's fog, a lone woman named Tam Nok now stood in an abandoned guardhouse made of large blocks of finely fit stone. The guardhouse was high on a ridgeline overlooking the fog that delineated the edges of the gate. But the fog, normally a swirling grayish yellow mixture, was now very dark, almost black, and more solid than anyone remembered since fleeing Angkor Kol Ker.

Tam Nok stared out over the jungle at the unearthly fog, toward where she knew the city lay. She was a priestess from Angkor Wat, taught all the knowledge that remained in the Khmer's collective memory of the Ones Before and the Shadow. Sadly, and dangerously, that knowledge was incomplete. She had traveled here on foot to see the Shadow for herself, and because the first stop of her journey lay inside the darkness in front of her.

Tam Nok was tall and slender, wrapped in a finely woven black cloak with red trim. Her eyes were slanted, her

skin dark brown. Her black hair was cut short for function-
ality rather than style. At her waist a dagger hung in a
sheath, and on her back was a leather pack, containing what
she would need to begin her journey. A bamboo case stuck
out the top of the pack, both ends corked with a piece of
wood. Inside lay precious documents, handed down
through generations of priestesses.

Looking at the darkness, the priestess accepted one
thing: The end was coming. The end for every living thing
on the planet. The writings of the ancient ones indicated
that the signs they were now seeing indicated they were
approaching the point where danger would come again. The
presence of the Shadow, darker than ever before over Angkor Kol Ker, backed up those writings. The earth was rumbling every so often, giving warning that the gods
underneath were disturbed. There had been a great explosion in the ocean to the southeast. Ash had fallen for days
afterward, and a dark cloud darkened the day. The sky was
still red as the sun set every night.

The writings handed down about the Ones Before said
there was a way to survive, to fight back against the
Shadow. But again, unfortunately, the writings were not
complete. There was a Shield that the ancient ones had been
given by the Ones Before. A Shield that worked against
the creatures and beings in a gate, that could even shut a
gate. But the Shield had been lost in a great battle, lost
where the Khmer's ancestors had come from. The ancient
ones had won the battle but in the process lost their home
and much of their knowledge and most especially, the
Shield they had used to win the battle. Tam Nok would
have to travel back the way they had come to search for it.
The path was long and hard, and she was uncertain of exactly where it was she was to go. She only knew where
she was to start from.

On each corner of the guardhouse was a statue of a
Naga, the seven-headed snake from the creation myth of

the Khmer. The Khmer who did not honor the Ones Before.
Who had lost the truth in the telling of the story over the
years dissolving into legend. Even among the priests and
priestesses, Tam Nok was aware that much of what she had
been told had to be viewed warily to separate fact from
fiction.

The inside walls of the guardhouse were covered with
carvings and drawings. Some were the scratchings of bored
soldiers, but other markings obviously were the work of
skilled artisans. They told parts of the history of the Khmer,
stretching back to the ancient ones and the Ones Before.

Tam Nok had been here four days studying the writing
and drawings. According to the words, the Khmer had established Angkor Kol Ker, the city now abandoned in the
fog, over 5,000 years ago. The ancient ones had come from
an island located in the sea beyond the sea. That had caused
Tam Nok to sit and think. There was a great sea to the east,
one that no sailor in known memory had ever crossed. To
think there was a sea beyond the land that no one had ever
gone to caused her some concern, because she knew that
her destination lay far away.

According to the writing, her ancestors left their island
to escape the Shadow. They traveled far before settling
here. For many generations, they thought they had succeeded in their evasion, and because of that feeling, much
ancient wisdom had slowly been forgotten. And then the
Shadow had come here.

Tam Nok knew about the failure here. The story of the
coming of the Shadow over Angkor Kol Ker was too recent
to have faded into legend. She was more interested in the
island in the sea beyond the sea. It was described in some
detail: rings of land and water, surrounding a central hill
on which was a mighty temple and palace. Even at Angkor
Wat where she had come from, the use of rings of water
to protect those within was preserved.

But the water had not saved the ancient ones. The island

was attacked by fire from the dark Shadow and decimated so completely it disappeared beneath the waves of the sea, and the people scattered.

Tam Nok knew her people had come from the ocean, from the direction of the rising sun. But the ability to cross that sea had been lost or perhaps deliberately forgotten as the generations passed. She could not go east. The writings had told her there were others who had escaped and gone in different directions. And that she would have to find some of those others in order to uncover what she was looking for.

As the sun rose in the east, she shouldered her pack. She climbed down the stone stairs on the interior of the watchtower. Tam Nok turned toward the Shadow and began walking into the valley.

If she survived this first part, she still had a very long journey before her.

Three

THE PRESENT

Dane peered out the window of the helicopter, and all he
saw was open ocean. He held Chelsea's leash tightly and
scratched behind her ears to calm her down. She had been
on helicopters before when they worked search and rescue,
and she had never liked the ride. The high pitch of the
turbine engines caused her great discomfort. She strained
against the leash, her tail thumping against Dane's leg.

Keeping tight hold, Dane slid down the red web seating,
closer to Sin Fen, the only other occupant of the cargo bay
of the two-bladed Chinook helicopter other than the crew
chief. The middle of the cargo bay was full of two pallets
of tied-down gear.

Before getting on the chopper, they had taken a Navy
transport from Andrews Air Force Base to Roosevelt Roads
Naval Air Station on the eastern tip of Puerto Rico.
Throughout the trip, Sin Fen had maintained her silence,
working on her laptop computer. Dane had spent the early
part of the flight napping, catching up on lost sleep, and
then reading, going through several books he had purchased
at the post exchange before they took off, when he had

been able to shake Sin Fen for a few minutes.

Chelsea squeezed between Dane and Sin Fen and promptly collapsed, her belly on the toes of his shoes, her chin resting on her front paws, somehow feeling comforted lying in that spot.

"What's the fallout from the nukes in the Atlantic?" Dane asked.

"I received the latest report from Foreman over the modem before we took off," Sin Fen said. "The bombs all detonated on the ocean floor, at depths between one thousand and three thousand feet. The Navy has sent ships and subs to do a survey, but we have to assume there was damage to the line between the plate tectonics. I think this was a test—like the United States used to test nukes in Nevada and the Russians in Novlaya Svetlanya. Checking yield and effect. The fact that the Shadow tested along the junction of tectonic plates shows their electromagnetic surveillance of those joints definitely has a purpose.

"There was, of course, quite a bit of radiation released. Given the prevailing currents that run northeast, some of that is going to brush along the coasts of Iceland, Ireland, and England. What the effect will be is hard to say at this point, although there's no doubt fisheries throughout that area will be affected negatively."

"Affected negatively?" Dane didn't bother to wait for an amplification. "In other words, we don't know much more than we did before eight nuclear bombs were exploded. Mind telling me exactly where we're going?" he asked.

Sin Fen still had her laptop open, and her almond eyes shifted their gaze from it to him for a second before returning. She typed in a command and then showed him the screen. A ship was displayed. "That's our next stop."

"What is it?" Dane had never seen anything like it.

A massive ship was in the middle of an empty sea, a large wake indicating it was moving. A huge derrick took up the entire center of the ship, towering over it. Two helicopters sat on a landing pad on the stern, dwarfed by the derrick, giving an idea of how large the ship was. There was room on the pad for the Chinook they were on to land with some to spare.

"It's the *Glomar Explorer*," Sin Fen said.

"A Navy ship?"

Sin Fen shook her head. "It was built in 1973 by Howard Hughes for the CIA."

Dane saw the long arm of Foreman involved in that somehow. "To do what? Oil exploration?"

"The cover story that Hughes gave the press was that the *Glomar Explorer* was built to mine minerals off the ocean floor. That's even what he told the people building it.

"It was constructed at York, Pennsylvania, and is over two hundred meters long. Hughes spent about four hundred million of the government's dollars on the thing without the taxpayers knowing about it. And that was in 1973 dollars. A recent refit just cost over six hundred million. To get it to the Pacific, they had to sail it around South America because it wouldn't fit through the Panama Canal.

"While the ship was built on the East Coast, a companion craft was built in California called the HMB-1, Hughes Marine Barge. It's about a hundred meters long and built like an underwater aircraft hangar.

"The barge and the ship work together when needed. While the *Glomar* is the surface platform, the HMB-1 is submergible. It's got a giant claw, remote TV camera, and lights. It can dock with the *Glomar* in the well of the ship underneath the derrick.

"The *Glomar* and HMB-1 were actually built to be part of a secret CIA mission called Project Jennifer. The purpose of that project was to recover a Russian submarine that had gone down in the Pacific with all hands. They went after the sub in 1974."

"Did they recover it?"

"Part of it," Sin Fen acknowledged. "The claw grabbed hold, and they started bringing it up, but the submarine broke. They only got about a forty foot section. Enough to recover some cipher codes and manuals, along with two nuclear torpedoes."

"Why would they spend that much money to get a Russian submarine?" Dane asked. "Our technology was ahead of theirs. There isn't much we could have learned."

"Recovering the cipher codes for the Soviet fleet was the priority," Sin Fen said.

"How long between the Russian sub going down and the *Glomar* pulling up that piece?"

"A year and a half."

"Then recovering the cipher codes is bullshit," Dane said. "The Russians would have changed their ciphers the day after they lost the sub."

"But the CIA still had tapes of all the classified traffic that had been transmitted using those codes while the sub was still sailing," Sin Fen said. "Even going back and breaking year-and-a-half-old transmissions can still reveal a lot of intelligence about fleet operations."

Dane glanced out the porthole at the open ocean. "The cover story was undersea mining," he said. "And the story you're telling me is that the CIA wanted to recover a Russian submarine for the cipher codes. Now, tell me the real reason the *Glomar Explorer* was built."

Sin Fen closed the laptop. "You are very distrusting, aren't you?"

"I'd be stupid not to be," Dane said.

Sin Fen nodded. "I apologize. Old habits die hard. I am so used to lying and telling cover stories. Working with Foreman all these years, not knowing what the gates were, we had to be very careful. We also had to manipulate people to do what we wanted without ever letting them have a hint what the real reason for their actions was, or it was most likely they would not do what we wanted."

"Like sending my recon team after a downed spy plane in Cambodia," Dane said.

"Yes, but there was a downed spy plane," Sin Fen said.

"Downed because it was flying a mission for Foreman, concerning the Angkor gate, not supporting our war effort in Vietnam," Dane noted. "And he wanted more than just the black box from the plane recovered. He wanted my team and his man, Castle, to check out the gate on the ground."

"Please believe that our motives are good, although our means might be deceptive."

"Right," Dane said in such a tone that Chelsea lifted her head and regarded him with her golden eyes for a few seconds, before pushing her head against his knee, earning a scratch behind the ears. "Back to the *Glomar*," Dane said.

"The real reason for the *Glomar Explorer* was to recover the Russian submarine."

"But why did Foreman want the *Glomar* to do that?" Dane asked. "He was never interested in old cipher codes or Russian subs, was he?"

"He was interested in submarines when they went through a gate," Sin Fen said. "This particular vessel disappeared for a week in 1973 during passage through the area known as the Devil's Sea off the coast of Japan. The Russian Navy got a bit excited about losing a nuclear-armed sub, as you can expect.

"Then the submarine suddenly appeared a week later, exactly where it had disappeared, as if nothing had happened. Except it wasn't answering any radio calls. Then, less than an hour after reappearing, it goes down in very deep water. Too deep for the Russians to rescue anyone or even recover anything from the wreck with the technology that was available at that time."

"But not too deep for Foreman to try," Dane said.

"Correct. He was able to get the CIA to fund the *Glomar* on the possibility of getting those cipher codes and classified manuals. Give the Navy an idea what the Russian nuclear submarine capability was. Plus he got Howard Hughes to help. Mr. Foreman has always been very good at getting wealthy individuals in the private sector to aid his cause."

"Did Foreman learn anything from the wreckage he did recover?"

"What Foreman was really interested in was the nuclear power plant and the nuclear weapons. The *Glomar* wasn't able to get the power plant, and he only recovered two of the fourteen nuclear weapons it had on board."

Dane waited.

"Some of the nuclear weapon berths were empty," Sin Fen finally allowed.

"Meaning the weapons were removed from the sub."

"Correct. And the two weapons recovered had been worked on."

"Worked on?"

"Casings taken off. Parts removed."

"That helps explain how the nukes from the *Wyoming* were aimed, fired, and detonated," Dane noted.

"Indeed it does," Sin Fen said.

"What else?"

"You are persistent, aren't you?" Sin Fen didn't wait for an answer. "They recovered some bodies off the Russian submarine."

"That's to be expected."

"Not these bodies," Sin Fen said. "There was a total of eight in the section recovered. Four were Russian crew members. The other four—well, three were Japanese and one was, as near as could be determined, an American."

"What were they doing on a Russian submarine?" Dane asked.

"That's a good question. A couple of years ago, Foreman made some discreet inquiries with his counterpart in Russia—a man named Kolkov—who was investigating what he called vile vortices—their name for the gates.

"Kolkov confirmed that when this Russian submarine sailed, there were no foreigners on board. Foreman is of the opinion that these strangers came on board while the sub was in the Devil's Sea gate."

"Sort of the way I was transported on board the *Scorpion*?"

"Perhaps. Or perhaps these people were inside the gate to begin with. Even more interesting is that we were never able to identify the American nor could the Japanese identify the other bodies. However, one of the Japanese bodies had some work done on his teeth that was indicative of the state of dentistry in Japan in the early 1900s. Yet the body was in his prime—no more than thirty."

"We know time is different on the other side of the gates," Dane said.

"We know that now," Sin Fen corrected. "We didn't know it then."

"Is it possible that the Shadow can use people?" Dane asked.

"The Ones Before used Flaherty, so it is possible the Shadow can use humans."

Dane rubbed his hand across his forehead, feeling the onset of a headache. "Why did the submarine sink?"

"That's another intriguing thing," Sin Fen said. "It appears that the Russians had quite a few ships of their fleet in the area, searching for the sub. When it reappeared, rather than recover it, the Russians seem to have sunk it."

"Why?"

"We don't know. We couldn't even get Kolkov to confirm that."

"Because of the foreigners on board?" Dane wondered.

"Perhaps."

"Or perhaps because of the nukes on board?"

"Or the nukes not on board," Sin Fen said with a slight smile.

Dane could pick up the aura of her emotion. He could

tell she knew how frustrated he was by the lack of clear-cut answers to the many mysteries surrounding the gates.

"Is that why Foreman is so worried about the *Wyoming*?" Dane asked. "Even though the crew took a fatal dose of radiation, he's concerned there might be others on board."

"Yes."

"But the sub would still be hot, wouldn't it?" Dane asked. "Anyone going on board would receive a fatal dose."

"Yes, but—" Sin Fen shrugged to indicate this was another mystery beyond her. "That Trident was launched from the *Wyoming*, there's no doubt about that. Whether there's anybody alive on board is kind of moot now."

"Why didn't they recover the rest of the Russian submarine?" Dane asked.

"They tried to, but the weather was getting bad and the Soviets were starting to sniff around. The CIA pulled the plug."

"So there's nukes unaccounted for there, also," Dane summarized.

Sin Fen nodded. "It's very highly classified, but not counting the recent loss of the *Wyoming*, there are over two hundred nuclear weapons from submarines and aircraft that have disappeared in or around the gates unaccounted for."

"That will help me sleep better at night," Dane said.

"The *Wyoming*'s Tridents are certainly the most powerful weapons and delivery systems."

"What's the status of the *Glomar Explorer* now?"

"After Project Jennifer, it was docked at Sausalito, California, for over a decade. When the Cold War ended in '89, we even tried to sell or lease it to the Russians to help recover their other lost subs. The Russians weren't interested. Then it was bought by a civilian corporation and refurbished a year and a half ago."

"Let me guess—" Dane said. "Since Howard Hughes

has been dead for a while, I would guess Michelet Technologies?"

Sin Fen nodded. "Yes."

"It's headed for the site we're going to?"

"Correct."

"And what are we supposed to do when we get there?"

"Try to find the Shield," Sin Fen said.

"And we need this ship in order to do that?" Dane was beginning to get a uniquely bad feeling about this mission.

"Using other resources, Mr. Foreman has determined that the place we have to look is on the bottom of the ocean floor at that spot."

"Of course," Dane said. "Why should it be easy?"

Dane felt her mental probing, and he blocked it. During the mission into Cambodia, he had been able to communicate with her through mental images, something Dane had had all his life. He had just never encountered anyone else with the ability. He found it both intriguing and disconcerting.

"Very good," Sin Fen commented. "You have learned much."

"Who are you?" Dane asked abruptly.

"I work for Mr. Foreman."

"It's not that simple," Dane said.

"No, it is not."

"You told me you grew up in Cambodia, near the Angkor gate," Dane said.

"Yes."

He probed her mentally and was easily deflected. "How did you gain this ability?"

Sin Fen shrugged. "How did you? I know as much about my past as you do about yours."

Dane felt Chelsea stir slightly against his feet, then settle down.

"I read your classified files," Sin Fen said. "Even if I didn't, I have a very good idea of your background. You were an orphan. You have no idea who your biological parents are. Neither do I. You moved from place to place as a child. So did I. You joined the Army at seventeen and went off to war. I became involved in black market activities in Phnom Penh when I was but a child—anything to avoid being forced into the prostitution that the other girls at the orphanage were pressed into. I was contacted by Foreman. You were recruited by Foreman when you were in Vietnam. And here we are now."

"How did Foreman find us?" Dane asked.

"I think Foreman is able to find us because he is one of us," Sin Fen said. "You've tried to get into his mind. It is a wall, just as yours is to me now. He has some sort of connection to the gates, just as we do. Do you know about his brother?"

Dane shook his head.

"Foreman's brother disappeared into the Devil's Sea gate off the coast of Japan in the last month of World War II while flying an attack mission. Foreman was in the same squadron and was on the only plane that avoided disappearing."

"He sensed it was dangerous," Dane said.

Sin Fen nodded. "And then he got assigned to Fort Lauderdale Naval Air Station. He was supposed to be a member of Flight Nineteen."

"The flight of TBM Avengers that disappeared into the Bermuda Triangle," Dane said.

"Yes. He didn't go on that flight and watched them disappear on the radar screen."

"So he knows enough to avoid going into the gates," Dane said, "but he's not afraid to send others in."

"He has dedicated his life to finding out what the gates are and who is on the other side. To do that, he has searched for others like him."

"What are we?" Dane asked.

Sin Fen shook her head. "I don't know. I told you before

about the two hemispheres of the brain and how we might be genetic throwbacks to the days when humans had a telepathic capability. That is what Foreman believes. That the speech capability on the right side of our brain is fully developed and functional, unlike normal humans, and that is how we are able to do what we do."

"What do you believe?" Dane asked.

"I agree with him that we are genetically different. But I think the reason is more than just a piece of the brain working. I believe we hear the 'voice of the gods.' Throughout history there have always been those who could hear something others couldn't. Priests and priestesses, the Oracle at Delphi, various saints and messiahs, the world's religions are full of such accounts. They can not all be false. I think we are modern prophets."

" 'Modern prophets'?" Dane repeated. "Of what?"

"It appears to be of doom," Sin Fen said, "since we are connected somehow to the gates."

"A lot of prophets who heard voices have been burned at the stake," Dane noted.

"And locked in mental institutions in more modern times," Sin Fen said.

"What is on the other side?" Dane asked. "We've seen some of the creatures that come through but never whoever or whatever is behind the intelligence—just the gold beam."

"Don't forget the blue beam that helped you," Sin Fen said. "I think there is a war being fought on the other side, and it's spilling over into our world. Our scientists are still trying to figure what exactly the gates are."

"So, are the good guys on the other side the gods we hear?" Dane asked. "And maybe the bad guys are the devil?"

"That I don't know," Sin Fen said. "Maybe there are voices from the other side. Maybe it is our own subconscious picking up something that our conscious brains can't."

Dane wasn't quite sure he believed her. "It has to be connected to these gates somehow. I was able to go into and come out of the Angkor gate when others were killed. I could sense more than others could. Hell, I can sense things here in our world that others can't. Have *you* ever been inside a gate?"

"Yes."

"Angkor?"

Sin Fen nodded. "When I was young, I accompanied a group of scavengers—people who raid ancient sites for the artifacts. They had heard the legend of Angkor Kol Ker and wanted to loot it. Looking back now, I realize it wasn't coincidence that I ended up with that group. They searched me out. And I know now that Foreman was the one who gave them the information about Kol Ker—and me.

"The lure of treasure overcame our fear of monsters of legend.

"We went north where the stories had Kol Ker located. To the place where people feared to go. We crossed into what I now know is a gate area. Into the fog." Her eyes had unfocused, staring at a point somewhere over Dane's left shoulder. "All in my party were dead within five minutes. Monsters. Like you met. Beasts I had heard of only in legend and whispered stories late at night attacked us. And the gold beam of light. That, too. And the blue. I barely escaped. I ran back the way I had come. Within a week of returning to Phnom Penh, Foreman had contacted me."

"He set your party up," Dane said.

Sin Fen's eyes refocused. "Yes. I know that now. I didn't know that then."

"He uses people to test his theories. To probe the gates. He used you. He used me and my special forces team. He used the *Scorpion*. How many people has he killed probing the gates?"

"I don't know," Sin Fen said.

Dane shook his head. "And we're here, still doing what he wants."

"It is war," Sin Fen said. "In war there are casualties."

"Do you really believe that?" Dane asked.

"You're the ex-soldier," Sin Fen said. "You must have believed it once."

"I went to Vietnam because—" Dane stopped in mid-sentence. He had no desire to explain himself to Sin Fen.

"Foreman has his own demons," Sin Fen said. "His parents died in Germany, in the camps. They sent the boys to live with relatives in the States in the late thirties but stayed in Germany to keep their business open, hoping that the country would go back to the way it had been. A foolish hope seen through the eye of history."

"Foreman must have sensed the danger," Dane said. "He must have felt guilty because they wouldn't listen to him."

Sin Fen shrugged. "He does not talk about it much. I only found this out when I checked his classified file at Langley."

"You did not trust him either then," Dane noted.

"No, I didn't."

Dane looked out the portal, and he could see the real version of the picture on her laptop rapidly approaching. The derrick centered over the deck of the *Glomar Explorer* towered three hundred feet over the smooth ocean and the ship. Over two football fields long and 116 feet wide at the beam, the ship dwarfed the two navy destroyers that slowly circled it.

"Do you trust Foreman now?" Dane asked.

"I trust that he will do all he can to battle the gates," Sin Fen said.

"That doesn't bode well for the foot soldiers in the trenches," Dane said.

Four

999 A.D.

The cold wind howled down from the rocky crags over-looking the fjord and cut into the flesh like a hundred spear points hurled by screaming warriors. It chilled to the bone, no matter how many blankets and furs Ragnarok Blood-hand tucked around his body. It was not as bad as the wind of a thousand spear points that he had experienced on the northern seas when the winds took the sea spray and froze it as it smashed over the bow of the longship, cutting into exposed skin as if the sea god Aegir himself was telling them to go back.

But it was not the cold nor the wind that had woken Ragnarok. He had slept through much worse. Indeed, he was known as something of an oddity among his crew be-cause he slept not under one of the dozen large wooden benches that stretched across the width of the longship but rather on top of the forwardmost bench, exposed to the elements. The ship was drawn up on the pebbled beach along the narrow strip of land that gave them access to the fjord and the sea beyond.

They had pulled in here before dark, not so much because of the coming night but rather due to a dense fog that had suddenly appeared, enveloping the ship. Ragnarok and his men had traveled through heavy fog before, but this one was unlike any they had ever encountered. It was very thick, allowing them to see barely twenty feet past the carved dragon prow. And it felt sickly on their skin, leaving a wetness unlike that of the ocean or fresh water. Even the color wasn't right, not quite gray but rather a yellowish haze with streaks of black in it.

This followed sighting a burning mountain earlier in the day to the east, a most bizarre occurrence that had rattled the crew. The volcano was atop a dark cloud that clung to the shore and mountain in a most unnatural way. The earth was unquiet, that had been clear for the past year as earthquakes and volcanoes rumbled and burned all over the area of the world Ragnarok and his men traveled.

At Ragnorak's order, they had carefully worked their way along the shore, making constant soundings even though the ship drew less than three feet, and finally turned into this fjord. The fog had faded slightly inside the fjord, but another very strange aspect was that it was not affected much by the fierce wind, something that had the crew muttering among themselves as they settled in for the night. It was unnatural, and Ragnarok had posted a guard and had the boat pulled onto the shore to wait out the strange weather.

Awake now, Ragnarok didn't jump up; rather he opened his eyes to tiny slits and peered about the boat as his ears strained to hear something beyond the wind. It was dark, but he could still see a certain distance and there was no one on board other than his crew. He knew every piece of wood on the ship, and he knew no one could move without him hearing the wood react. The rumble of assorted snores reached him, carried by the wind.

Satisfied he wasn't in immediate danger, Ragnarok stood up, furs and blankets dropping from his body. He was an imposing figure, six and a half feet tall with broad shoulders upon which long black hair fell in dirty, uncombed curls. His face was square, with a formidable jaw. A thick red scar ran down the left side, from the temple, just in front of the ear, to end at the jaw. His eyes were startlingly blue, an inheritance from his mother. Unlike most Vikings, he did not have a beard. He cut the hair on his face every week or so with a sharp knife, leaving a coarse black stubble peppering his face.

He wore leather trousers, the color of which meandered somewhere between the original brown leather and the black grime encrusted by years of wear. A tunic covered his barrel chest, this garment in much better shape with a red piping in the symbol of an eagle sewed into the back. His arms were bare, and the muscles rippled as he picked up his ax—Skullcrusher—from where it had rested next to his head.

The Danish ax was a weapon not many men, even few Vikings, could wield effectively in combat. Skullcrusher had a haft over four feet long of three-inch-thick oak. The base of the ax ended in a metal point, much like a spear, so it could be wielded either way. The head—the normal business end of the ax—was huge, with a single edge that Ragnarok honed every day as conscientiously as many fair-haired Viking women combed out their long hair. Opposite the cutting edge, the head ended in a four-inch-thick blunt surface, the part of the weapon that gave it its name. Ragnarok had smashed many a head with a mighty swing, knocking shield and sword out of the way to find his target.

Ax in hand, he remained perfectly still. His eyes looked toward the beach. There was nothing moving. He looked past the beach. A high wall of rock angled up, disappearing into the fog. Ragnarok had climbed many such ridges surrounding fjords, and he knew that the likelihood of an enemy doing that was slim. Then he turned in the direction Vikings always looked—to the water.

The black surface was ruffled by the wind in an almost hypnotic pattern. To the left, the fjord narrowed, eventually running into a glacier coming from the inner mountains. To the right, the fjord led to the sea, a narrow, fifty-foot opening between two high outcroppings of rock the only way in and out. They had rowed in through that opening shortly before nightfall seeking landfall. No ship's wake disturbed the surface of the water, no oars dipped into the water. All was still.

Ragnarok tensed. All was still now, the wind dying down, the water becoming mirror flat. The winds of the north were fickle, with a mind of their own to betray and confuse even the most experienced sailor, but to suddenly cease like that—Ragnarok shook his shoulders, pushing away a chill.

The fjord was on the west coast of Norway, north of even the most northernmost Viking settlements, where during winter the sun was little more than a glow on the horizon for a few hours each day, and the rest of the twenty-four-hour cycle was spent in darkness. It was early spring, and while the beach was free of snow, patches of white still clung to the elevations just above.

There was nothing moving he could see. Nothing to indicate what might had woken him. There was also no warrior standing guard on the small wooden ledge six feet up on the main mast that served as the lookout post for the ship.

Ragnarok strode down his boat, stepping over sleeping bodies, pausing at the large rudder. He gently kicked one of the forms under the last bench.

"Eh?" a deep voice grumbled.

Ragnarok bent over and kept his voice low. "Hrolf, get up."

Hrolf the Slayer pushed aside his blankets and sat up, head twisting to and fro.

"Who is supposed to be on guard?" Ragnarok asked.

Hrolf cursed as he looked down the boat and saw the empty post. "Duartr. I will whip him like a dog for—"

Ragnarok held up a hand, head cocked as he heard something, almost the same pitch as the howling wind that was now gone, but deeper, more threatening, coming from a single point in the distance. "He is not in his sleeping place."

Hrolf stood, grabbing his sword and drawing it out of the scabbard. He was a foot and a half shorter than his leader, but broader, a keg of a man, with muscle layered on muscle and a tremendous belly under his leather tunic. The sword was as long as half Hrolf's height, and very thick. The end was blunt as a Viking fought not by jabbing but by slashing. The edges on both sides were razor sharp, and with the weight of the sword and the muscle Hrolf could put behind each stroke, the sword was capable of beheading a large bull with one slice.

"What was that?" Hrolf's head turned toward the landward side.

"I don't know," Ragnarok said. "Get the crew awake—quietly—and the boat afloat."

Ragnarok climbed onto the gunwale and jumped onto the beach, the pebbles making a very slight noise giving way under his leather boots.

The distant howling set the hair on Ragnarok's neck to rise. Not wolves, he did not fear them. Some of the blankets he slept under were made from the fur of wolves he had killed with ax or spear. Something different, something he had never heard before. Ragnarok had sailed the north sea to Eire Land, Iceland, and even beyond to the land Eric the Red had so deceitfully christened Greenland. He thought he had seen all there was to view in the great white North. The unique sound told him there was something more he had not yet met, and his heart leapt at the thought, but he had given the order to Hrolf to float the ship as a Viking always protected his ship and his village before any other pursuit.

Ragnarok's right hand tightened on the haft of the ax. The sound had come from over the ridge behind the beach. He kept his eyes focused on the steep walls as he crossed the beach to the scree pile of large stones deposited at the base of the steep rock wall.

Something was lying where the ground rose precipitously. A body. The top half jammed between two boulders. Ragnarok knelt next to the corpse. Ragnarok frowned. The man's sword was gripped by both dead hands. He recognized the engraved cross-guard—it was Duartr's. A good Viking death to have one's sword in hand, but who could have killed him before he gave an alarm? Ragnarok reached down and pulled the body back from between the boulders.

The head was gone. Even in the darkness, Ragnarok could see the white of the spine poking up above a bloody hole. Whatever had taken the head off had not done so cleanly. And the chest and stomach had been ripped open, as if a beast had feasted on Duartr's innards.

Ragnarok let go of the body and stood. He could hear the boat being pushed out, wood scraping against pebbles and into water, hushed voices hissing orders. He looked up, scanning in short arcs, trying to see through the clinging fog.

His efforts were rewarded when he saw something moving about two hundred feet above and to the right. Someone was climbing down. The strange screaming came again, closer this time, from near the top of the ridge, not from the climber.

Ragnarok growled, the sound coming softly from deep in his chest. He felt the blood pounding in his head, the battle fury rising with each accelerated heartbeat.

The figure was lower now, less than a hundred feet above his head, climbing with skill and speed. The body was covered with a black robe that dangled below it. Ragnarok climbed higher on the scree pile, closing the distance.

He reached a large slab, about eight feet wide and long, that had broken off the ridge and was now lying almost horizontal. Putting his feet wide apart, Ragnarok lifted up his ax and rested it on his left shoulder.

The figure was less than fifty feet away now, but Ragnarok's focus was higher, searching for the source of the chilling screams, which were coming more often now, every few seconds. Ragnarok stepped back slightly as two screams, one right after another whipped by him. They had come from slightly different directions. And there was still the matter of what had happened to Duartr's head and body—whoever or whatever had done that was already in the area.

The figure had altered direction slightly and was now climbing down directly toward Ragnarok. The black cloak swirled as the figure reached the slab and turned about, facing him, a deep hood covering the face, two hands up-turned, empty of any weapon.

"Who are you?" Ragnarok asked.

The screams were getting closer, and Ragnarok could feel the threat in them.

He was surprised at the voice that answered him: a woman's! "Perhaps you would be better to worry about what is making that noise?" The woman spoke Norse with an accent the Viking had never heard before.

"They sound like dogs from hell." Ragnarok slipped the ax off his shoulder and held it in front of him with both hands.

"They are," the woman said. "Valkyries and their creatures of the night."

All Vikings knew of the Valkyrie, the demon-goddess of the lord of the underworld, who did his bidding on Earth, who feasted on the corpses of those killed in battle.

"Then I will die bravely fighting the demon bitches,"

Ragnarok said, the moonlight glinting off the edge of his ax.

"It would be better to flee quickly," the woman said.

"A warrior does not flee battle."

"You can not stop them." The woman stepped forward and placed a hand on his heavily muscled forearm. "They have killed many brave warriors like you."

The howls were getting closer. Ragnarok had heard stories of the Valkyries and many other strange and frightening creatures from his mother, but he had never seen any of them. He had no doubt that such creatures existed though—or else his mother would not have told him of them. And he had seen Duartr's body. To fight an emissary of a god—even a demon god—would be quite a challenge. If he won, there would be glorious stories to tell. If he lost, the gate to Valhalla would surely be open to such a warrior.

"I cannot run," Ragnarok said.

"I am a disir." The woman pulled her hood back. Her hair was pure white even though her face was young and unlined. Ragnarok had never met someone with skin so dark. And the eyes! They were angled as if the skin on the side had been pulled back, unlike any he had ever seen. "My name is Tam Nok. I demand your assistance in escaping my enemies."

Ragnarok needed time to think, but as in all battle, there was no time. "I thought it was the other way around—disirs are supposed to help us."

Tam Nok stepped closer. Ragnarok knew there was danger close by, but his gaze was drawn to her eyes, their strange slanted shape. Deep black, even darker than the night around them, they drew in his very being.

"I am trying to help more than just you," she said. "Every Viking—all of mankind is in danger. If I die here, we all die. Make your decision now, Ragnarok Bloodhand."

A distant part of Ragnarok's mind wondered how she knew his name. "I cannot—" He whirled as an unearthly growl ripped the air to his left, the ax leading the way. The blade impacted in the chest of a beast in the midst of its leap. Ragnarok had a brief glimpse of bared teeth, a thick body, outstretched arms with claws at the end as he followed through the swing, throwing the body past him. A serpent's tail flickered by, narrowly missing his face, as the beast made a dying attempt to kill.

Ragnarok shoved his boot into the creature's chest and pulled the ax out with a cracking of bones. It had the body of a lion, the tail of a serpent, and the head of a monster with fanged teeth. Ragnarok had never seen the like.

"We need to leave," Tam Nok pulled on his arm. "Now!"

Looking past where the creature had come from, Ragnarok could see a tall figure—over seven feet in height—cloaked in red, with bloodred hair cresting over its shoulders. The face was white and long and hard. No mouth that he could see, just two red eyes that bulged outward. The Valkyrie's scream chilled Ragnarok's blood, although there was no mouth from which the sound could emanate. The scream came from the entire being, twisting the air that surrounded it. Ragnarok squinted. The air was shimmering next to the Valkyrie in a way he had never seen. The creature held up its right hand toward him. The hand was covered in the same sort of white armor as the face, with a bright gold stone held in the palm.

As Ragnarok stepped forward toward the Valkyrie, both hands holding the ax over his head, Tam Nok cried out, "No!"

A gold beam flashed up from the Valkyrie's hand, hitting Ragnarok in the chest, searing through the leather. He screamed in agony and staggered back. The hand pointed toward him once more. Tam Nok stepped between them, whipping something shiny from under her cloak. The gold beam hit the object and ricocheted off into the darkness.

Tam Nok jumped back, into Ragnarok, and the two of them slipped off the stone, falling.

The pain in Ragnarok's chest was forgotten as he tumbled down the rocky slope. He came to an abrupt halt at the bottom, Tam Nok on top of him. Both were bruised and battered but still alive. He rose up, pulling her along with him.

"They can not see well," Tam Nok hissed. "We must go now!"

There were voices below, the men on the boat, alarmed by the commotion. Ragnarok looked across the pebbled beach. His longship was in the water, oars manned, several warriors standing behind their shields slotted along the side, arrows notched to bows, peering into the fog and dark.

"Let us go," he ordered, but Tam Nok was already moving. Ragnarok frowned and hurried after her. Something flashed out of the dark, and Ragnarok reacted instinctively, pulling the ax up in front of him. What looked like a red rope lashed around the haft. There was a sizzling noise and the ax head fell off, the haft cut through.

Ragnarok stared in the direction the rope had come from. A very dark shadow, a pitch-black huge blob in the darkness, was about twenty feet away on the shore. More rope, arms grasping for a victim, came lashing out. Ragnarok threw what remained of his war ax, spear tip forward, at the dark mass. He rolled under the groping arms and came to his feet, running full-out now, after Tam Nok. Several arrows flickered by, just missing him, aimed toward the monsters behind him.

The scream of the Valkyrie behind was echoed to the left and right, other Valkyries closing in. Something leapt out of the darkness at Ragnarok, a small whirring ball of claws and teeth that he caught and threw over his shoulder, feeling a slice of pain along his right shoulder.

He scooped Tam Nok under his right arm, tossed her over his shoulder, and splashed into the water as his bowmen continued to shoot over his head, their eyes wide at the glimpses of the inhuman targets that they could make out in the dark.

Ragnarok tossed Tam Nok over the edge of his boat and jumped up, Hrolf grabbing hold of his arms and hauling him aboard.

"Row!" Ragnarok yelled. "Row!"

Ragnarok peered backward. The beach was disappearing into the dark. The howls of the Valkyries echoed across the water, as they discovered their prey had escaped. The wind was picking up again as abruptly as it had stopped earlier.

"Drop the sail," Ragnarok ordered Hrolf. Ragnarok wrapped both large hands around the worn wood for the rudder, adding his strength to that of Bjarni, the helmsman.

The old warrior looked worried. It was a dangerous move in the narrow fjord with such a strong wind blowing, but he did as ordered. The wind grabbed hold of the cloth and the ship picked up speed. Ragnarok leaned into the rudder, helping Bjarni steer a course directly between the outcroppings that defined the entry into the fjord.

Hrolf threw his powerful shoulder against the wood, helping Ragnarok and Bjarni as the wind pushed them farther to the left, toward the southern rocks. Ragnarok was surprised when Tam Nok joined them, her lean form next to Hrolf.

A chill ran down Ragnarok's spine. He looked up.

"Beware!" Tam Nok screamed.

Ragnarok let go of the tiller and spun about. One of the Valkyries swooped out of the dark fog, clawed hands outstretched, ruby eyes glistening in the otherwise blank face. It was closing rapidly on the ship.

Ragnarok grabbed a spear and held it up, braced against his chest. The Valkyrie swerved at the last second, narrowly missing being spitted on the spear, and flew along the left side of the ship. Thorlak the Hardy swung at the beast with his sword, his shield held in his other hand, and the beast dipped a wing under the metal. A clawed hand grabbed Thorlak's extended arm and snatched him off the deck as a mother might grab a child. Thorlak swung with his iron-rimmed shield even as his feet cleared the edge of the boat.

The metal connected with a hollow clang, as if it had hit fellow metal, and the creature abruptly rose straight up. Then the free hand, claws extended, sliced down and neatly separated Thorlak's shield arm from his body at the elbow. The Valkyrie disappeared back into the fog, Thorlak hanging below, his screams fading.

"Ragnarok!" Hrolf yelled.

The Viking leader turned his attention back to the boat. The longship was heading straight toward rocks. Ragnarok threw his shoulder back into the tiller, every muscle straining to bring the boat about. Warriors in front of him were grabbing bows, spears, and shields, their frightened eyes scouring the fog, tensed for a reappearance of the demon.

Slowly, the dragon head on the high prow swung to the right. They cleared the southern promontory with less than twenty feet to spare, the howls of the Valkyries fading as they sailed into the open sea.

Five

THE PRESENT

Night or day no longer mattered as soon as the elevator began going down. The electric lights on the top of the cage reflected off the dark walls, showing the layers of rock going by as the elevator descended. Professor Nagoya had made the trip many times, and it held little interest for him. He'd already called ahead with the coordinates to be checked, and he knew his team would be hard at work.

He'd taken the bullet train north from Tokyo, traversing the two hundred kilometers in less than an hour. A helicopter had been waiting in the parking area of the station he got off at and had whisked him here.

Rock walls on four sides guided Nagoya straight down. The Kamioka Mozumi mine was the deepest in Japan. Its lowest level was over three miles below the surface of the Earth. At a steady rate of four hundred feet per minute, the cage descended. Nagoya had to switch cages three times and cross three horizontal tunnels to get to the deepest shaft that led to his destination.

These last three vertical miles took him almost as long as the 120 horizontal miles from Tokyo. At long last the final cage thumped to a halt. Nagoya impatiently pulled aside the gate. A young woman was waiting for him, Ahana, his assistant. She bowed as she greeted him.

"What have you found?"

"We are still coordinating with the Americans," Ahana said, "but the results are looking positive. There is *something* at the coordinates we were given by Mr. Foreman."

Nagoya felt his pulse quicken. After all these years, every little discovery about the gates and those on the other side was like a drink of water to a man in the desert. They knew so little. Given that he had managed to get his government to invest over a hundred million dollars in this project, it was good that it was finally showing results. Of course, the project had ostensibly been done for other research reasons; indeed, it was used for various research projects by numerous organizations, and it paid dividends that way, but Nagoya had been the one who had accomplished what many had said couldn't be done.

They walked down a corridor carved out of solid rock, over eight feet wide and ten feet high. After 200 yards, the tunnel opened into a large natural cavern that had been discovered during drilling years ago, before the mine was tapped out. The cavern, over eighty meters deep and eighty wide, had been exactly what Nagoya had been searching for.

The tunnel came out near the very top of the cavern. A steel grating extended out over the open space, with several workstations where the crew that manned the site worked. Underneath, a highly polished stainless steel tank, sixty meters wide by sixty deep, had been painstakingly built, section by section. Along the walls of the tank over 20,000 photomultiplier tubes (PMTs) had been attached. PMTs were extremely sensitive light sensors that could detect a single photon as it traveled through water and reacted with it. They were all linked together with the output displayed on the computers in the workstation.

The tank was filled with very pure water. The surface was black and mesmerizing. Nagoya often found himself simply sitting and staring at that totally smooth surface, lost in thought.

"What do you have?" he asked once more as Ahana took her place at the main console.

"The computer is still processing the data, sir." Ahana typed in some commands. "Another few minutes, please."

Nagoya put his hands behind his back, trying to appear calm. The entire complex went by the name of Super-Kamiokande. In technical terms, it was a ring-imaging water Cerenkov detector. Foreman, Nagoya's counterpart in the United States, called it the Can, a rather simplistic term, in Nagoya's opinion, for a device that was the only one of its kind.

Cerenkov light was produced when an electrically charged particle traveled through water. The reason the Can had to be so far underground was to allow the miles of earth and rock above it to block out the photons emitted by man's devices on the surface of the planet. Thus researchers could study the much stronger cosmic rays given off by the sun, which could pass through the rock in an almost pure environment, much like astronomers put their telescopes on the highest mountains.

The other reason—and one that only Nagoya knew of—that it was deep underground was to look in the other direction, into the Earth. Since charged particles should not be emitted by the Earth itself, no other researchers even considered that a possible use. The Can looked for a particular charged particle that Foreman had stumbled across as being significant to the gates and the effect they produced.

For that reason, Nagoya did not mind the name the American CIA man had given the Super-Kamiokande, which had been developed as a joint U.S.-Japan research project. Both Nagoya and Foreman had tweaked their governments into doing something even the governments didn't really understand the need for at the time.

Nagoya knew that Foreman, over the decades after World War II, had focused on various locations where strange things seemed to happen: The Bermuda Triangle was only the most prominent to the public. There was also the Devil's Sea off the coast of Japan, the area that had first drawn Nagoya's interest. There were many more spots on the face of the Earth that propagated strange electromagnetic and radioactive properties.

The Russians, interestingly enough, had been the foremost investigators of these areas, looking beyond the spots inside their own borders. At a secret meeting brokered by Foreman shortly after the Berlin Wall fell, Nagoya had finally been able to meet his Russian counterpart, Kolkov, and learn much history and theory.

The Russians had lost a submarine in the Devil's Sea and two inside the Bermuda Triangle gate during the Cuban missile crisis. Additionally, the Soviets had sent ground recon elements into the Angkor gate area in Cambodia in 1956 and 1978, losing both groups without a single survivor. Only Kolkov knew how many people the Russians had lost over the years into the gates inside their territory, three of which Nagoya knew certainly existed: Tunguska, in the waters of Lake Baikal, and near the Chernobyl reactor.

Indeed, survivors from the gate were few and far between. Foreman had two of them working for him, the man named Dane and the woman Sin Fen. Nagoya had never met Dane, but he often wondered about the woman, whom he had met several times. She made him feel very nervous, as if her dark eyes could see into him, into parts he himself wasn't aware of.

Nagoya also knew that the Russians were greatly interested in the gates for some very specific reasons. First, there was the natural tendency for paranoia on the part of every Russian. Numerous invasions over the years and betrayals had engendered a certain mind-set in that country. Second, the Soviet government had supported Kolkov with tremendous amounts of resources once it was determined that a gate opening in the vicinity of Chernobyl had caused the disaster at that nuclear power plant. There was also considerable speculation that the massive explosion in 1908 at Tunguska had somehow been associated with the gates.

Like Foreman and the CIA, Kolkov had worked in the dark hallways of the KGB for decades, searching for answers when no one was even sure what the questions were.

Nagoya, with less resources but more technical expertise at his beck and call, had focused on scientific answers to the gate anomalies. Over the centuries, the Japanese had lost ships and more recently planes in the Devil's Sea gate and there were many legends about the area.

Nagoya wanted to step forward and look over Ahana's shoulder to see how the data was progressing, but he knew to do so would cause her some loss of respect among her peers, so he forced himself to continue waiting, standing over the tank, looking down at the totally smooth black surface.

The Super-Kamiokande—the can—had been developed because Foreman had discovered something rather strange about the gates. Using research money that poured down from the United States government to various universities for projects, some of which even the American public considered quite arcane and bizarre, Foreman had had the Bermuda Triangle gate checked with just about every type of scanner science had ever invented in the desperate hope of uncovering any information that might yield data on what exactly the gates were and what was on the other side. Up until a year ago, the gates had been simply a black hole to all imaging and sensing devices, recording nothing.

But last year, one of those research projects discovered that the gates discharged muons, which was strange infor-

mation indeed. As a physicist, Nagoya knew the history of
the muon.

In the 1930s, physicists had been very confident that the
building blocks of matter were the proton, electron, and
neutron. There were three other basic particles that scientists were aware of but knew little about: the photon, neu-
trino, and positron.

But there was a problem with the physics of the time.
Scientists also knew that the protons in the proximity of
the nucleus, holding equal charges, should strongly repel
each other, yet they remained there. Nagoya was very proud
that it was a Japanese scientist, Hideki Yukawa, who came
up with the answer and was awarded the Nobel Prize for
his brilliance.

To explain why the protons were held in place, he pro-
posed a new force in the nucleus formed by a new particle,
which he called the meson. He also determined that the
ratio of the force of this new particle was inversely pro-
portional to its mass, which made the meson 200 times
more massive than the electron.

Other scientists around the world searched for mesons,
mostly by studying cosmic radiation from the sun, the
strongest electromagnetic field they could find, infinitely
more powerful than anything man could produce. The researchers discovered that it wasn't quite as Yukawa had
predicted. There was more than just a meson, there were
two particles under that heading. One held the strong charge
with little mass—now named the pion—and the other held
a lot of mass with little charge—now called the muon. Both
the pion and muon were very unstable and decayed rapidly
when separated. The muon decayed into an electron, a neu-
trino, and an antineutrino.

These discoveries were the beginning of particle physics,
which opened the doorway to quantum mechanics as well
as a new perspective on special relativity and Einstein's
energy-mass relation.

The fact that the gates emitted muons that did not decay as rapidly as established equations for physics predicted they would was troubling to Nagoya and the other scientists who were investigating the gates. Fundamentally, it meant that the physical rules on the other side of the gates were different than that on the Earth side—or, and this was even more troubling—it meant that whoever or whatever was on the other side was manipulating particles at the very basic level in order to make the gates work. Nagoya thought it was likely both. He also felt that the gates were tears in the very fabric of the Earth's physical nature and were deliberately caused by some force at another place, probably another dimension.

It was a staggering concept and one that Nagoya was determined to resolve. He had to admit that the Russians had suspected as much before anyone else, seeing a link between the gates. In the 1960s, three Russian scientists had published an article in the journal of the Soviet Academy of Sciences titled, "Is the Earth a Large Crystal?"

It was not taken seriously by scientists in the West, being lumped with articles in the same journal on psychic power and other matters most scientists considered the work of the lunatic fringe. Only in the last several years were those scientists beginning to realize the error of their ways and were opening their minds to possibilities they had never considered before. That awakening was not due to acceptance of the Russian theories but rather new discoveries in physics that demolished old, accepted beliefs.

The three Russian scientists who wrote the article had backgrounds in history, electronics, and engineering, and they threw aside their differences and preconceived notions to explore the world around them. They started with an earlier, widely debunked theory that a matrix of cosmic energy was built into the planet at the time of its formation and that the effects of this matrix were occasionally evident in modern times in areas that were now known as gates.

The Russian scientists divided the world into twelve pentagonal slabs. On top of those slabs they delineated twenty equilateral triangles. Using this overlay, they postulated that these triangles had a great influence on the world in many ways: fault lines for earthquakes lay along them; magnetic anomalies were often recorded; and ancient civilizations tended to be clustered along the lines.

They called junctions of these triangles vile vortices. It just so happened that these vile vortices were in many of the same places as the gates that Foreman was investigating. Thus, while the rest of the scientific community ignored the Russian paper, Foreman was very interested and passed it along to Nagoya in the mid-1960s.

The Russians had even postulated a mathematical harmony to the crystalline structure that formed these vortices to explain the rhythmic nature of the disturbances associated with them.

Nagoya, upon receiving the paper from Foreman, and being a scientist, had had two reactions. One was that the Russians were onto something by connecting the vortices. The other was that the crystalline theory was grasping for an explanation that current science couldn't give. Nagoya knew that the lithosphere, the outer surface of the planet, which is where these vortices were located, had been moving for millions of years. He even knew of Einstein's theory of crustal displacement, which was not commonly accepted. Regardless, he knew that any crystal formation would be so disfigured by this movement as to make the fixed nature of the patterns the Russians postulated impossible over any period of time. Also, Nagoya knew there was no evidence of the planet having any sort of massive crystalline structure.

But during the recent expansion of the gates, there had been no doubt they were connected as they linked along the lines delineated by the Russians with electromagnetic and radioactive propagation and were only stopped at the last minute by Dane from completely covering the planet.

The recent information from Foreman about the lines of propagation from the gates that flowed along the intersection of the world's tectonic plates gave more validity to the Russian theory. The movement of the plates, continental drift in laymen's terms, was the most powerful force on the surface of the planet. It could bring forth devastating earthquakes, volcanoes, tsunamis, create the tallest mountain range on the surface in the Himalayas, and crack open the deepest depths of the oceans in the Marianas Trench.

Nagoya also believed tectonic plate intersection had been used to destroy a continent and civilization. His first contribution to gate theory was a historical one, based on his fascination for ancient cultures and civilizations. During his undergraduate years, he had had dual majors in history and physics, only deciding to go into the latter when he accepted that it was the more factual of the two, able to be proved, whereas history, the more he studied of it, presented itself as fact but was often wrong.

Nagoya had always been fascinated by the legend of Atlantis. First mentioned by Plato in the *Timaeus* and *Critias*, two of his dialogues, historians had widely felt it was just a device used in the oratories and not based on an actual place. Nagoya had found that assumption rather naive. Connecting that legend with archaeological finds that were often suppressed and alternative theories of the development of civilization, Nagoya believed that a highly advanced human civilization had once existed in a place known as Atlantis and the gates had opened—as they had just a week ago—destroying it to the point where it was now only a legend.

Besides Plato's mention, Nagoya believed in the existence of Atlantis for other reasons. The discovery of large stone blocks, closely fitted together in about fifty feet of water off the coast of the island of Bimini in the Bahamas had excited him. He felt that it might be actual, physical evidence of the existence of Atlantis or more likely, given the location, an outpost of Atlantis.

Another area he found fascinating—and one that the writing on the *Scorpion* had resurrected—was the similarities in early writing among ancient cultures. The Viking runic alphabet was not that much different from writings he had studied in South America, Mexico, Africa, even on Easter Island.

Nagoya believed these similarities were because they stemmed from a common ancient writing system that predated the oldest recorded language that was generally accepted by historians. That interest had led him to the diffusionist theory of the development of civilization.

The historically accepted concept of the development of civilization was the isolationist one. Isolationists believed that the ancient civilizations all developed independent of each other. The cities of South and Central America, Mesopotamia, the Indus Valley, China, and Egypt all crossed a threshold into civilization at about the same time, the third or fourth century before the birth of Christ. When looking at the vast time line of the existence of the planet, and even mankind, that was a rather remarkable coincidence.

Nagoya knew, of course, that there were explanations for that coincidence, the largest one being natural evolution. The many common discoveries in the archaeological finds of these civilizations, such as the similarities in written language, were explained by isolationists as due to man's genetic commonness. Nagoya called that the "great minds think alike" theory, and he didn't buy off on it one bit. An isolationist would say that there were ancient pyramids in South America, in Egypt, in Indochina, even in North America—some made of stone, some of earth, some of mud, but remarkably similar, given the distances between those sites and the traditionalists' insistence that those sites had had no contact with each other—all that was because each society as it developed had a natural tendency to do the same thing.

Nagoya was much more a fan of the diffusionest theory of civilization. He believed that those widely separated civilizations developed at roughly the same time in roughly the same way because those civilizations were founded by people from a single earlier civilization, survivors from the destruction of Atlantis.

Isolationists over the years had scoffed at the diffusionest theory on two counts. One was the very existence of Atlantis. The second was the issue of how survivors could have gotten from Atlantis to such remote locations around the world. In response, Nagoya pointed to the fact that modern scholars, sailing on reconstructed vessels, had crossed both the Atlantic and Pacific Oceans. Whether is was a balsa-wood raft of Polynesian design named *Kon Tiki* or the longship of the Vikings, the ocean had been crossable in ancient times.

There were archaeological facts to support the theory that the ancients had indeed crossed those oceans: artifacts found in places where they had not originated. There was an entire group of people devoted to the field of what was known as forbidden archaeology—investigating things found in places where conventional archaeology said they shouldn't be.

Nagoya, as a scientist, had not been overly surprised to learn that there were many discoveries made by archaeologists that were suppressed. He knew that scientists tended to bury evidence that contradicted their own theories. There were locked rooms in almost every museum around the world where artifacts that could not be logically explained were hidden away from the public's eyes.

Nagoya believed that if one accepted that there was an Atlantis—a civilization 7,000 years before the accepted rise of civilization—many of those hidden objects could be explained.

Even the destruction of Atlantis around 10000 B.C. was recorded in almost every culture around the world. There were many records of a great flood at about that time. Not only in the Bible but in such tomes as the Tibetan Book of the Dead, which described a large landmass sinking into the sea at that time. The Mayans called Atlantis Mu. The northern Europeans called it Thule. And a large landmass sinking into the ocean would produce tsunamis—waves— hundreds if not thousands of feet high, which would race around the world's oceans inundating low-lying coastal planes with such devastation that it could easily be inter- preted as a worldwide flood.

There was no doubt in Nagoya's mind that Atlantis had existed, and there was also no doubt that the world was now facing the same threat that had destroyed it. He thought it was important to study as much as was known about that ancient culture and how it was destroyed.

While many modern scholars and scientists scoffed at ancient writings as more fiction than fact, Nagoya took the opposite view. He'd read translations of the early docu- ments, such as Solon's dialogue, which first mentioned At- lantis, placing it in the Atlantic. The description of the destruction of Atlantis fit in with what would happen if tectonic plates were manipulated to unleash their terrible force, resulting in earthquakes, volcanoes, giant waves, and, ultimately, disappearance under the waves. The Greeks even said that where Atlantis had been, parts of the ocean were blocked by mud and underwater plants.

"Another five minutes and we will have the complete readout." Ahana interrupted Nagoya's thoughts.

He acknowledged the information with a nod. Nagoya and Foreman believed the latter part about the impassable sea might refer to the Sargasso Sea, which was north of the Puerto Rican Trench and where they now knew was close to where the Bermuda Triangle gate opened.

Beyond Atlantis, Nagoya had read extensively about any

theory regarding earlier civilizations. The Vikings had had a land they called Thule, a land of fire and ice where creatures and gods lived, separated from the real world by a deep chasm. Another interesting legend was that of Mu, a lost continent of the Pacific Ocean. Some claimed that Mu predated even Atlantis. A French scholar in 1864, translating one of the few surviving texts of the vanished Mayan civilization of Central America, uncovered references to a place called Mu, which the text described as a ancient landmass with a bustling civilization that sank into the sea after a catastrophic volcanic explosion.

Another French archaeologist, examining Mayan ruins and translating some of what he found, added to the story of Mu. It had been a civilization that ended when two brothers fought for the right to marry the queen. When the continent was destroyed, the queen fled to Egypt where, with the new name of Isis, she built the Sphinx and began civilization in that part of the world.

These Frenchmen placed Mu not in the Pacific but in either the Gulf of Mexico or the Caribbean, and Nagoya believed they might have stumbled across records of Atlantis under a different name and from a Western Atlantic perspective rather than an Eastern perspective.

Looking around at the sophisticated scientific equipment that surrounded him, Nagoya knew there was a tendency for scientists to be very conservative and overly reliant on equipment rather than the power of their own minds. Nagoya firmly believed the human mind to be the most intricate device on the face of the planet but also the one that the least was known about.

The person Nagoya was most fascinated with was a man who was neither scientist nor philosopher but the son of a Kentucky farmer: Edgar Cayce. Born in 1877 and dying in 1945, Cayce left behind a legacy of visions, many of which regarded Atlantis.

Like Plato, Cayce placed Atlantis in the Atlantic. But

Cayce provided much more information, gathered while he was in a trance state, about the legendary island kingdom. He claimed that people lived on the island for thousands of years, and it experienced three major catastrophes, only the last of which was the ultimate devastation that wiped it off the face of the earth. Also, Cayce said the Atlanteans were highly evolved, using electricity and flying aircraft. He also spoke of a strange element he called "firestone" that generated energy. First mentioned by Cayce in 1933, Nagoya found that early writing very intriguing in that the description given by Cayce of firestone was very similar to how one would describe radioactive materials—and this a decade *before* the first public recognition of atomic energy.

Nagoya believed there were nuggets of truth in every legend, and now that there was no doubting the reality of the gates, he also had to wonder how much truth there was to Cayce's visions and predictions. Cayce had also said that the first Atlanteans were spiritual beings, lacking physical form. It was after they began achieving physical form that the troubles began. Nagoya wasn't sure how much to make of Cayce's visions, but he kept an open mind, more so since the assault out of the gates.

Nagoya had no doubt that Earth had been threatened by the gates in the past as it was being threatened now. And he also believed that although Atlantis was destroyed, that was only a defeat in a battle in which the war had yet to be decided. Somehow, the invasion through the gates had been stopped years ago. And however that had been done, it was necessary to find those same means to stop it once again, even more so now that the Trident had been fired in the Atlantic and the nuclear weapons exploded along the fault line.

Nagoya took hope from the fact that someone on the other side of the gates was obviously on mankind's side. The fact that Foreman's man Dane had been contacted by his former teammate Flaherty, both before he entered the

Angkor gate and after he was at the ruins of Angkor Kol Ker, were positive signs. The return of the *Scorpion* with the map etched into its metal was also positive.

Somehow, that site marked on that map, which coincided with the location of the deepest spot in the Atlantic, the Milwaukee Depth, was important. And that was the data he was waiting for from Ahana. As soon as he'd been alerted by Foreman about the map on the *Scorpion*, he'd had the computers that recorded data from the Can focus on that spot almost on the other side of the world, recording the muons that came out of it.

"We've centered and plotted the muon emission pattern." Ahana spun her seat about. "Very strange, sir."

"How so?" Nagoya asked.

Ahana stood, indicating for Nagoya to take her place. "This," she said, pointing at the screen, "is the muon level reading. Note that the Bermuda Triangle gate is steady as we've always noted. This is the level we've been scanning around the world to map the gates. We never noticed anything different until you directed us to do a more thorough search of that specific area. I fine-tuned the sensors to record any muon activity down to one-tenth of the current gate reading."

Her finger touched the monitor screen. "Note this very thin trace going from the Bermuda gate south? It ends exactly here, the same spot noted on the side of the *Scorpion*."

"So they are indeed connected," Nagoya said.

"Yes, sir. We not only have a longitudinal and latitudinal reading, but because we are reading this through the mass of the Earth, we were able to get a depth reading. That spot is at the very bottom of the ocean. And at that location, it spreads and encompasses an area on the ocean floor over eight miles in circumference and a half mile in height that has low levels of muonic activity."

"What do you think it is?"

"It's not a gate," Ahana said. "It's on our side, in our

world, but it has some qualities like a gate."

Nagoya knew his assistant did not want to make a foolish guess, but one thing he had learned over the years was that no guess could be too wild when dealing with anything associated with the gates. "A theory?" he prompted.

Ahana bit her lip, then spoke. "I think it is some sort of statis field surrounding an open space."

"Holding what?"

"I don't know."

The submarine cut the water smoothly, the special rubberized absorbing material attached to the outer hull leaving minimum disturbance in the ocean it passed through. The specially designed propellers gave off little signature, making it the quietest submarine in the ocean. At full speed, this vessel was quieter than any other submarine built simply sitting still in the ocean.

At one thousand feet, the sub had at least another fifteen hundred feet of ocean to spare below it before the modular hull would experience any pressure problems. Speed was perhaps the most important aspect of the ship's design as its nuclear power plant allowed it to cruise at thirty-five knots, almost forty miles an hour.

The *Seawolf* was the U.S. Navy's most modern and most expensive submarine. Designed from first deckplate to the top of the sail as an attack submarine, the *Seawolf* had one priority mission: kill other submarines. At over two billion dollars' cost, it incorporated every advance in underwater warfare ever developed. Not only could it kill other subs with its Mark-48 torpedoes, it was also armed with Tomahawk cruise missiles, enabling it to target 75 percent of the Earth's land surface. Three hundred and fifty-three feet long, the *Seawolf* was actually not much longer than the first U.S. Navy sub given that name during World War II. However, its forty-foot beam was almost twice the diameter of those earlier vessels.

The rear two-thirds of the submarine were taken up with the nuclear power plant, engine room, and environmental control systems. The crew of 14 officers and 120 enlisted men worked and lived in the forward third. Not as cramped as earlier submarines, the *Seawolf* still required a special type of man willing to work in tight quarters and live under the surface of the water for extended periods of time.

An example of the lack of space was the fact that the commander of this ship, Captain McCallum, had to hold meetings with his officers in the wardroom, where they also ate their meals. There was barely room for the twelve officers—two remaining on watch in the operations and engine room—to fit.

Since their abrupt departure from their home base in Groton, Connecticut, earlier in the day, the entire crew had been wondering what was up. The sub was sailing due south at flank speed. There was also the factor of a strange man being brought on board and kept isolated in the captain's stateroom since sailing.

"At ease," McCallum called out as he squeezed into the officers' wardroom. The captain sat at the end of the table, placing a file folder with a Top Secret cover in front of him.

"Gentlemen, we're currently operating under direct orders from the National Command Authority. You can read into that, that the president himself has authorized this mission. Our mission is to proceed with all speed to designated grid coordinates north of Puerto Rico and remain on-station until further orders. Our task is to destroy the USS *Wyoming*, which is currently missing, if it reappears with hostile intentions, before it can launch any of its ballistic missiles."

"Sir—" his executive officer, Commander Barrington, began to protest, but McCallum cut him off.

"Before disappearing, the *Wyoming*'s crew received a fatal dose of radiation. If it reappears, you can be assured that it would not be manned by our fellow sailors."

McCallum could see the shock on his officers' faces. He knew it was best to hammer home the situation and let them sort it out afterward.

"Gentlemen, there is a strong possibility that the *Wyoming* might reappear with people other than the crew on board. In the '70s, a Russian submarine that disappeared into the Devil's Sea gate reappeared a week later. The Russians sank it. When our people tried to recover the wreckage, they pulled up a section that had bodies of men who were not part of the crew on board. The nuclear warheads had been worked on, and some are still missing as far as we know. No one knows how these non–crew members got on the ship, but the fact is they were there.

"And, as you all know, a Trident, which had to have come from the *Wyoming*, was fired out of the Bermuda Triangle gate yesterday and nuclear warheads were detonated in the Atlantic Ocean. That leaves twenty-three Tridents unaccounted for.

"And something else tells us subs can come back out of this gate, sometimes long after they've disappeared."

McCallum reached to his side and opened the door. Another officer wearing the same rank stepped in; the only difference was that this officer's uniform was outdated, not worn since the Navy upgraded in 1975.

"Gentlemen, this is Captain Bateman of the USS *Scorpion*."

Given that the *Scorpion* had disappeared in 1968, the appearance of the ship's captain—and his relatively youthful appearance belying thirty years—made the officers of the *Seawolf* forget even military formality for a few seconds before belatedly springing to their feet, as required when the captain of a ship entered the room.

"At ease, gentlemen," Bateman said.

As the officers retook their seats, Captain McCallum opened the file folder and pulled out some pictures. He passed them around the table. "This is the *Scorpion*. It is currently being held under cover in the pens at Groton. As you can see, it appears as it did on the day it disappeared over thirty years ago." McCallum pointed to his right. "As you can also see, so does Captain Bateman. Gentlemen, he doesn't know why any of this happened or even how, but because he is sitting here in front of you, we have to accept that it has happened. Captain Bateman is here to assist in whatever way he can as we patrol near the anomaly known as the Bermuda Triangle gate.

"We know little about this area, which you can see on the satellite imagery defined by the black triangle. Captain Bateman's ship was part of an experiment in 1968 to learn more about it. While an SR-71 Blackbird reconnaissance plane entered a similar area over Cambodia called the Angkor gate, the *Scorpion* entered the Bermuda Triangle gate to attempt to make radio communications with the Blackbird. This would prove that there was a link between the two sites. I'll let Captain Bateman tell you what happened."

Bateman was a short, balding man, his face pale. His eyes held a distance to them, and as he spoke, he kept them on the table, not making contact with anyone. His left hand had a tremor to it, and he gripped the edge of his chair to keep it still.

"We entered the area. We didn't have much information about what we were doing, other than crossing into a certain area and attempting to make communications via a surface buoy. We were on a heading of nine-zero degrees at a depth of two hundred feet. Our location was about sixty miles north of the northwest end of Puerto Rico.

"We began transmitting on high-frequency radio. We made contact with the Blackbird, even though it was over Cambodia, which was not possible unless the signal was traveling through the anomaly we were in directly to the anomaly the aircraft was in.

"The Blackbird began reporting systems trouble." Bateman's voice was almost a monotone. "We were ordered to abort. I told the helm to come hard about. Then we got pinged."

"Sonar?" McCallum asked.

"It was like someone was using sonar on us, but the tone was slightly different. I didn't have much time to dwell on that because we then had a problem in the reactor. Instruments indicated a coolant line failure. I ordered the reactor off-line.

"Then we picked up something very big coming in our direction on radar. Very big." Bateman looked up from the table for the first time. "I'd never seen anything other than a landmass that large on the radar screen, except this object was moving. I ordered us to emergency surface."

Bateman fell silent.

"And then?" McCallum prompted.

"And then nothing," Bateman said. "I blacked out. Everyone on the crew did. When we came to, we were cruising at two hundred feet in the same general area we had been in before. Except it was over thirty years later, the reactor was fine, and we had people on board who had come through what you call the Angkor gate. That's all I know."

"Our concern is to stop anything coming out of the gate," McCallum said. "There are no plans to go into it. We are to stand off at a safe distance and be ready to engage targets."

"What if the large contact my ship picked up comes out?" Bateman asked.

"We will engage and destroy it," McCallum said.

"I think you need to be prepared for system failures," Bateman said. "I didn't have time to even think about combat when we were attacked. This boat is very nice, and you have very sophisticated devices, but I recommend you come up with a plan to fight if you lose all your sensors and targeting equipment."

"Our master computer has a backup," McCallum said to

Bateman. "It's also shielded to survive the electromagnetic pulse generated by a nuclear explosion."

The captain turned to his officers. "You have your orders," McCallum said, ending the meeting. The officers filed out of the wardroom.

McCallum went to his stateroom. Built into the wall, next to his small desk, was a safe. It held the key that allowed the captain of the *Seawolf* to launch nuclear weapons. It also held sealed orders McCallum had been handed by a CIA man just prior to sailing.

McCallum opened the safe and retrieved the envelope holding the orders. He cut through the seal and slid the piece of paper out. He read through it twice, then ran the paper through his shredder. He picked up the phone on his desk and ordered the officer in charge of navigation to make a slight change to their course and destination.

Six

999 A.D.

Ragnarok turned the rudder over to Bjarni and sat down on the rearmost bench. He peeled back his tunic to check the wound on his shoulder.

"You must clean it out," Tam Nok said. "The wounds of these creatures can be poisonous."

Her comment irritated Ragnarok, as if he had never been wounded before. Every weapon could cause poison to grow in the body. The skin had been sliced smoothly. Ragnarok squeezed around the edges, forcing more blood to flow out. He called out for Askell the Healer. The old man, bent from years behind an oar, made his way down the ship and peered at the wound with sad, gray eyes.

He checked Ragnorak's chest. "A burn. It is already clean. It will heal," was the brief summation. "I will work on your shoulder."

He reached into the large pouch hanging at his side and brought out what he would need. As Askell pressed a poultice onto the opening, Ragnarok considered his situation. They were holding course away from land. Bjarni the Far-sighted was excellent at being able to keep the ship moving in a straight line without benefit of landmarks. Ragnarok wasn't quite sure how he did it, but the skill had been proven over and over again during the years they had sailed together, so he had implicit faith in the helmsman. Fog still surrounded them, although the wind had died somewhat. Nothing was visible in any direction except dark gray. Most men dared not sail out of sight of land for fear of becoming lost on the open sea, but Ragnarok knew once the sun rose, they could always reverse course and sail in the direction the sun came from to find land once more. He had sailed up and down the coast of Norway many times, although never this far north.

He had come along the coast looking for arable land, a valuable commodity in this part of the world. All he had found were steeper hills, worse weather, the burning mountain, fog and, subsequently, the encounter the previous evening.

There were rumors going around the Viking world of strange things happening. Traders from the south talked of earthquakes that killed many. The religion of the Christians had taken over much of the world south of the Vikings and even now was claiming many a Norseman converted. And there were many Christian monks who were warning of the coming of the millennium since the birth of one they called God, that there was to be a second coming after much devastation.

Ragnarok didn't believe in the Christian god. They claimed they had only one, yet they spoke of three, which he didn't understand. And while some of the priests of this religion claimed pending doom, others said nothing of it. He had participated in raids on several monasteries in England and Eire Land and, while he didn't accept their religion, he did respect the fortitude of the monks he encountered who wavered not the slightest in their steadfast belief in their god, even as they died on the sword.

Ragnarok believed in the Norse gods of his mother, but

they were not the most important thing in his life. The ship that swayed under his feet was the center of his life and had been for years.

The longship was over eighty feet long and fifteen feet wide at the center beam, a large but not overly big longship. Ragnarok had heard that King Olaf Tryggvason in Norway had had a ship built the previous year over 160 feet long, twice the size of his ship. Ragnarok wished he could see such a massive ship, but he also knew that if he ever came across the king's ship on the water, it would be the last thing he would ever see, unless he could outrun it.

The keel of Ragnarok's boat was hewn from a single large oak tree and curved using the strength of many men. The keel beam was carved in a T shape, the thinner end of which extended into the water. Long experience at sea had taught the Vikings that this shape aided in steering a true course.

The ship's ribs were also of solid oak to give strength and stability. The outside of the ship was constructed using inch-thick sections of overlapping oak planking called strakes. The strakes were nailed to the ribs and also tied with spruce-root bindings. The total effect was a very strong yet flexible ship, able to take on the batterings of an open ocean sailing yet drawing such little water that it could easily be pulled up on a beach and then pushed back into the water.

The mast was actually not very tall for such a long ship, only twenty-five feet high, hewn from a single tree. What the sail lacked in height it made up for in width, being over forty feet wide. That unique design allowed the sail to be raised or lowered quickly. It was made of a double layer of coarse wool, a dusky gray color except where a large bloodred hand silhouette had been painstakingly dyed into the cloth.

Supplies were carried under floorboards that gave access to the low-lying space beneath them and the keel. Just be-

hind the mast, an iron pot was hung over a large hearth-
stone where, when the sea was totally calm and conditions
favorable, a fire could be used to cook meals. Those conditions were few and far between, and the crew usually
subsisted on dried meat and stale bread while they were at
sea. Caskets and barrels were lashed here and there, containing other supplies and, most importantly, drinking water.

The crew was totally exposed to the sea at all times, the
only shelter coming when they slept under the nominal
cover of the rowing seats, three feet wide, that stretched
across the width of the ship. There were fifteen seats, ac-
commodating thirty rowers. Over each row station, shields
hung on hooks. At the prow of the boat, a dragon head had
been carved, the beast's eyes searching the sea ahead.

The rudder was also a uniquely Viking invention, fixed
to a large block on the right side of the rear of the boat.
Bjarni steered the boat using a tiller bar. On the opposite
side of the tiller, two vertical wood poles were set into the
top of the hull, which the men held onto, rears sticking
over the sea, in order to void their bowels.

The ship was all Ragnarok had, and he had helped build
it over the course of three years as a young man. He had
sailed it for the past ten years, and it had been his only
home for the past four.

A voice came from the front of the boat. "We're clear
of the fog!"

Ragnarok looked up, and the front of the boat was
bathed in the early morning light. They slid out of the fog.
Ragnarok looked back. The fog was like a wall behind
them, the gray surface covering the horrors they had experienced.

"We're safe now," Tam Nok said.

Of more interest to Ragnarok than his wound was his
passenger. The one who called herself a disir, an emissary
of the gods, sent to Earth to help man. At least that was

the role of disir in the stories his mother had told him. Other than deflecting the golden beam from the Valkyrie, she had done little to show her powers. That there were gods and that those gods sent their minions to Earth to interfere in the affairs of men, Ragnarok had no doubt. There were too many unexplained things, too many wonders and horrors for it all simply to be a matter of chance. The Norse believed the gods had made man, and thus they could play with him as they willed. Man could fight the gods to the best of his abilities and sometimes even win if one was brave and true enough.

And if one lost fighting the gods, the gate to Valhalla would certainly open. For a Viking there was no greater honor than dying bravely in battle, weapon in hand. A man who lived to an old age and died in his bed was viewed with disdain, a drain on the resources of his village, a coward who had simply not sought out that last fight that brought honorable death.

Valhalla was the hall of chosen slain where men dined and drank deeply at the table of the gods. Every evening, the warriors fought each other to the death, and then their wounds and bodies were healed so they could repeat the same the following day. It was the kind of afterlife that every Viking warrior dreamed of.

Ragnarok's mother had been a storyteller, one who knew all the tales, and on the long winter days and nights, the entire village used to gather around her to hear her voice. Thus Ragnarok knew of the disir and the Valkyries—unnatural women who meddled in the affairs of men. Even the monsters he had caught glimpses of in the fjord had not shocked him. He had seen strange things on and in the ocean during his journeys and heard tales from men he believed of even stranger creatures. Now he had his own tale to tell, although he knew he never would—because he had left the enemy standing on the battlefield.

Like many in this part of the world, Ragnarok knew the

world was a much larger place than what he saw and experienced. There was always more water and lands beyond the horizon, and he had a burning desire to see as much of it as he could before his end came in battle.

Despite all that, he had never had someone who claimed to come from the gods on his boat. The disir who called herself Tam Nok—a strange name indeed—was seated on the same bench, on the other side of the longship, five feet away.

"Where are you from?" Ragnarok asked.

Tam Nok pointed in the direction of the rising sun. "A long way, a very long way in that direction."

"Rome?" Ragnarok had met a man in Denmark once who claimed to be from that land of legend. Where it was supposed to be warm almost all the year and the sun was always high at noon. An ancient kingdom which had once conquered all of Gaul and Germany and most of England. The man had had several gold coins that he claimed were Roman, and Ragnarok had never seen the like before.

"Beyond Rome. Beyond Persia. Beyond India."

Ragnarok could only stare at the woman. Other than the white hair, she looked much too young to be speaking of traversing lands he knew of only in legend. She reached into her cloak and pulled out a long tube of a wood he had never seen.

"Bamboo," Tam Nok said, catching his questioning look.

"Bamboo?" Ragnarok repeated.

She tapped the wood. "This is bamboo. It grows where I came from. Tall. As tall as your tallest trees. It is hollow but very strong."

Ragnarok glanced across the woman at Hrolf, who shrugged. They had heard many tall tales, some true, some made up by braggarts—except she had the wood in her hand, and he saw no reason why she would lie about such a thing.

She removed a plug in the end and carefully pulled a piece of parchment out of the wood. She unrolled it on the bench between her and Ragnarok.

"What is this?" Ragnarok was staring at the lines drawn on the paper.

"A map."

"Of?" Ragnarok was trying to locate some place he knew, but the scale was strange.

"The world. Most of the world." She tapped the map with a long, thin finger. "We are here."

Ragnarok focused on that point, then expanded his view. He recognized the coast of Norway, the inlets, but if that small part was Norway, this map covered so much more. He felt excitement such as he had never known before, different than a battle rage, a yearning to know what lands and seas those lines represented.

"This is Denmark!" Ragnarok pointed. "And England where the Saxons are. I have been there on raids. Iceland. I have been there, also, and beyond—here to the land called Greenland by Eric the Red. I traveled there two summers ago."

The map ended on the left with Greenland. Ragnarok had heard of lands beyond, but he had never seen a map so detailed. What amazed him were the lands that extended across the map to the right.

Tam Nok nodded. Her finger slid way across the map to the east. "I am from here."

Ragnarok was astounded. Her finger had gone across Norway, past Kiev, across the lands of the steppe horsemen, fierce fighters of whom Ragnarok had heard amazing stories, and many times farther than that to a land that abutted a sea he had never heard of.

"My kingdom is called Khmer. My city, Angkor Thom. I am a priestess of the temple of Angkor Wat."

"I have never heard of these places," Ragnarok whispered. "You told me you were a disir, a maiden of the gods of Asgard."

"The gods—" Tam Nok swept her hand around her head taking in the world—"have different names in different places, but they are the same gods. You would call me a disir; in my own land I am a priestess.

"I have traveled for over a year to get here, and I have much farther to go." Her finger slid back across the map to where it ended in the west. "I must travel beyond the edge of this map."

"To where?" Ragnarok asked.

"I do not know exactly where yet."

"Why are the Valkyries after you?" Ragnarok asked.

Tam Nok didn't even raise her head, her voice coming from inside the folds of her hood. "They want to stop me."

"Why?"

"I have knowledge they want no one to have. Knowledge that can help man defeat them and the Dark Ones of the Shadow who send them."

The sound of the water against the hull helped erase the last of the battle rage, and Ragnarok turned, putting his back against the hull, his feet stretched out. He was trying to work all this new information into his mind.

Askell shifted around and continued his work. Having cleaned out the wound, he now was preparing to close the gash. Numerous scars crisscrossed Ragnarok's body, and he was used to the pain of wounds.

"How did you know my name?" Ragnarok asked.

Tam Nok's head came up, and she pushed back the hood. Those dark eyes peered at Ragnarok. "Like the knowledge the Valkyries wish to destroy, I know many things without having to be told." She looked about. "Where were you going before you met me?"

Ragnarok laughed, even as Askell pierced his shoulder with a bone needle. "You just said you knew many things without being told."

"I am tired," Tam Nok said. "I do not have the energy for word games."

The smile left Ragnarok's face. "I do not like running, woman."

"It was not a battle you could have won," Tam Nok said.

"That is not the important thing," Ragnarok said. "It is more important to fight bravely."

"I will tell you what is important," Tam Nok said.

"Be still!" Askell hissed as Ragnarok's boots slammed into the bottom of the boat. The rage had returned, but he bit back his hasty retort. He forced himself to remain still as Askell finished the last stitch.

Askell used his teeth to cut the animal-gut string he had used to sew up Ragnarok's shoulder. He put the needle back in his bag and went back to his place. The other men close by all tried to appear as if they were not listening, but Ragnarok knew they were. There was no such thing as privacy on a longship. He pulled the tunic up over his shoulder and tried the arm. Some blood seeped through the stitches, and there was pain, but he could use his arm; that was all that was important. The burn on his chest was an ache he had already gotten used to.

Then he returned his attention to the woman, keeping his voice low. "You do not scare me, priestess. This is my ship. One of my crew was killed back there by your demons. He did not receive a proper burial, but at least he died with his sword in his hand, a good death. Another of my crew was taken away. They were both good men, brave warriors. You say you are a disir, but that is only your word. You will have to do much more to convince me that you are what you say you are."

"Where are—" Tam Nok paused and rephrased her question and changed her tone. "Captain of this fine ship, where were you headed?"

"The Faroes, and from there, Iceland," Ragnarok said. He pointed on the map to the two locations.

She also referred to the map. "I must get to this place."

"England," Ragnarok said. "That is south of here and dangerous. We have spilled much Saxon blood over the years. They fear us, but if they catch one ship alone, they will be on us like dogs. And it has been well plundered. There is no longer much treasure close to the shore that can be easily taken. It is not in the direction we—"

"I will pay for the transit."

Ragnarok could sense the interest from those of his crew who could hear. "How?"

Tam Nok reached inside her cloak and pulled out a small leather bag. She slid it across the bench toward Ragnarok. He picked it up and loosened the tie, peering inside. Not quite sure what he was seeing, he spilled the contents out on his palm. Stones and ingots glittered in his palm. Gold and jewels. He had seen such before, during raids on the English and French coasts, but he had never had such a large share.

"I could throw you overboard and just take these and continue on my way," Ragnarok noted.

"You won't," Tam Nok said. "It is not your nature."

Ragnarok frowned at that and put the stones back in the bag. "Why England?"

"As I said, I am looking for something beyond the edge of the map. But in England I will get more information. That is the first place I must look."

"What are you looking for?"

"A Shield."

"It can stop the Valkyries and their creatures?"

"It can do much more than that."

"How do you know this Shield exists?" Ragnarok asked, intrigued by the concept of such a powerful weapon. His ax—Skullcrusher—had been most formidable and had never been broken in battle, until now. A weapon even more powerful than that would be worth more than any gold or jewels. He had seen how Thorlak's shield had not even slowed the creature in the slightest, even though he had seen such blows in battle split a man's head wide open. The white armor the Valkyries wore was something he had never seen before, as was the golden beam that had burned him.

Tam Nok pulled another piece of parchment out of the tube and tapped it against Ragnarok's chest just above his burn. "The runes on the writing inside this tell me that. They tell me the Shield to stop the Valkyries and the ones who will come after the Valkyries exists."

"Let me see," Ragnarok said. His mother had taught him the runes, something his father had reluctantly allowed.

Tam Nok unrolled the scroll.

"These are not runes," Ragnarok squinted at the lines drawn on the paper.

"Not the runes you know," Tam Nok agreed. "Nevertheless, they are runes of another people. An older people. They tell how they defeated the Dark Ones of the Shadow. And how they—the ancient ones—had a weapon. But I do not know where the Shield is. I do not have the map for that. For that, I need to go to England and find someone who can give me the rest of the map, the piece that is missing. The piece that shows the lands beyond Greenland, over the sea."

Ragnarok had heard stories of land beyond Greenland. Vikings who had been caught in a storm while trying to reach Iceland or Greenland and come upon a strange land, where trees came down to the shore. Where there were strange people, Skraelings, who were unlike any people in Europe. As was Tam Nok, Ragnarok thought.

"You are sure there is someone there who has that?" Ragnarok asked.

"I have been told to go to England to find out," Tam Nok said.

"You trust whoever told you this?" Ragnarok asked.

Tam Nok pointed up. "I was told by the gods. I hear

their voices. They have always led me in the right direction."

"Why can't the gods tell you where the Shield is, then?" Ragnarok felt pleased with himself for having thought of that, "and skip having to go to this other person?"

"You would not understand," Tam Nok said. "It is the way things are."

Ragnarok leaned back once more on the seat, considering what she requested. With favorable winds, the northern part of England was two days' sailing away to the southeast. The Faroes were a day and a half to the north and east. He looked at the map. To think there might be another map showing the lands that Eric the Red had sailed to a generation ago!

"Bjarni," Ragnarok called to the helmsman. "South, by southeast."

Seven

THE PRESENT

"We can maintain position using our global positioning receiver and a series of thrusters," Captain Stanton explained as he led them through a long corridor leading from the helipad on the rear of the *Glomar Explorer* toward the center of the ship. "Once we arrive on a site, we can stay on position within six inches."

Dane was impressed. The *Glomar Explorer* appeared even larger when one was actually on board. Chelsea kept close to Dane's side as they walked along the steel-decked corridor. The hum of heavy machinery was in the air, and the ship vibrated slightly.

The corridor ended, and they walked onto a gantry way that angled around a large open pool in the center of the ship. The pool was over a hundred feet long by sixty wide. Above their heads, the derrick poked over three hundred feet into the bright blue sky. The walls of the pool were hung with hundreds of lengths of pipe. The dark surface of the ocean lay calm in the pool at the bottom of the opening. Above, the derrick towered over their heads.

"We are capable of lowering seventeen thousand feet of

pipe," Captain Stanton said. "That's over seven thousand feet deeper than the next best thing available on the market. Better than any standard rig. And we're much more mobile than any rig."

"How long until you're in position?" Sin Fen asked as they crossed the gantry way over the well.

"Another six hours." He opened another hatch on the far end. "We have a briefing ready to get you up to speed. This way."

Dane and Chelsea followed the captain and Sin Fen into a conference room. Ariana Michelet was sitting at the head of the table. The only daughter of Paul Michelet, the founder of Michelet Technologies, Ariana had not only had the good taste to be born into one of the richest families in the world, she had also been graced with good looks. Tall and slender, she had olive skin, very little of which was showing given she was wearing a set of black coveralls that looked like a flight suit. A patch on the shoulder showed a silhouette of the *Glomar* with Michelet Technologies written in script around the edge.

She stood and smiled, reaching down to pet Chelsea. "It is good to see you—both of you," she said to Dane.

"I'm a little surprised to see you here," Dane said.

Ariana straightened and stared at him. "Why is that?"

"After the way your father and Foreman tricked you into going into the Angkor gate—and nearly being killed there—I would think you'd be a little leery of getting involved in anything either of them set up."

She sat down, indicating for them to take their chairs. "I would think the same of you. Foreman got you to go into the Angkor gate *twice*. I only went once."

Dane smiled. "Good point."

"Besides, we own this ship." She waved her hand to take in the *Glomar*. "The technology is all ours."

"So what exactly is the plan?" Dane asked. "What are

we going to do? Drill in the middle of the ocean and hope we come up with something?"

Ariana reached forward and hit a couple of buttons. The room darkened, and a map appeared on the wall behind her. "We are heading for this spot, about one hundred miles northwest of Puerto Rico. It also happens to be part of the deepest section of the Atlantic, a thousand-mile-long valley in the ocean floor known at the Puerto Rican Trench."

"Why am I not surprised at that?" Dane asked.

"It's called the Milwaukee Depth." Ariana pointed down. "The bottom there is twenty-seven thousand four hundred and ninety-three feet that way. You could dump Mount Everest in there and only about fifteen hundred feet of it would stick out of the water."

"But the good captain here," Dane pointed at Stanton, "said you could only drill to a depth of seventeen thousand feet."

"We're not going to drill," Ariana said.

Dane waited.

Ariana hit the Forward button on the machine, and a new slide appeared. It showed a drawing of the *Glomar Explorer* with the pipe going down below it into the ocean. At the end of the pipe, three vertical cylinders were grouped around a thinner central cylinder.

"We plan to go down in stages. We will lower a deep-sea habitat on the end of the drilling pipe to the maximum depth of seventeen thousand feet. That will be our base camp, so to speak, if you wish to reverse the concept of mountain climbing. The habitat, *Deeplab IV*, is Navy. It will meet us at the site."

"Where's it coming from?" Dane asked.

"The Navy Undersea Warfare Lab at Norfolk. It was flown to Roosevelt Roads Naval Station on board three C-5 transports, and from there it was cross-loaded onto a sub tender and is being assembled as we speak. It will arrive on-station over the Milwaukee Deep just about the same time we do."

"Has the lab ever been down that far before?"

"*Deeplab* is rated for twenty-thousand feet," Ariana said.

"Has it been down that deep?" Dane repeated.

"Not yet," Ariana said.

"Better and better," Dane commented.

She clicked a button, and another version of the map appeared. An outline of the Atlantic, from Bermuda in the north to Puerto Rico in the south, to the U.S. mainland in the west, with a black triangle in the center. A much larger yellow triangle covered it. "At its widest propagation, the Bermuda Triangle gate was just short of touching the Bahamas, Puerto Rico, and Bermuda. Its current size is much smaller, a triangle centered about forty miles to the north of our destination."

"So the place we're going to isn't inside the gate now?" Dane found that unusual.

"No," Ariana said, "but—" She paused and turned to Sin Fen.

"Give me the good news," Dane prompted.

Sin Fen spoke up. "The Navy has been surveilling the Bermuda Triangle area for a while at the behest of Mr. Foreman, using SOSUS in addition to constant surveillance from overhead satellites."

"What's SOSUS?" Dane asked.

"A sound surveillance system that tracks submarines," Sin Fen answered. "The initial SOSUS systems were laid along the Atlantic coast in the '50s and '60s as the threat of Soviet ballistic submarines increased. Over the years, the Navy expanded the system into the Pacific and closer to the Soviet Union.

"Basically, each SOSUS line consists of a bunch of extremely sensitive listening devices on the ocean floor connected by cable and reporting to an onshore tracking center.

The Navy has constantly been upgrading the system and trying new listening devices."

"Even after the Cold War ended?" Dane asked. He was always alert for parts of explanations that didn't quite fit, and although he couldn't "read" Sin Fen, he could read the way Ariana and Captain Stanton were reacting to her words and he knew he was, as usual, only getting part of the story.

"Even after the Cold War," Sin Fen replied. "The navy isn't stupid. They got money to continue working on SO-SUS by tying it in with several civilian and government agencies to do a variety of tasks other than track submarines. SOSUS now listens for underwater earthquakes, volcanoes, and even tracks whales for biologists."

"Very interesting," Dane said. "What did SOSUS pick up?"

"Even before Mr. Foreman investigated and we got the map off the *Scorpion*," Sin Fen said, "the area known as the Bermuda Triangle has always raised quite a bit of speculation. Over the centuries, numerous ships—and more recently, planes—have disappeared while in this area."

"Bull," Dane said in mild voice.

Sin Fen simply raised an eyebrow.

Dane amplified his objection. "As you may have noticed, I did some reading on the way down here. The insurance company Lloyds of London—who ought to know since they insure ships and planes—did a study and found that the area delineated as the Bermuda Triangle had no statistically significant higher losses than anywhere else. Also, many of the ships and planes that people claim disappeared into the Bermuda Triangle were nowhere near the area when they disappeared. Some were hundreds if not thousands of miles away from that triangle you're showing."

"You are quite correct," Sin Fen said. "However, there *is* something in the Bermuda Triangle. It is not so much that ships and planes enter the gate and disappear. We think it is more that something from the gate goes to the ships and planes and makes them disappear."

"What is this thing?"

"We don't know—yet," Sin Fen said. "What we do know is that something comes out of the gate and travels to the depths of the Puerto Rican trench every once in a while and returns to the gate."

"Why this spot?" Dane asked.

"We don't know," Sin Fen said. "However, special imaging using a muon detector in Japan, has—"

"A what?" Dane asked.

"I'll explain it to you later," Ariana said. "Suffice it to say that this detector can pick up a gate and the gate's influence in our world."

"OK, go ahead," Dane said.

Sin Fen indicated for Ariana to change the slides. A new picture appeared, showing the Bermuda Triangle gate outlined in red. A thin red dotted line went south from it to the Milwaukee Depth, where there was a red circle drawn.

"A muon-active area eight miles in diameter is located there," Sin Fen said.

"Another gate?" Dane asked.

"Not a gate," Sin Fen said. "An area in our world influenced by the gate."

Dane thought about that. "That means whatever is on the other side can pass through the gate and come into our world."

"Yes, or send something into our world that manages to survive," Sin Fen said.

"That's a change," Dane said. "At Angkor, the gate was a mixture of our two worlds. There were animals from both sides in the gate. And water stopped the creatures from their side."

"The creatures, yes," Sin Fen said, "but whatever the intelligence is on the other side—and there is no doubt there is some sort of intelligence over there—it has been able to send radioactive and electromagnetic rays through the gate and take over our satellites. Who's to say they can't also come out in other ways? Much like astronauts exploring another planet. They definitely showed the ability to send our own equipment back at us by releasing the *Scorpion* and firing the Trident.

"We think they may have developed vehicles or suits capable of coming into our world. Maybe the gates that are located in or over water on our side are located in or over water on the other side." Sin Fen was speaking rapidly, and Dane had the impression this was a matter of some conjecture on her part. "It's even possible some of their water life can pass over and survive in our water as long as a gate encompasses the area. So water might not be a barrier to such creatures but rather their natural environment, just as we have land and water creatures on Earth."

"As usual," Dane said, "we don't have a clue what's going on."

"Several times, SOSUS has picked up a bogey," Sin Fen continued, "and each time, it originates from the gate and returns there."

"The same bogey the *Wyoming* picked up?" Dane asked.

"Yes. And the *Scorpion*. Something very big that moves very fast. It's real and larger than anything we've ever put under the water."

"Does it go to the spot we're going to?"

"Sometimes."

"OK," Dane said. "*Deeplab* gets you down to seventeen thousand feet. There's still a long way to the bottom."

Ariana hit the button again. An elongated craft appeared, like a plane with stubby wings. The front of it was curved. Halfway back, another circle poked above and below the main body. There were also short wings at the rear, along with two vertical fins. One thing Dane noted immediately was that there were no portholes or glass that he could see.

"This is *Deepflight II*. We call it a fixed-wing submers-

ible, a very radical design departure for deep-sea submersibles. That's what will get us from *Deeplab* to the bottom
of the Milwaukee Depth."

"How deep is it rated for?" Dane asked.

"Thirty-seven thousand feet," Ariana answered. "More
than enough to get the job done. It's a four-person craft—
two in the forward pressure sphere . . ." She used a laser
pointer to highlight the forward part of the craft. ". . . and
two in the rear sphere. Each sphere is made of titanium and
seals separately."

"How does the pilot and crew see out?" Dane asked.

"Video and imagers," Ariana said. "To keep the pressure
integrity of the craft, there are only two breaches to the
titanium sphere: one is the hatch, which is titanium, also,
and basically a titanium hatch closely fitted to the rest of
the sphere, and one reinforced access port for the electronics and controls."

"What's the point then?" Dane asked.

"What do you mean?"

"If we can't see out, why put people inside? Why not
just use an RPV?"

"You can see out," Ariana said. "Using the low-light-
level television, LLTV, and other imagers such as sonar
and radar, you'll be able to 'see' better than using your
eyes. It also makes the craft less intrusive, as you don't
need to light up the ocean with bright lights in order to be
able to see. The *Deepflight II* has conventional searchlights,
but it also has infrared searchlights."

"Will we have the ability to pick up these muon things?"
Dane asked.

"Not yet, but we're working on that," Ariana said. She
continued, using the laser to highlight the screen. "The craft
is twelve meters long by four wide by four meters high.
Each pressure sphere is three point five meters in outside
circumference, two point eight meters in inside circumference.

"Maximum speed is six knots, descent rate is four hundred feet per minute, ascent seven hundred feet per minute. The dual engines are powered by a series of batteries. Flight endurance is twelve hours, life support is ninety-six. Outside of the spheres it is a 'wet' submersible, which means the engine, everything other than where the crew is, will not be pressurized and will be open to the water."

A cell phone rang, and Sin Fen pulled it out of her belt. She turned her back and spoke in a low voice for several seconds, then closed the phone. "Captain Stanton and I have work to do. I'll leave you to complete the briefing."

Stanton and Sin Fen left the room, leaving Dane and Ariana alone.

"How have you been?" Dane asked before she could go back to her slides.

"As good as can be expected," Ariana replied.

"Which means?"

"Pretty crappy." Ariana stood up, walked over to a porthole, and stared out at the ocean. "We both were lied to, and we both were used."

"And we're both here now," Dane noted.

"Of course," Ariana said. "Where else would we go? Walk away? Pretend what's happening in the gates isn't real? Pretend that Trident didn't land in the Atlantic? Those bombs didn't explode?" She turned and faced Dane. "Foreman and my father know us better than we know ourselves. They're both experts at using people. They don't have consciences, but they know how to manipulate people who do." She shrugged. "And besides, the threat is real. Foreman has had to do whatever he could to fight it when no one would believe him."

"But not your father," Dane noted.

Ariana sat back down. "He's old and he worked hard—"

"Don't make excuses for him," Dane said.

"He got you to rescue me," Ariana noted. "I think you're being a bit hard on him."

"I'm a bit hard on everyone," Dane said. "Why are you here?" he asked. "Besides the fact that your company owns this ship."

"Because some of my friends were killed in the Angkor gate." She looked up at him. "Is that good enough for you?"

"Yes."

"And there's the threat," Ariana said. "You know about the lines of propagation along the plate tectonics?"

Dane nodded. "But Foreman said that was just a reconnaissance. Imaging."

"So far," Ariana said. "But I'd say the nuke attack went a bit further than a reconnaissance."

"Sin Fen said that was a test."

Ariana nodded. "Yes, but one hell of a test, don't you agree? The interior of the Earth is my area of expertise, and what the Shadow is doing scares me. Most people feel solid ground beneath their feet and think Earth is a big rock with a molten core deep inside, but that's not the way it is at all.

"The Earth is a dynamic planet. The very outside of the planet, the crust, is called the lithosphere. It's around a hundred kilometers thick under the landmasses. And relatively cold and stable. Under the oceans, there are places where the lithosphere is only six to eight kilometers thick. That's like a sheet of paper wrapped around a basketball. This is especially true where tectonic plates meet." She pointed down. "Like in the Milwaukee Depth.

"Below the lithosphere is the asthenosphere. It's hotter, less solid, and moving very slowly. Plate tectonics results from the lithosphere moving over the asthenosphere."

Ariana went over to the slide machine and clicked through until she came up with the same image Foreman had shown Dane: the world with lines drawn across it.

"There are six major plates and several minor ones. These plates move relative to each other at various speeds, anywhere from one centimeter to twenty centimeters a year.

Now, that doesn't sound like much, but given the unbe-
lievably large masses involved and the instability of the
asthenosphere below, it can produce some rather dramatic
results, both long and short term.

"Where plates are pulling away from each other, you
have an opening into the asthenosphere that results in a lot
of volcanic activity. Where plates converge or smash into
each other, one plate usually slips beneath the other along
an inclined plane known as a subduction zone. These result
in mountain ranges. The Himalayas are the result of such
a subduction zone where the Indian Plate is sliding under
the Asian Plate. There is a third type of action, a transform
fault, where the plates are sliding against each other. The
San Andreas Fault is a good example of a transform fault."

"What makes these plates move?" Dane asked.

"That's a good question," Ariana said. "We don't really
know for sure, but the best theory is the slow churning of
mantle rock, what's called mantle convection. That's where
mantle rock deep inside the Earth is driven toward the surface by the extreme heat of the planet's core. As it gets
higher, it cools, until eventually it starts to sink back down.
Sort of a very slowly boiling pot using rock instead of
water. Another theory is that the weight of the plate itself
is slightly tipped, causing it to move in a certain direction.
This theory is called slab-pull. We're not really sure which
causes plates to move, and in reality, it might be a bit of
both."

"You're joking," Dane said. "We don't know what's under our feet and how it works?"

"I'm not joking," Ariana said. "Up until thirty years ago,
there were those who thought the Earth was solid. There
were others who thought the Earth was hollow and you
could get inside through entrances at either of the poles.
Hell, there are still people who think the Earth is hollow
and there are large cities populated by strange beings under
such places as Mount Shasta in California.

"The only way we have any idea what's going on under our feet is through remote imaging. The deepest probe ever sent into the Earth hasn't even come close to going a tenth of the way through the lithosphere, so everything below that is just conjecture."

Ariana shut off the slide projector. "What scares me is the possibility that while we may not know much about plate tectonics, whoever's on the other side of the gates may know exactly how they work and how to manipulate the enormous forces involved."

"If they do?" Dane prompted.

"If they do, they have a whole range of options. They can bring forth volcanoes. Cause massive earthquakes. Landslides thousands of miles long. If any of those events happen underwater, then the follow-on result would be tsunamis.

"Let me give you an idea of the threat I believe we're facing, and you'll understand why I'm here. Have you ever heard of Krakatoa?" Ariana asked.

Dane nodded. "A big volcano in the southwest Pacific that exploded in the 1800s?"

"May 20th, 1883," Ariana said. "The island, which is located in Indonesia, had been exhibiting signs of activity for several years. It lay along the meeting of the Eurasian and Pacific Plates, right on the Pacific Rim.

"On that last day, it finally erupted. At ten oh two in the morning, local time, the top literally blew off the volcano. It was the largest explosion in recorded history. The biggest atomic or hydrogen bomb we've tested doesn't even compare.

"The blasts knocked down walls over two hundred kilometers away. The explosion was heard on Rodriguez Island, over four thousand six hundred kilometers from Krakatoa, a thirteenth of the world's circumference.

"The resulting waves were over forty meters high. They devastated shorelines thousands of miles from Krakatoa.

Over a hundred and sixty-five villages were destroyed and thirty-six thousand people killed. Since the island itself was uninhabited, most of these deaths were the result of the tsunami.

"Before the eruption, the island had been nine kilometers long by five wide. After the explosion, only a third of the island was still left above water.

"Ash fell on Singapore eight hundred kilometers to the north. When the ash reached high altitude, winds circled the Earth, producing such vivid red sunsets that fire trucks were called out in New York City. It blocked out the sun to the point where global temperatures fell by over a degree in the year following the eruption and took five years to get back to normal. And that was just one volcano. Think of dozens, hundreds of eruptions like that."

"What's the worst-case scenario?" Dane asked.

"Worst case? If the Shadow knows how to use those nukes we gave them—which they just indicated they do— and knows exactly where to place them—which I hope they're still working on—they can split this planet wide open. Which means the end of every living thing on the planet."

Eight

999 A.D.

The trip down the east coast of England had been un-eventful. No English boat cast off to challenge them, and the few fishing ships they saw quickly got out of the way when they spotted the large sail and the distinctive shape of the Viking longship. Ragnarok didn't find that unusual. For over two hundred years, since the raid on the monastery at Lindisfarne in 793 A.D., the English people had learned to fear the longships that ravaged their coast. Even one Viking ship, sailing alone, was enough to raise fear along the east coast and cause the people to hide behind their castle walls.

Eight years previously, in 991, Ragnarok's ship had been one of ninety-three in Olaf Tryggvason's fleet, which conducted an extended raid of the lands they were now passing. They defeated the Saxons in battle and exacted a handsome ransom of 10,000 pounds of silver. Three years later, in 994, Ragnarok sailed with King Svein Forkbeard all the way up the Thames to London, where another large ransom, this time of 16,000 pounds of silver, was handed over by the Saxons.

After that raid, though, Ragnarok had had enough of working for someone else. The ransoms were rich indeed, but the amount that trickled down to the ship captains that made up those large fleets made it hardly worth the time or risk. The following year, Ragnarok began sailing on his own and waging trade not war. He found a lucrative business plying between Greenland, Iceland, and Scandinavia with a few essential goods. Not that he wasn't averse to taking down a ship or isolated village if the opportunity presented itself.

Ragnarok was opportunistic, and meeting Tam Nok had fueled his interest. However, Ragnarok knew little more than he had two days ago when he had first met the strange woman. She kept to herself, a difficult task on such a small ship with a crew of thirty men crowded on board. But the fact that the crew viewed her as a disir, a holy woman, helped considerably. There was also Ragnarok's glower if any of the men came too close to the woman.

The men were happy that they had earned more than enough for the season from Tam Nok's gold and jewels. Ragnarok knew there were some who would not even want to make the originally planned trading trip to Iceland after they parted ways with Tam Nok. They viewed running into the disir as a mixed blessing. Duartr had been killed, his body not given a proper burial, left for the Valkyries to feast on. And Thorlak had been taken away into the darkness—and he had been a popular shipmate. On the other side of the sword blade, they had already earned more money than they had expected for the season.

The stakes were raised a little higher early in the morning when Tam Nok made the announcement that England was too general a destination. She needed to be escorted to a certain point—in the middle of the Salisbury Plain, over thirty miles inland from the south coast of the island, due north from the Isle of Wight.

Being on the sea was one thing, but a Viking warrior

on land, far from his boat, was like a fish kept out of water too long. Tam Nok had solved Ragnarok's hesitation with another leather purse of gold.

In addition to the pending land journey, that act made Ragnarok uneasy. About half of his crew were old hands, men he had known for years. But the others, sixteen of the thirty, were men who had signed on for the first time this spring. Recruited from villages along the coast, they were outcasts simply for the fact they were willing to leave their clans and villages behind.

The first bag of gold had been like the scent of meat to a hungry dog. The second was blood on the snow, a trail leading them to want to slake their hunger even more. Still, Vikings respected their gods and their women, and Ragnarok hoped those dual loyalties would keep the crew in check.

His crew, like him, were mostly men without homes. For various reasons, they all had no place to go other than the ship. For some, it was a case of being outlawed and banished. For others, feuds in their home villages had made staying impossible. A few, like Hrolf, Bjarni, and Askell, were from the same village as Ragnarok, and when he left, they went with him out of loyalty.

Ragnarok planned to return home one day and claim what was rightfully his, but he knew that he needed more power in order to do that. Revenge burned in his heart, a simmering heat that he lit only to aid his battle lust and tried to avoid at all other times. Betrayal and treachery had cost him everything he held dear other than his ship and his close companions, and he planned to repay that treachery threefold. It was a topic he rarely spoke about, not even with those who knew what had happened to his family, but it had molded him into the leader he was, one who believed loyalty was the paramount virtue of a warrior.

The sun was low over the land off their starboard bow, but Ragnarok planned on sailing through the night. He had let Bjarni the Farsighted sleep during the day and the experienced helmsman would take them through the sand bars off the southeast corner of England and past the white cliffs. Although they had only sailed through the English Channel four times before, Ragnarok trusted Bjarni to be able to do it, even in the dark. The man had an incredible memory; if he'd sailed someplace only once, he remembered it as if it were a daily route.

There was more danger in the channel, as the Saxon pigs were better organized the farther south one went. There was even a king in London who claimed much of the island as his own. The king's ships might not be as fearful of a lone Viking wolf prowling through their waters. Another reason to continue on through the night.

Tam Nok was tucked under the forwardmost—and narrowest—bench, the cloak pulled around her, the hood over her face. Ragnarok was in the rear, his back against the side of the longship, a knife in his hand as he carved a long, thick stake of oak. He wanted a new haft ready. He planned to find a metalworker in England to make him a new head for another war ax.

He had a sword, the one his father had wielded, but Ragnarok preferred the power of the ax to the sharpness of the sword. He was also proficient with spear and bow but used those mostly to hunt, not for battle. He had men on board who were designated bowmen. Their job was to give a long-distance punch to the ship, but Ragnarok knew a leader's place was always in the forefront, and using an ax had allowed him to break through several shield walls and lead his men to victory.

When it became too dark to work, he stood next to Bjarni for a while. The shore to the west was so faint in the darkness there were many times Ragnarok could not see it, but Bjarni was steady on the rudder till.

Hrolf joined them, the three most experienced members of the crew now together around the rudder block.

"We will not be the first ship to arrive in Iceland this spring," Hrolf noted.

"We've made more than enough to make up for that," Ragnarok said.

"Enough to make up for Duartr being dead?" Hrolf asked.

"He would be dead whether we were heading for Iceland or England," Ragnarok said.

"And abandoning Thorlak?" Hrolf was the only man on board who would dare say that.

"What should I have done?" Ragnarok asked. "Flown after the Valkyrie bitch on my wings?"

"I think you trust this woman too much," Hrolf said. "Perhaps she lured Duartr onto the beach in the fjord. All this talk of gods and Valkyries and weapons—" Hrolf spat over the side of the boat.

"She was not near the beach when I went ashore," Ragnarok said. "She was climbing down the rocks. One of those strange beasts got to Duartr in the dark. And it is not a question of whether I trust this woman. It is a risk, but if this weapon she speaks of exists, it must be very powerful."

There was only the sound of the sail taking the wind and the water against the hull for several minutes.

"You think we might be able to return home?" Bjarni finally asked.

"If the weapon is powerful enough," Ragnarok said, "it might be possible."

"This is our home," Hrolf said, slapping a callused hand on the side of the boat. "This is your home," the old warrior continued. "Even if you went back, you would return to the sea as quickly as you could. This is what you know and what you love. It isn't about going home for you, my friend, it is about vengeance."

"So it is," Ragnarok agreed, surprised at what amounted to a speech for Hrolf. "And what is wrong with that?"

"Nothing," Hrolf said, "except vengeance for you springs out of loyalty, and I would recommend you consider how much your desire to revenge the dead will hurt those who are still living and loyal to you." Hrolf pulled his cloak tight around his broad shoulders. "I am tired, and the words come out without thought. I must sleep." He climbed over the bench and made his way to his place.

Ragnarok glanced at Bjarni in the twilight. The navigator had said nothing, his eyes focused ahead, turning to the right every so often to check the coastline that was sliding by.

"Do you want to go home?" Ragnarok asked him.

Bjarni's hands were steady on the tiller, so solid it was difficult to tell where the wood ended and the flesh began. "As Hrolf said, this ship is my home. We are here with you because our families are dead, and we were loyal to your father and we are loyal to you."

"But vengeance—" Ragnarok began, but Bjarni's low voice interrupted.

"My Captain, we can spend the rest of our lives seeking vengeance. And if we achieve it, will not those we achieve it on have someone in their family seek vengeance on us? When does it end?"

"Ah—" Ragnarok spat over the side of the boat. "You old men have gotten soft."

"That may well be," Bjarni agreed.

"I am going to sleep." Ragnarok lay down, pulling his blankets tight around his body.

He woke to the not so gentle nudge of Bjarni's boot in his chest. Ragnarok rolled to his knees, looking in the direction the dark silhouette of Bjarni pointed. Someone was moving forward along the left side of the ship, a dark lump barely visible against the almost pitch-black night sky. Ragnarok got to his feet, pulling his sword out of its scabbard.

Ragnarok dropped all pretense at stealth as there was a flash of metal from the dark form—an upraised knife. Ragnarok sprinted down the ship, leaping benches and bodies. The knife struck downward near the first bench. Sparks flew as it hit metal coming up.

Ragnarok roared a battle cry, leaping the next to last bench, then came to a complete halt. Tam Nok was on her feet, parrying the next thrust of the would-be murderer with her long knife. She spun, almost faster than Ragnarok could follow, and he heard the thud of her knife striking home in the man's chest. The man staggered back, hands groping for the blade. Ragnarok grabbed him and pulled him backward, hearing the man's spine crack as he thrust his knee into the man's back.

By the faint light he could finally see the face. It was Eric Thorren, one of the men who had just signed on two weeks previously. The light faded from Thorren's eyes and the body went slack in Ragnarok's hands. He dumped it to the floor, then stepped over it.

"Are you all right?"

Tam Nok knelt down and pulled her blade out of Thorren's chest, wiping the metal clean on his cloak before sliding it into the sheath. "I am fine," she said.

"He was a new man," Ragnarok explained. "He wanted your money. Then he would jump overboard and swim for shore. We wouldn't be able to follow with the ship in the dark as there are many sandbars. I will—"

"I don't need explanations." Tam Nok settled back down in her place under the forward bench, pulling her hood over her face once more. "I just need you to get me where I want to go."

Ragnarok bit back his angry reply. He was mad at himself for having even tried to offer an explanation. Since when did a captain have to explain himself to a passenger, and a woman at that? First Hrolf and Bjarni, and now this. Things were not the way they should be.

Ragnarok turned from her. He slid a hand inside the man's tunic and pulled out the small leather pouch that hung there on a cord around the neck. Ragnarok opened the pouch and emptied it into his hand. A single ingot of gold fell out.

It was Ragnarok's gold; a piece that he gave to every man on his crew. It was the offering to be made to Aegir's wife. Aegir was the Norse god of the sea, and his wife controlled the entrance from the depths of the ocean to Valhalla. A good Viking captain always made sure every member of his crew had a piece of gold so that if a mishap occurred during the voyage and the man died, his body lost at sea, he would have the offering needed to cross over.

Ragnarok put the gold piece in his own pouch, then slid Eric's body overboard. He watched it disappear into the dark water, then stared at Tam Nok for a few seconds before returning to his place in the rear of the boat.

Thorlak the Hardy spat, the glob hitting the creature in front of him and slowly sliding down the white, hard face. There was no reaction to his act of defiance. The Valkyrie had been standing in front of him, not moving for hours, like a piece of stone.

Thorlak had no idea where he was. He had vague memories of traveling through the dark fog, dangling in the creature's claw. Then darkness. Then awakening in his present situation. Which was not good.

His arms were pinned back on a flat, vertical surface with metal clamps tight over his one hand and the stump of his other arm. His legs were similarly locked down. He was naked, his clothes lying a few feet away in a dirty pile. The air was strange, thick, clammy, and cold on his skin. Despite that, a trickle of sweat ran down his forehead.

The arm that had been severed had been cauterized, and no blood seeped through anymore. Thorlak felt woozy from the loss of blood and knew without his sword arm, Valhalla would most likely not open its doors for him. But he had to try. He could wield a sword left-handed, and maybe the gods would smile on him for fighting against such great odds.

All he could see was the unmoving white-faced monster in front of him, the unblinking red eyes staring at him: and beyond, a large cavern, the ceiling and near walls he could see, but the far wall not visible in the dim light.

"Let me have my sword and a brave death." Thorlak's words echoed into silence, bringing no response. "You are pigs. Cowards." His voice sounded weak in such a large space.

There was movement, and Thorlak squinted to see. Another Valkyrie floated into view, the bottom of the cloak just a few inches above the rock floor. It was carrying something shiny and large—some sort of package. It placed the package on a stone table twenty feet away and swung up the lid.

Thorlak's eyes widened as the creature used its right hand to twist off its left arm, all the way back to the elbow. It placed the removed appendage on the table and picked up something from the package. It was another arm but one that did not end in the clawed hand but rather a single blade eight inches long. The red light reflected off the metal, making it appear as if already tinted with blood.

The Valkyrie turned and floated over toward Thorlok, the other one finally moving, getting out of the way. Thorlak searched for more spit, but his mouth was dry. The Valkyrie stopped less than two feet away, the dead red eyes dispassionately regarding him.

"Give me a warrior's death!" Thorlak screamed.

The left arm, blade on the end, came forward. The tip touched him on the breastbone.

"A sword in my hand!" Thorlak begged. "To go to Valhalla!"

Thorlak's breathing was very shallow. If he took a deep breath, the blade would pierce his skin. Sweat was pouring off his forehead, trickling down his naked flesh.

The second Valkyrie reappeared, carrying something, a metal band. It reached up and placed the band on top of Thorlak's head, as if crowning him. He felt small jolts of pain all around the top of his skull. A wire led from the band to a square box the creature held in its hands.

While Thorlak was still puzzling over what the band and box were, the blade at his chest moved forward a fraction of an inch, slicing flesh like a rudder through water, and down his chest to his stomach.

Thorlak bit back his scream, not willing to let his enemies know his pain. He had once seen a captured Saxon lord go through the bloody eagle without ever uttering a whimper of pain. The Norse torturer had cut through the Saxon's back, removed several rib bones, then pulled the man's still-breathing lungs out through the hole. They lay on the man's back, inflating and deflating with each breath like a pair of bloody wings. The Saxon had bit through his lip to keep from screaming in agony and stared defiantly at his tormentors until he died.

If a Saxon pig could do such, Thorlak knew he also ought to be capable of the same bravery. The blade sliced left along the bottom of his stomach, then back across to the right. With the other hand, the Valkyrie peeled back the skin along the T-shaped incision.

Thorlak thought to his youth, to the hills above the fjord of his village, green with grass and the bright flowers that fought their way to sunlight for the brief summer. A young girl whom he had gone with through the fields to the—

The blade cut along the side of Thorlak's face, now horizontal to the surface, peeling away the skin in one fine swipe and jerking Thorlak's mind back to the present.

The blade did the same to other side of the face. Then the scalp, taking care to pass over the metal band, until Thorlak's head was nothing but a bleeding skull covered with exposed muscle and ligaments. Still he did not cry out.

Memories would not work. Thorlak forced his mind onto a task. Rowing. He had pulled so many strokes on board Ragnarok's ship that it was as natural to him as breathing. His hands were on the oars, his muscles straining. Pull. Lift. Push. Down. Pull. Lift. Push. Down. Pull.

The litany got Thorlak's brain into a rhythm as the Valkyrie continued its ghastly work. It went on until all of Thorlak's skin, except for the tiny strip under the metal band, was gone. Blood pooled at his feet, mixing with the sweat that had been there and staining the pile of peeled skin.

The Valkyrie paused in its work and simply hovered. Thorlak's mind was rowing, steady, helping to pull Ragnarok's ship through the ocean water. The pain was there, but not so close as it was before.

There was a tingling in his head. A very strange feeling. For a few seconds, the pain faded even more. The two Valkyries hung in the air, simply watching. Thorlak faltered with the oar in the air. The wood disappeared from his hand. He was back in the cavern.

The pain came back. He gave up. His mouth opened to scream, but nothing came out.

He felt weak, tired. He had been called the Hardy because he could stay awake and row after all others on the ship collapsed, but he knew he could not row much farther now. The journey was nearly over. He reached for the oar, wrapping his hands tight around the wood, feeling the comfort of the known.

The blade, now crimson in the red light, came forward once more. Thorlak let go of the oar and surrendered to the darkness.

Nine

THE PRESENT

Dane was impressed with the efficiency of the *Glomar* crew. They could snatch a new section of pipe off the wall of the pool, use a crane to pull it up to the top of the derrick, then two men would clip safety lines around the pipe itself and bolt it to the section below while the entire thing was moving down at a steady rate. Just before the pipe went into the water, two other men clamped the power, oxygen, and communications cables to the side of the pipe, continuously unreeling the cables while making sure there were no snags.

Two hours earlier, *Deeplab IV* had been attached at the bottom of the very first section of eighteen-inch pipe. Lieutenant Sautran had waved once before disappearing into the hatch at the top of the central corridor. The hatch was screwed shut, final checks were made, and *Deeplab IV* disappeared beneath the waves.

As the pipes continued to be connected and pushed *Deeplab IV* deeper and deeper, Dane noticed something strange: the thick pipe that extended down from the derrick was moving up and down very slowly, independent of the ship. It was mesmerizing to watch.

Captain Stanton caught the look and explained. "It gets to you, doesn't it? We have to keep *Deeplab* stable. Can't have it bobbing like a cork on the end of the pipe. So we use an inertia dampener." He pointed to where the pipe was clamped between several rollers. "The ship is what is actually moving with the swell. The pipe is staying perfectly still. You should see that when we get rough water. The hydraulics attached to those rollers can move the pipe over thirty feet vertically if necessary. What feels weird is that you think you're standing still and it's moving, but somewhere in your mind, your body knows you're moving."

Dane's attention was diverted as a large Navy helicopter appeared on the southern horizon, something large slung below it.

"*Deepflight II* is arriving," Ariana said. She turned for the rear of the ship. "Let's go check it out."

Dane followed her and Sin Fen across the gantry and through the passageways until they reached the edge of the large helipad. By that time, the chopper had arrived, hovering fifty feet above the deck. Dangling below, attached by two cables, was the deep-sea submersible.

It was long and looked more like a plane with two bulging bubbles, one at the front and one in the middle, than a submarine. Several *Glomar* crew members ran out and insured the submersible touched down gently on the deck, then unhooked it. The helicopter moved away while they hooked *Deepflight*'s harness rig to the ship's rear crane. It was lifted once more and swung around the side of the ship. Dane and the others waited as the helicopter came back and settled down on the helipad. A man got off, and the chopper lifted and was gone.

Ariana led the way to greet the new arrival, a young-looking man in a bright red jumpsuit. He was tall and well-built, with thick black hair. Besides the jumpsuit, he wore a New York Yankees baseball cap, bill back, on his head.

"Jimmy DeAngelo at your service." He stuck his hand

out to Dane, and then each woman as they introduced themselves to him.

All the while, his eyes kept shifting to the submarine
teetering in the air, following it until it disappeared into the
well. "How soon are we going down?"

Dane glanced at Ariana, who shrugged. "As soon as
you're ready to take us."

DeAngelo nodded. "I'd say in forty-five minutes. I did
all my checks prior to coming here, but I want to make
sure all the handling hasn't damaged anything."

Three hundred and fifty feet below the lowest level of the
Pentagon proper was the Joint Chiefs of Staff's National
Military Command Center, commonly called the War
Room by those who worked there. It had been placed inside
a large cavern carved out of solid bedrock. The complex
could only be entered via one secure elevator and was
mounted on massive springs on the cavern floor. There was
enough food and supplies in the War Room for an emergency crew to operate for a year. Besides the lines that went
straight up to the Pentagon's own communications system,
a narrow tunnel holding backup cables had been laboriously
dug at the same depth to the alternate National Command
Post at Blue Mountain in West Virginia.

When it had been built in the early '60s, the War Room
had been designed to survive a nuclear first strike. The ad-
vances in both targeting and warhead technology over the
past three decades had made that design obsolete. There
was no doubt in the minds of anyone who worked in the
War Room that they were high on the list of Russian and
Chinese nuclear targeting, and that they would be vaporized
atoms shortly after any nuclear exchange. Because of that,
it had been turned into the operations center for the Pentagon.

The main room of the War Room was semicircular. On
the front, flat wall, there was a large imagery display board,

over thirty feet wide by twenty high. Any projection or scene that could be piped into the War Room could be displayed on this board, from a video of a new weapons system to a map of the world showing the current status of U.S. forces or a real-time downlink from an orbiting spy satellite.

The floor of the room was sloping from the rear to the front so that each row of computer and communications consoles could be overseen from the row behind. At the very back of the room, along the curved wall, a three-foot-high railing separated the command and control section where the joint chiefs and other high-ranking officers had their desks. A conference table was off to the right side of that. Supply, kitchen, and sleeping areas were off the rear of the room, in a separate cavern. The War Room had had its first taste of action during the Gulf War when it had operated full-time, coordinating the multinational forces in the Gulf.

Since the gates had activated, the War Room had been the central clearing point for all information regarding them. Foreman found that ironic, given that for over fifty years he had been the voice that cried in the wilderness against the danger he saw posed by the gates. Of course, he had not known they were gates or what the danger was for many of those years.

Foreman had been forced to use guile, deception, and even blackmail at times to keep his small section in the covert ops section of the CIA alive. In the beginning it had not been so hard as he was one of the founding members in 1947. But as the years went on and the old guard retired or died, it had become more of a struggle.

Claiming that Earth was being invaded by a strange force through gates he could not explain had caused many doors to be shut in Foreman's face, and he had learned to use deception more often than the truth, especially since he didn't know exactly what the truth was. As one of the founding members of the CIA, Foreman was an expert in the covert world, able to manipulate government agencies and millions of dollars of black budget money to support his activities over the years.

The activation of the gates and the nuclear attack out of the Bermuda Triangle gate had been a double-edged event for Foreman. The threat had been real and disaster narrowly averted by Dane destroying the propagating tower in Angkor Kol Ker. On the more positive side, Foreman was finally being taken seriously.

As he sat at one end of the War Room conference table, Foreman realized being taken seriously had its drawbacks. He was now part of the system, and as such, there were a lot of people asking a lot of questions, and the information flow had increased very dramatically to the point where he wasn't sure he was getting what he needed. Although he was expert at manipulating and operating in the gray covert world, Foreman knew he was not as adept at dealing with the massive bureaucracy of official Washington when it was brought to bear on a problem.

At the present moment, he was listening to the various services argue about the best way to stop a Trident if another was fired out of the Bermuda Triangle gate.

Half-listening to the military men argue, Foreman checked the computer display that was inset into the table in front of him. All seemed to be progressing well at the *Glomar. Deeplab* had passed through 10,000 feet.

On the other side of the world, Professor Nagoya had been underground for over twenty-four hours. It simply consumed too much time to go back to the surface, and all the work he needed to do could be done at the Super-Kamiokande control center. Ahana and the rest of the crew also remained there. Several bunks were attached to the wall in the outside corridor, and each person snatched sleep when they absolutely couldn't keep going any longer.

Several things were going on at once, and since there was only one Can, each series of experiments and surveillance data gathering had to be perfectly planned so that when time was allocated, the task could be accomplished in the most efficient manner and the next task begun as quickly as possible.

Besides monitoring the Bermuda Triangle gate every fifth task, the scientists under Nagoya's leadership were checking the other gates, trying to determine their exact configuration and whether they also had traces of muon activity extended outward in any form. Besides that, there was the basic research of trying to figure out what exactly the fact that the gates and gate-affected places outside of them gave off muon activity meant.

Nagoya believed that if he could figure out how the gates worked, he could figure out how to shut them.

The simple fact, which irritated Nagoya to no end, was that even though the gates emitted muons, the Can shouldn't be able to pick them up. A muon had a life span of only 2.2 microns when measured in a reference frame that was at rest with respect to them. Even given that the Can wasn't in rest—moving at the speed of Earth's rotation—the life span of the muon wouldn't be much longer, even in relative terms. They should be able to travel only about 600 meters before decaying into something else.

Yet thousands of miles away, the Can was able to trace out muon images from the Bermuda Triangle gate and other gates as they were scanned. Scientists Nagoya consulted with were struggling with issues like this that didn't neatly fit into hard physics. Quantum and wave physics had begun to explain some of this strange data, and Nagoya felt the key to understanding the gates, the essence of them, was to understand the physics surrounding them.

Nagoya was studying the data they'd accumulated in just the past few days, comparing it to the little they knew about muons. He'd been one of the members of a team that, in

1976 at the European Council for Nuclear Research (CERN) in Geneva, had tried to determine why even muons that were caused by the sun's rays hitting the atmosphere traveled farther than their life span indicated they should. Muons were injected into a large ring, reaching speeds of .999 the speed of light. At the time, the muons themselves could not be detected, but the electrons produced when the muons decayed could be, and thus the distance and rate of travel of the muons prior to the decay could be deduced.

The first thing they discovered was that moving muons had a life span almost thirty times longer than stationary muons. The reason for that lay in time dilation, according to the theory of relativity. Simply stated, time dilation meant that from a stationary observation point, a moving clock ran more slowly than an identical stationary clock.

That old data, combined with the new data Nagoya was now looking at, suggested several things to him. First, he assumed that the gate-emitted muons were not a cause but a by-product of some other action at the subatomic level. Second, whatever that action was, it was continuous, as all the gates they were now checking showed muon emission.

The problem Nagoya faced was analyzing real data as opposed to data generated under the controlled condition of a laboratory—on top of the rather large problem of possibly dealing with a totally new world of physics from the other side. He had to work his data while taking into account the Earth's rotation, mass of the Earth between the Can and the target site, distances; the list went on and on to the point where Nagoya almost despaired of coming up with anything coherent.

With his strong background in research, Nagoya had slanted the use of the Can more to gathering data than to surveillance of the gates. Because of that, despite the fact that Foreman was launching a mission near the site, the Can oriented on the Bermuda Triangle gate only once every six tasks, meaning there could be over two hours between peeks.

The Can had just finished a peek at the Bermuda gate, noting nothing out of the ordinary. It moved on to a peek at the Russian gate under Lake Baikal to gather data. It would not reorient on the Bermuda Triangle area for two hours, six minutes, and thirty-four seconds.

The rays of the sun are no longer visible to the unaided human eye deeper than 1,600 feet below the surface of any ocean. Even in the clean, blue water north of Puerto Rico, this law of the sea and evolution held true. Just over one-quarter of a mile below the surface of the ocean, darkness ruled.

Humans, of course, have always found ways around the laws nature tries to impose on them.

During World War II, submarines went no deeper than 400 feet, well within the range of the sun's rays, in what oceanographers called the sunlit zone, extending to 600 feet. Next was the twilight zone, which went from 600 to 3,000 feet. Then came the midnight zone, where darkness ruled.

Technology had come a long way since the diesel-fueled submarines of the Second World War in allowing man to penetrate the ocean depths. Modern military submarines now could go down to 3,000 feet and remain submerged for months at a time. Exploration submersibles had been used to photograph the wreckage of the *Titanic* in over 12,500 feet of water. The Japanese had sent a remotely piloted vehicle to the very bottom of the Earth's surface, the Challenger Deep in the Marianas Trench in the Pacific Ocean, at a depth of 10,911 meters or over 33,000 feet down. *Deepflight* was the cutting edge of the next generation of vehicles designed to explore the depths of the world's oceans.

Dane was in the front sphere with DeAngelo while Sin

Fen and Ariana had crawled into the rear one. There were no seats, but rather an inclined, padded frame on which Dane and the pilot lay stomach-down. Tethers went around their bodies, giving them some freedom but preventing them from hitting the walls around the couches.

The curved wall directly in front of their faces was a series of flat TV screens that showed the view outside. Other flat monitors gave instrument readings so DeAngelo could pilot the craft. Right now, they were still on the surface of the ocean next to the *Glomar*.

Besides numerous gauges and displays surrounding his position, DeAngelo had two levers in front of him with a short bar between them. He turned to Dane.

"It's really very easy. Each lever controls the propeller on that side. Push forward and that blade goes faster, pull back and it goes slower. There's a point right about here—" he pulled back both levers—"where the blade stops. Then, as you go farther back, it reverses direction, so if you want to pull a hard right turn, you max forward speed on your left, and max reverse on your right.

"You have to be careful though," DeAngelo added. "*Deepflight*'s center of mass is determined by the computer. It's checking right now, and we'll make trim as soon as we're released. This thing turns on a dime. It doesn't take much to flip her. Which is why you really need to make sure you tether in or drive very carefully.

"Then this center bar is ascent or descent. It controls the horizontal plane between the two propellers. Push forward and you go down. Pull back and you go up."

"And what if we lose all power?" Dane asked.

DeAngelo pointed to his right to a red cover, about two inches square. He lifted it up. A keyhole was underneath. "Put the key in, turn it, and we drop enough weight that we will go up."

"Who has the key?" Dane asked.

"It's around my neck on a chain."

"Can we talk to Ariana and Sin Fen in the rear sphere?"

DeAngelo flipped a switch. A view of the inside of the second sphere, Ariana and Sin Fen on their stomachs, looking up, appeared. Dane noted that there was a small camera above the screen that showed them, so he imagined they had the same view in reverse. DeAngelo handed Dane a headset and put one on himself.

"How are you ladies doing?" DeAngelo asked.

Ariana looked at them. "We're fine."

DeAngelo checked one of his displays. "We're in the water, but still slaved to the ship. The divers will release us in a minute or so. I'll get us trimmed, and then we'll start heading down.

"*Deepflight* is the most advanced submersible in the world," DeAngelo said as he checked instruments and threw switches. "It's more like flying an underwater plane than the traditional concept of a submersible. We also have redundancy on every major system, so it's extremely safe."

Dane felt the absence of Chelsea very keenly. De-Angelo's confidence did little to allay Dane's concerns about the upcoming mission. The thought of being cooped up in a confined space—whether in the submersible or the habitat—he found less than appealing. After returning from Vietnam and before being found once more by Foreman, Dane had spent over twenty years working in search and rescue. He had an uncanny ability to sense out people who were trapped, whether it be inside destroyed buildings or someone lost in the woods. The former had always been his least favorite mission while the latter was what he lived for.

He'd been in many confined areas while crawling through the ruins of buildings, but always with Chelsea. She was supposed to be the search and rescue dog and find the bodies, but in reality, it had been Dane's uncanny mental sense that allowed him to find those still alive. He'd relied on Chelsea for emotional support to get him through those difficult rescues.

He tried to block out his growing anxiety by studying the information packet on *Deeplab IV* Lieutenant Sautran had given them before departing for the depths.

The habitat was configured in three pressure-resistant modules connected by a center, vertical corridor. Each module was actually three pressure-resistant spheres set inside the outer protective cylinder wall, so there were a total of nine spheres, each independent of the others as far as pressure integrity goes. The only way into each sphere was through a hatch oriented toward the main corridor. The bottom of the main corridor had a hatch in it, allowing access to the ocean and submersibles.

Total living space was about 4,000 square feet, which when Dane divided by nine, didn't make him feel any better. And square was the wrong term to use as there seemed to be an obsession for round shapes in all the designs from habitat to submersible. Dane understood that was the best shape to handle the enormous pressures they would encounter, but understanding didn't necessarily entail happiness.

A new voice came through the headset: Captain Stanton. "*Deeplab* is in place at seventeen thousand feet. They report everything is working fine. You're cleared to descend and link up."

"Roger that," DeAngelo said.

"Godspeed and good luck," Stanton said. The cable link, their only means of communication, went dead as the divers on the outside disconnected it.

There was sudden movement.

"All right, we're free." DeAngelo's hands were wrapped around the two levers. "What you're feeling is the swell. That will be gone in a minute." He let go of the right lever and pushed the center bar up. Dane felt out of balance, as if his head were lower than the rest of his body.

"We're going down," DeAngelo said. "I want to get clear of surface effect, then I'll trim us out."

A minute passed, and the bobbing motion was gone. "OK," DeAngelo said. "I'm getting us balanced." He continued speaking as he worked. "The ship has several small ballast tanks placed around the hull. I'm shifting air to give us neutral buoyancy and also to balance us exactly, fore and aft." He held a hand over the mike. "I could have done it by computer, but I've learned never to ask a lady her weight. It's easier to do it manually."

Dane glanced up at the screen showing the rear sphere. Sin Fen and Ariana were trying to get as comfortable as possible.

"Done," DeAngelo said. "We're heading down." He pressed forward on the center bar, then pulled back on both levers, the right one farther back than the left. "We're going down in a half-mile left-turn spiral."

"How long until we're there?" Dane asked. The only sound since they slipped under the surface of the water had been the hum of the engines and DeAngelo's running commentary. At least there was none of the creaking and cracking noises Dane associated with going deep underwater, a legacy of too many World War II submarine movies.

"We're going down at four hundred feet a minute," DeAngelo said. "To get to seventeen thousand feet will take about forty-five minutes."

"Have you been in the lab before?" Dane asked.

DeAngelo shook his head. "I didn't even know something like *Deeplab IV* existed before Foreman lined all this up. The military must have kept it deep in the black." He smiled. "No pun intended."

"None taken," Dane said. He studied the outside camera view relayed on the screens in front. The blue water quickly became dark green, then began fading to black.

"Lights on." DeAngelo flipped a switch, and a halo of light surrounded the sub. To Dane, it felt as if they were suspended in a black void, with no sense of movement, totally cut off from the rest of the world.

"The pipe is off to our left," DeAngelo said. "I'm going to spiral down around it but keep it at a safe distance."

On the surface above *Deepflight*, Captain Stanton was settled into his command chair, a large, deep, leather seat bolted to the deck directly behind the helmsman station. There was the traditional wheel at the station, but more importantly, an extremely accurate ground positioning receiver currently getting input from five GPS satellites. Next to the GPR was a series of controls for the thrusters that kept the *Glomar* in position. They were run by computer, insuring that the large ship stayed within half a foot of the same spot on the surface of the ocean.

With the automated positioning system and the automated dampening system on the pipe, there was little for those on board the *Glomar* to do other than wait. It was a situation Stanton was used to. He reached into the pocket on the side of his chair and pulled out a paperback. He had just opened it to the first page when his radar man broke the silence.

"Sir, I have a contact!"

Stanton put the book down. "Where?"

"Directly below. Depth twenty-seven thousand feet."

Stanton stood and walked over to the radar console. "That can't be."

"It just appeared on-screen, sir."

"What is it?"

"It doesn't fit any known profile, sir. It's big!"

"What about the profile we were given from the *Scorpion*?" Stanton asked. The thought of something six times the size of a Soviet Typhoon class sub staggered even the captain of a ship the size of the *Glomar*.

"It could be, sir. Matches up in size. It's not like anything I've ever seen before."

"Where did it come from? How come you didn't pick up something that big earlier?"

"I don't know, sir. It just appeared."

"What's it doing?" Stanton asked as he went over to the communications array.

"Ascending, sir. Toward *Deeplab*."

Stanton picked up the phone that linked the *Glomar* to *Deeplab* through the cable attached to the pipe. "How quickly?"

"Very fast, sir! Depth twenty thousand feet and rising!"

Stanton picked up the phone. "*Deeplab*, this is *Glomar*."

The phone crackled with static. Stanton thought he heard something, a voice, but he couldn't be sure. "*Deeplab*, this is *Glomar*," he repeated.

"Eighteen thousand feet and rising!"

Stanton's hand tightened on the phone. "*Deeplab*, this is *Glomar*." He pointed a finger at his communications officer. "Get me Foreman."

"Seventeen thousand feet. Holding."

"*Deeplab*, this is *Glomar*." The only sound in the receiver of the handset was static.

"I've got Foreman on SATCOM." The com officer held out another phone.

Stanton paused as he grabbed the phone. The entire ship shook, and there was a loud screeching sound from the derrick.

"We're deeper now than the *Titanic*," DeAngelo said.

"Is that supposed to cheer me up?" Dane asked. He shook his head, trying to ease a pounding in his left temple. "Sin Fen?" he said into the boom mike.

"Yes?"

Dane looked up at the screen displaying Ariana and Sin Fen. "How are you feeling?"

"My head hurts."

"Mine, too," Dane said. "Something's not right."

DeAngelo scanned his gauges. "Everything's reading correctly."

"Not here," Dane said.

"*Deeplab,*" Sin Fen said.

Dane nodded. "Something's wrong."

"Should I turn back?" DeAngelo asked.

Dane closed his eyes and was silent for a few seconds. "No. We keep going."

"Get me Nagoya!" Foreman ordered. He turned back to the microphone that linked the War Room with the *Glomar Explorer*. "Status?"

"The contact is descending." Captain Stanton's voice echoed out of the speakers that lined the roof of the cavern. "Twenty thousand feet and going down as quickly as it came up."

"*Deeplab?*" Foreman asked.

"Readouts from the umbilical say everything is functioning fine, but no one is answering the phone. It's stable now."

"*Deepflight?*"

"We have it on radar," Stanton said. "Passing through fifteen thousand and still descending on the planned glide path."

"There's no way to communicate with it?" Foreman asked.

"No, sir," Stanton replied.

An Air Force officer thrust a SATPhone at Foreman. "We have commo with Dr. Nagoya."

Foreman took the phone. "Nagoya, what readings do you have in the Bermuda Triangle gate?"

"We're not currently oriented toward the Bermuda Triangle," Nagoya replied.

"Damn it!" Foreman slapped his hand against the top of the conference table. "I've got people down there. Reorient now!" He hit the off button for the phone as Captain Stanton's voice echoed out of the speakers.

"Object is gone. It just blinked out at twenty-seven thousand feet."

"What about *Deeplab*?" Foreman asked.

"Still there. Still no communication."

"Nagoya," Foreman yelled into the radio, "get me some readings!"

Deeplab reminded Dane of a hornet's nest, hanging from a thin branch. The sub's lights highlighted the lab against the surrounding dark ocean. A single lamp glowed where the pipe was bolted into the top of the lab.

"Shouldn't there be more lights?" Dane asked.

"Why?" DeAngelo had brought them out of the spiral and was slowly approaching the habitat dead-on. "They have no windows. They do have cameras and infrared imagers, but there's usually no need to have them on. What are they going to see at this depth, anyway?"

Dane glanced up at the screen showing the interior of the rear sphere. Sin Fen had her hands against the side of her head, eyes closed in concentration. Dane closed himself off to the space around him and opened his mind as Sin Fen had taught him.

The habitat was less than forty feet in front of them. DeAngelo went into a slight dive to come up under the central access.

"Something happened," Dane said.

"What?" DeAngelo was concentrating on piloting, eyes shifting between the forward display and his radar, which was counting down the feet between them and the habitat.

Dane opened his eyes. Sin Fen was staring at him in the screen. "Do you know?" Dane asked her.

"No."

"What's going on?" Ariana asked.

"I feel something very strange," Dane said.

"Hold on," DeAngelo warned as he shifted the imager view to the top camera. They were directly below the habitat, the bottom hatch less than five feet away from the top of the forward sphere, and closing. With a slight thud, they made contact and came to a halt.

"We'll go in first," DeAngelo said, "make sure it's secure, then I'll come back in, move forward, let you out, go back, and anchor us in. I'm pressurizing the lock," he added.

The difficulty of even the slightest maneuver or operation at deep pressure reminded Dane of the missions he had conducted in Special Forces in extreme cold weather environments. There, every little task had to be thought out thoroughly before being attempted, and then it would take two to three times as long to conduct than it would in a more temperate zone. A mistake that would normally cause no more than a minor inconvenience could be fatal in such an environment.

"I've got a seal." DeAngelo was reading his gauges.

For the first time since they were lowered into the water, he let go of the controls and turned onto his back, then sat up. He reached up and slid open a control panel on the side of the hatch.

"I confirm a seal," DeAngelo said as a green light came on in the panel. He looked at Dane over his shoulder and smiled. "If we open this thing without a seal—well, we wouldn't even know what killed us."

Dane heard him, but he was concentrating, trying to get a feel for what lay above. When he had searched for people, Dane had always been able to pick up people's auras, the projections from their conscious—and even at times, subconscious—minds. Now he was reading nothing other than a vague sense of shock and fear.

"Releasing secondary lock." DeAngelo threw a switch.

Dane reached out to Sin Fen with his mind. He felt her presence and she reacted to his probe, confirming she was picking up the same disturbing impression from the habitat.

"Do we have a weapon on board?" Dane asked.

"A weapon?" DeAngelo was momentarily confused. "Why would we carry a weapon? You shoot a gun down here, it's the opposite of shooting one in an airplane with a hundred times worse results. You puncture or even weaken the hull around us, we don't depressurize, we pressurize, which means we implode. Besides, what do we need a weapon for?"

Dane shook his head. "Forget it."

DeAngelo went back to his checklist. "Secondary lock disengaged. Equalizing pressure." He hit a button.

Dane felt his ears pop.

"Primary lock disengaging." DeAngelo hit a red button.

There was a solid thud as the locks in the hatch cycled back. DeAngelo unbuckled his harness, and Dane did the same.

"Give me a hand." DeAngelo was now on his knees, hands on the hatch handle. "Push."

Dane did as instructed, and with a slight hesitation, the hatch swung up into the lock. A splash of water came in, hitting both DeAngelo and Dane.

DeAngelo now used the handle as a step to get into the lock. Five feet above their heads was the bottom hatch for *Deeplab IV*.

"We're here guys!" he yelled. He looked down. "They'll open as soon as they're sure we're open and secure."

Dane looked up. "No, they won't."

DeAngelo frowned. "Why not?"

"Because there's no one alive in there."

Ten

999 A.D.

As far as Ragnarok was concerned, the only good thing that had happened since setting foot on dry land was that he had gotten a new ax head made by a Saxon blacksmith. Other than that, the trip had been misery. Traveling only at night to avoid raising an alarm, Ragnarok plodded after Tam Nok as they went north. The only weather that England seemed to have was cloudy and rainy. They slept during the day, or tried to sleep, Ragnarok too concerned with security to get more than a few minutes of slumber here and there. He wasn't used to walking so much, and his leather boots had chafed the skin raw at several places on his feet.

They had beached the longship along the coast to the west of the Isle of Man. As soon as Ragnarok and Tam Nok were ashore, Hrolf had the crew push the craft back into the water. Ragnarok had stood on the beach, watching his ship disappear into the night. They would meet back at the same place in six days.

Two of those days had already passed, filled with nothing but walking through forests and over hills and fields.

Ragnarok could tell by the stars they were going northward, but he had no idea how Tam Nok was choosing their path or what their destination was. When he questioned her, she told him the gods were leading her, and she would know where they were going when they got there; neither a very satisfactory answer.

He had managed to persuade her to halt long enough for him to enter a village early one morning and find a blacksmith. The man had been half-frightened out of his wits to see a hulking Viking appear in the low doorway to his smithy, but a few gold pieces had induced him to bring out a large ax head, such as the Saxons used to kill cattle, and spend all that day on the forge and anvil fashioning it in the shape Ragnarok wished.

"I will call it Bone Cutter," Ragnarok said, taking a slash with the ax through the air in front of him. It was dark, and the land was growing flatter. Tam Nok was at his side, walking with a steady stride that never seemed to grow weary. She carried a pack with an equal share of the food and water without the slightest complaint. Ragnarok had to fight hard to keep from limping.

"What?" Tam Nok didn't pause nor did she even look at him.

Ragnarok waved the war ax. "I said I will call it Bone Cutter. It has a good feel, and that Saxon oaf did a good job with the edge. It is much sharper than my last one. It will slice through flesh and bone."

"Is a name for your weapon important?"

Ragnarok was mystified that she would even ask such a question. "Of course. In battle, a good weapon is a man's closest friend."

"I have been in battle and I have killed," Tam Nok said, "but I do not view my weapons as my friends."

Ragnarok shrugged, the gesture lost in the dark. "That is because you do not see battle for what it really is."

He waited for her to ask the inevitable question but the

next couple of miles passed in silence. Tam Nok was the strangest woman he'd ever met. Not only because of her dark skin and strange eyes but even more so because of her actions. Viking women were strong and well-respected, but even they did not travel by themselves or wield weapons except when absolutely necessary. A Viking woman was most concerned with family and children, yet there was no sense about Tam Nok of that.

The moon was full, making the traveling at night easier but also making them more vulnerable to being spotted. Ragnarok was not overly concerned at being found at night. Most men did not seek out trouble in the dark, and unless they had the misfortune to encounter a large armed force, he felt they would be left alone.

They crested a small hill, and Ragnarok scanned the terrain ahead. A large plain extended to the horizon, but sparks of light in the distance caught his eye.

"Torches," he said, pointing. They were too far away to tell how many lights there were or what the holders of the lights were doing.

"I see them." Tam Nok didn't break stride.

Ragnarok noticed something else unusual. "I do not like this," he said, tapping Tam Nok on the arm and pointing. Large, unnatural mounds dotted the plain in front of them, most around a hundred feet long by seventy in width by ten in height.

"What don't you like?" Tam Nok asked.

"Those are burial mounds. This entire plain is a graveyard. It brings bad fortune to walk through such a place."

Tam Nok spared him a glance. "We can not go around. They are between us and where we wish to go."

"The place with the torches?" Ragnarok asked.

"Yes." Tam Nok's voice held an edge of irritation. "The person I must talk to is there. We do not have much time."

"How can you know we don't have much time?" Ragnarok asked, not at all impressed with her pronouncements after strolling across England for over two days. "How can you know that is the place we are to go, and the person you want to meet is there?"

Tam Nok paused. "The people we are to meet are like me. They are priests and priestesses. Not of the new religions—Christian or Muslim—but of the old religions. Ones who worship the old gods—the Ones Before whom the ancient ones worshipped. Your legends, your gods, they came out of the legends of the Ones Before. You must let me deal with these people. I understand them. You will have nothing to fear if you do what I say."

"Since you answer none of my questions," Ragnarok said, "I have little choice but to follow your lead. But there is nothing I fear," he added.

"There are things you have not seen yet," Tam Nok said, "so it is not good to boast."

"I am not boasting," Ragnarok said.

"We shall see."

"I fought the Valkyries and their creatures," Ragnarok noted.

Without a reply, Tam Nok strode off into the dark, and Ragnarok followed, frustrated at her lack of acknowledgment.

They passed several of the large burial mounds. They were somewhat different than the burial mounds Ragnarok was used to. Vikings also interred their dead in mounds, usually shaped in the form of a ship, with rocks to delineate the edges. A Viking leader would be buried with his favorite ship inside a mound, a truly extravagant arrangement that indicated the honor owed that leader by his people. A slave girl might also be slain and put in the ship with him to make his journey to Valhalla more pleasant. Certainly more pleasant than this journey he was on, Ragnarok reflected. These English mounds were larger, and the tops were not decorated with stones. He also sensed they were old, very old.

Death was but a new beginning for a Viking who had led a life of honor and glory. It was the journey to Valhalla, where more battles, even more glorious than those on Earth, awaited the warrior. That was why it was essential that a warrior be buried with his weapons. Ragnarok knew the strange woman, even though she claimed to be a disir, would not understand. It was the reason his ax had a name and why regaining the weapon had been the most important thing for him to do as soon as they landed.

The lights were growing closer, numerous torches glittering in the crystal-clear night under the bright moon. There was a noise now, something Ragnarok couldn't quite make out. Almost like the cry of the Valkyries he had heard just before meeting Tam Nok, but different, of the Earth, although how he knew that, he could not say.

The silhouettes of two objects began to take form on the horizon, about a mile away. One was a towering tree, as large as any pine Ragnarok had ever seen, but this one stood alone on the plain and had leaves and many, many branches. The torchbearers were gathered all around the base of the tree in a wide circle.

The other, a quarter mile to the right, was not a tree—that was all Ragnarok could tell—although it was as tall as the tree. The sound seemed to be coming from that direction. Peer as much as he could, Ragnarok could not make it out, although it might have been some sort of guard or siege tower, rising sixty feet into the sky.

"There is someone just ahead," Tam Nok said. "Do not attack."

"What do you—" Ragnarok began, but then a figure, sword raised, suddenly loomed out of the dark, as if spat out of the earth itself, ten feet in front of them. The man barked out something in a strange tongue Ragnarok had never heard, obviously a challenge.

Ragnarok hefted his ax and prepared to strike, but Tam Nok stepped between. She spoke rapidly in the same tongue. It occurred to him that it was strange she spoke his tongue, coming from so far away. He wondered how many languages she knew and how she had learned them.

Those thoughts were brushed away as the stranger lowered his sword and replied to Tam Nok in the same tongue, then turned and pointed them toward the tree. The man disappeared into a fold in the ground, pulling a cloak over his body to help conceal his location. Ragnarok was not impressed. Hiding in a hole in the ground to ambush strangers did not seem very honorable.

The strange noise grew louder, and Ragnarok could now discern that there were two noises intermingled. One was coming from the tree ahead, a chanting of human voices, lower-pitched than the other sound, which was a terrible keening, worse than the cries of Viking women upon learning the ship their mates sailed out on would never be coming back.

"What is going on?" Ragnarok hissed at Tam Nok, but she waved a hand, hushing him.

He could see now that the torches were carried by white-robed men and women standing in a circle around the tree. There were about sixty of these. Inside of that outer circle was a second group of twenty, also holding torches, these robed in green.

Near the massive trunk of the tree, the light from the outer torches illuminated a group of ten people, eight robed in blue, and two others, one in black and one in red. They were all facing toward the tree and chanting. The red-robed figure turned toward Ragnarok and Tam Nok, as if waiting for them.

Tam Nok raised her hands and called out a greeting as they approached the white-robed circle. There was no reply, but the circle stood aside to let them pass, as did the ring of blue. The chanting still continued from both circles, and Ragnarok was now certain that the strange noise was coming from the other tall object to his right.

The figure robed in red who had watched their arrival broke from the group next to the trunk and came toward them. The rest of the group kept its attention on whatever it had been doing.

Tam Nok again spoke in the strange tongue. Ragnarok felt out of place. His ax was heavy, pulling his left arm down. The chanting was running through his mind, urging him to join in. He shook his head, dirty hair twisting in the wind, and growled. The tree seemed to be alive, the bark gnarled and twisted from hundreds, thousands of years of life, the branches drooping overhead, covering them. Drawing him into the earth, to be one with the soil.

"Your friend is restless." A woman's voice came out of the red hood, speaking in Norse.

"There is not much time," Tam Nok said.

The other woman pulled her hood back, revealing pale skin and fiery red hair. "I am Penarddun."

"I am Tam Nok, and this is Ragnarok."

Penarddun smiled. "A mighty warrior of the north seas. You travel in formidable company."

Ragnarok shifted his feet, trying to stay focused on the two women. He was not sure if she was referring to him or Tam Nok. The chanting was getting even louder. And that eerie noise was still floating on the air.

"I need—" Tam Nok began, but the other woman held up her hand.

"I know what you are looking for."

"Is it here?"

"No."

The chanting abruptly stopped. The black robed figure— a man, as near as Ragnarok could tell—yelled out something in the strange tongue and then headed toward the other tall object, the others falling in behind him.

Penarddun extended a hand toward the tree. "We worship the mighty oak, symbol of the Earth Mother." The slender hand continued toward the other tall object. "And

there we sacrifice to the Ones Before. Come." She followed
the last in line, and Ragnarok reluctantly followed. For
some strange reason, he had no desire to see the cause of
the terrible noise.

As he drew nearer—and the torches illuminated more of
it as the robed ones gathered round—he began to make out
the form. It was a huge figure made of wood and wicker,
over sixty feet high, formed in the image of a man. Two
legs rose to a thick body. Two arms hung at the sides, and
at the very top was a head, made of bent wooden staves.

Ragnarok's hand tightened on the handle of his ax. Inside the wooden confines of the structure were people.
Crammed in, some standing on others, arms poking between the beams, their supplicating voices the horrible
sound he had been hearing. The writhing forms captured
inside made for a bizarre spectacle, as if the wooden creature were alive, its skin crawling with some malignant dis-
ease trying to get out.

"What is this?" Ragnarok hissed at Tam Nok, but she
hushed him.

"It is their way," she whispered.

"Those captured inside are murderers, thieves, betray-
ers," Penarddun said as if she had overheard. They halted
about fifty feet away as the same circles that had surrounded the oak re-formed around the wicker man. The
voices of those inside rose even higher, begging for release,
for mercy.

"The gods listen best if the message is coated in blood,"
Penarddun said.

Ragnarok was surprised at such words coming out of
such a slight and beautiful woman. He had seen many horrible things done in combat, but this was something he had
never experienced.

"And the message is very important," Penarddun continued. She turned to Tam Nok. "Is it not?"

"I don't—" Tam Nok began, but Penarddun cut her off.

"The Shadow is coming once more. And we need the Ones Before to help us stop the Shadow." Her voice lowered so that only Tam Nok and Ragnarok could hear. "My fellow Druids believe this is the best way to get the help of the Ones Before. But you and I know there is another way. They do not hear the true voices of the gods, but we do."

The man robed in black took a torch from one of those in blue. He walked toward the base of the wicker man. The priest thrust the torch into one of the legs of the statue. One of the prisoners kicked it back out.

The priest turned and raised his arms, yelling something. The circle of Druids closed on the wicker man and flung their torches at it. In seconds, flames caught hold at a dozen places.

The screams of those trapped inside rose to a fever pitch. Ragnarok watched as limbs smashed against the wood in desperate attempts to escape, bones breaking almost unnoticed in the grip of the searing flames.

Ragnarok looked to his right. Penarddun's face was lit by the fire, appearing almost translucent. Tam Nok had also pulled her hood back and her dark eyes were watching the gruesome spectacle with no expression.

"Is this getting us any closer to our destination?" Ragnarok asked.

Both women turned to him in surprise.

"You said you knew what we were here for," Ragnarok said to Penarddun. "If it is not here, where is it?"

Penarddun turned from the fire. "Do you know what the 'it' is you are searching for?"

"You said you knew why I was here," Tam Nok said.

"I know why you are here," Penarddun agreed. "I know you need something I am to give you. I know where it is, but I don't know what it is. It is the nature of our position to only be given pieces of knowledge."

Ragnarok shifted his feet impatiently. "Where?"

Penarddun pointed to the north. "That way. Not far."

A man had broken through the wood, high up on the wicker man. He fell to the ground, his hair on fire. The body slammed into the earth, and the man feebly tried to rise. One of the Druids ran forward with a dagger and slit the man's throat, blood splattering the dirt. The wails and screams were decreasing as those inside succumbed to the flames. Ragnarok was glad the wind was at their back and that the odor of burned flesh was being blown away from them.

Penarddun finally turned from the dying flames. "Come." She walked to the black-robed man and spoke to him in the strange tongue. He looked Tam Nok and Ragnarok over, then replied. They seemed to be arguing about something.

"What now?" Ragnarok asked Tam Nok.

"He doesn't want her to lead us to wherever it is we must go. It is apparently a very holy site. He is scared," she added. "The Druids have many enemies."

"Not as many as they had before," Ragnarok noted, nodding his head toward the remains of the wicker man.

"The Romans tried destroying them for centuries, hunting them down like animals," Tam Nok said. "And now that the Romans are no longer here, it is those of the new religion, the Christians, who seek to destroy the old ways and replace them with their new beliefs. The king in London has been converted and is being urged to destroy the Druids."

"How do you know all this?" Ragnarok asked.

"I have listened while on my journeys," Tam Nok said. "Something I recommend to all who travel."

Before Ragnarok could reply to that, Tam Nok stepped forward, next to the two high Druids. She spoke to them in their tongue, then pulled out the bamboo section. She unstopped the end and showed them the map and writing she had shown Ragnarok on his ship.

The black-robed priest still seemed opposed. Tam Nok rolled the parchments up and put them back in her tube. She pulled something out of the neckline of her cloak, an amulet attached to a thin metal chain around her neck. It glittered in the reflected light of the dying fire of the wicker man. A blue glow suffused Tam Nok's hand and seemed to spread out over those close to her.

Penarddun and the priest dropped to their knees, bowing their heads toward Tam Nok. The other Druids, seeing their leaders, did the same until they were surrounded by supplicating figures.

Tam Nok spoke quickly in their tongue, and Penarddun stood. "Let us go," she said. They walked out of the circle of still-kneeling Druids toward the north.

Ragnarok started to ask Tam Nok what the amulet was, but she hushed him. He fell in step as they passed between two burial barrows. A slight breeze had started to blow, and Ragnarok caught the scent of burned flesh. He bowed his head and breathed only through his mouth.

Eleven

THE PRESENT

Dane had always let Chelsea find the bodies on their search and rescue missions. When she went after human scent, it usually didn't matter whether they were dead or alive. In fact, Dane knew Chelsea could usually smell a dead body more clearly than a live one, depending on the length of time since death. Dane, on the other hand, could only sense the thoughts coming from the live ones and nothing from the dead, so whenever they went into a search situation, he concentrated on trying to save the living while his golden retriever located the bodies and Dane marked them for recovery.

But Chelsea was over three miles above his head. And Dane had ordered DeAngelo back into *Deepflight*, to await the results of his reconnaissance. As he climbed up the ladder in the central corridor of *Deeplab*, the feeling in his gut reminded Dane of all his cross-border missions into Laos and Cambodia during the Vietnam War when he had been a member of the classified SOG (Studies and Observation Group) unit. Already a decorated Green Beret, Dane had been drafted into SOG, and then his team had been picked by Foreman to run a mission deep into Cambodia to search for a downed SR-71 spy plane.

Foreman had neglected to tell Dane's team—Reconnaissance Team Kansas (RT Kansas)—that the SR-71 had disappeared while flying over the Angkor Kol Ker gate. In fact, Foreman told Dane and his teammates nothing. And within minutes of crossing a stream and entering the Angkor gate, every other man in the patrol was dead or had disappeared.

Dane knew *Deeplab IV* wasn't inside a gate. He would have been able to feel that. But something had happened here. He'd felt it while they were descending, and he felt it now, a faint image, floating at the edge of his consciousness, like trying to remember a bad dream after a restless night.

Something had been here. And from the lingering sensations, it was something that had come out of the gate.

Dane climbed through an opening in a metal grate, then paused at the top hatches. There were three, evenly spaced around the cylinder. Green, red and blue, level 3. Red 3 was the command sphere. Blue 3 was communications. Green 3 was the escape pod. Dane checked the status board for Green 3. It indicated that the pod was gone.

Dane cleared the safety on the door for Blue 3. Once he had a blinking green light, he began manually turning the handle. It was cold in the central corridor, despite the glow of two electrical heaters, both at the bottom. After thirty seconds, the handle clicked and stopped moving. The light turned to a steady green. Dane pulled the hatch out on pneumatic arms. He pulled himself through the three-foot-wide opening into the communications sphere.

It was empty. Dane looked at the rows of blinking lights and dials. The overhead light began flashing, and if that wasn't enough, a metallic voice announced that the sphere was unsecured and the hatch needed to be shut.

Dane ignored both the light and voice. He went over to

a console and picked up the phone that linked the habitat with the surface.

"Is someone there?" The voice on the other end sounded anxious. "What's going on?"

Dane stared at the phone in his hand for a second, then put it back in place without saying anything. He went back out, shutting the hatch behind. He opened the door to Red 3, the command and control console.

He sat down in the commander's seat and swung the laptop computer mounted on an arm in front of him. It was on, a screensaver showing sharks and stingrays swimming across the screen. Someone with a sense of humor must have put that in, Dane thought as he hit the Enter key.

The screensaver disappeared and he was presented with an index showing the various parts of the master computer. Dane ran his finger across the touchpad until the arrow was centered over History. He double-clicked.

He was presented with a new set of choices. Dane choose Log for his first investigation. Lieutenant Sautran's voice echoed out of a speaker. It began with his initial confirmation of all systems positive and everything running in the norm as *Deeplab* was lowered into the water from the *Glomar*.

Dane began fast-forwarding, searching for a point at which things got out of the norm. He found it just after Sautran reported *Deeplab* arriving at its current depth.

"We have a contact," Sautran reported. "Directly below."

There was a burst of static, then Sautran's voice came back.

"It's ascending. Eight thousand feet below and rising rapidly. Very big. About the size of the *Scorpion* bogey. We're trying to make contact by pinging with sonar."

There were a few moments of silence.

"No reply," Sautran's voice was calm. Dane could only imagine what was going through the naval lieutenant's mind as something huge came up toward them from the deepest part of the Atlantic Ocean. "Lou, is it mechanical or living?"

Sautran must have left the log recorder on as he talked to one of his two crew members. Dane opened another window on the laptop screen. It showed the status of the members of the crew at the same time of the recording of the log.

Sautran's symbol was in the same sphere Dane was currently in. Lou Wilkins, the crew's imaging specialist, was in Green 1, on the lowest level, where the main imaging units all terminated. Bob Freeman, the habitat specialist, was in Red 2, the habitat's life systems sphere.

"Uh—" Wilkins's voice was in the background, coming over the intercom. "Hard to tell, L-T. It's moving straight up. All I've got is radar and sonar. But there's nothing on the planet that big and alive. Hell, there's nothing been built that big, either. I'm trying—" There was a burst of static.

"Lou?" Sautran's voice now had an edge to it.

"Five thousand feet and rising," Wilkins reported. "Geez, this thing is ascending fast. We don't have anything that can come up that quickly under control. Even the Japanese don't have anything that—" Static again.

Sautran was no longer talking to the log, leaving the recorder running as he dealt with this unexpected situation.

"Freeman, get out of there. Get to the pod. Everyone to the pod. ASAP!"

Dane nodded. Sautran was doing the right thing.

"Lou, give me something. What is this thing?"

"Two thousand feet below and still closing," Wilkins reported. "I'm turning on the IR searchlights and imagers. See if we can't get a look-see at—geez!" Wilkins's voice went up several octaves. "Everything's going nuts here."

"Same here, Lou." Sautran's voice was tight. "I'm reading major systems failures everywhere. Life support is—"

Static for several seconds. "—failure—" static "—divert-
ing—"

The recorder went dead, catching Dane by surprise, his
ears straining to try to hear through the static. Dane waited,
letting it play out for another minute, but there was nothing.

He checked the window that showed crew member
status. All signs had also blipped out. Total systems failure
across the board. Dane looked about the command sphere.
He wasn't an expert, but everything seemed to be working
fine now. He checked current crew member status. Nothing.
They were all gone. Or their crew indicator sensors were
gone. But Dane knew, without having to check the other
six remaining spheres he hadn't been in, that there was
nobody on board but him. At least they'd managed to escape in the pod. Dane assumed that the *Glomar* would recover the sphere once it reached the surface.

He got out of the chair and left the command sphere to
climb down and let Sin Fen and Ariana inside.

The National Security Agency was established in 1952 by
President Truman as part of the Department of Defense. Its
mission was to focus on communications and cryptological
intelligence, a field known as SIGINT, or signals intelligence.

While the majority of what the NSA did was highly
classified, it was widely accepted that the organization was
the largest employer of mathematicians in the world.

One of those mathematicians who had been with the
organization for over two decades was Patricia Conners.
She'd worked various jobs in the organization from code-
making to code-breaking. She'd moved over to remote imagery five years ago and was considered one of the top
people in the agency not only in interpreting data down-
loaded from the various spy systems the United States military employed but in the actual operation of those systems.

Conners was in her mid-fifties, a short, gray-haired lady,

whose benign appearance belied a razor-sharp mind. She had been involved in the gates when running imagery from spy satellites at Foreman's request.

Her office was two floors beneath the main NSA building at Fort Meade. She did all her work through the large computer that took up most of the desktop. On the left side of the computer she had a large framed picture of her grandchildren gathered together at the last family reunion, all six of them, two via her daughter and four from two sons. On the right side of the computer was a pewter model of the starship *Enterprise*, the one from the original TV series. Stuck on the side of her monitor were various bumper stickers from the science fiction conventions she religiously traveled to every year, ranging from one indicating the bearer was a graduate of Star Fleet Academy to another warning that the driver braked for alien landings.

In the past week, it seemed like science fiction had become science fact as the assault came through the gates and was only narrowly stopped at the last minute. But now there were triangular-shaped gates at locations around the world that resisted every type of imaging that had been tried.

Conners knew about the Super-Kamiokande, and right now, that seemed to be the primary way they could detect activity around the gates. She had a direct link to the Can and also to Foreman in the War Room. Her job was to maintain a watch with the regular imaging devices on the off chance something changed and they could see in, or, more likely, if something was detected coming out of the gates.

As part of that, she was linked to the Navy's SOSUS array, keeping an eye on underwater activity around those gates located in the water. SOSUS had picked up the disturbance coming out of the Milwaukee Depth, but the system wasn't fast enough to allow them to alert the *Glomar*. Besides, Conners knew the *Glomar*'s own radar and sonar couldn't have missed picking up something that big.

Conners was running through the programs, making sure they were all running properly, when something in the SO-SUS data caused her to pause.

She stared at the screen for almost ten seconds before realizing what she was seeing. "Goddamn," she muttered as she picked up the phone that linked her to Foreman.

Thirty miles to the northwest of Dane's position, the *Seawolf* was finally in its designated patrol area on the edge of the Bermuda Triangle gate.

Captain McCallum had the submarine surface so he could maintain a satellite link with the War Room. He climbed the ladder to the top of the sail along with the watch crew. Training his binoculars to the east, he could see the solid black wall that marked the edge of the gate.

Two decks down and to the rear of where McCallum was, Captain Bateman took several CD-ROM discs out of a large bank and stuffed them in his shirt pocket.

He stood up and left the wardroom and headed forward, passing through the command and control room. He noted that the hatch to the sail was open but continued on to the helm.

Three men were seated facing a bank of instruments and displays. A chief petty officer was in a higher chair directly behind them. Bateman watched them for a few seconds, then continued forward in the ship until he came to the combat systems' electronic space. Two men were over-watching banks of computers that ran every system in the ship.

Bateman shut the pressure hatch behind himself, the only way out of the room, and began turning the handle.

One of the ratings in the room cleared his throat. "Sir, that door is to remain open unless—"

Bateman pulled the pistol out of his belt, turned, and fired, cutting off the rest of the sentence and blowing the man's brains all over the gray-painted side of a computer hard drive. The other sailor stared in disbelief, which changed to shock as Bateman fired again, hitting him in the stomach. The man dropped to his knees. Bateman fired again, a shot directly to the heart, killing him.

Bateman clamped down the lock on the handle, insuring that he would be left alone.

Then he turned to the computers, pulling the CD-ROMs out of his pocket. He inserted the first one in a laptop and brought up the information he wanted. He used a screwdriver to pull the cover off one of the pieces of hardware and went to work.

Twelve

999 A.D.

They passed swiftly between more barrows, the unnatural formations forming small valleys between them. Ragnarok was glad to be putting distance between themselves and the wicker man, but his sense of foreboding didn't abate. This was a strange land and a strange folk. Worshiping oak trees and burning people as a gift to the gods, chanting in the darkness, all were things foreign to Ragnarok, and he longed for the feel of a swaying deck under his feet.

The two women moved like wraiths, their long legs swinging back and forth under their cloaks through the knee-high grass. Ragnarok followed, his ax resting on his shoulder, towering over both of them. He had done more walking in the last three days and nights than ever in his life.

"We must arrive before dawn," Penarddun said, "or else hide. The king's men will be searching."

"Why?" Ragnarok asked.

"Because he has sworn allegiance to the Christians," Penarddun said. "He has turned his back on the old ways. Every so often, when the bishop of the Christians squeals, he sends soldiers to hunt us down. Fortunately, there is not much profit in it, or else he would do it all the time."

"There are older ways than your beliefs," Tam Nok said.

"That is most likely so," Penarddun agreed. "But I only know what I know. Much has been lost over the years. Where we are going is part of that older way. If what you seek is not there, then I know not where it is."

Tam Nok suddenly halted, holding up her hand to indicate for the others to stop also. Her head turned, almost like an animal sniffing the night. Ragnarok looked to and fro, but all he saw were the barrows dotting the plains that surrounded them.

"They are coming," Tam Nok said.

"Who?" Ragnarok asked.

"The Valkyries. They are not close, but they are coming."

"I thought they could not cross the water or move out of the fog," Ragnarok noted.

"They have many powers," Tam Nok said. "We have time but not too much." She began walking even faster, and Ragnarok followed, his senses on alert.

They passed between two long barrows, and there were no more burial mounds. A long plain stretched to the horizon, and in the center of it, about half a mile away, was some sort of strange building unlike anything Ragnarok had ever seen.

Penarddun had halted upon first sight of the structure, and Tam Nok and Ragnarok flanked her. It was difficult to tell at this distance, but it looked to Ragnarok like a much larger version of the stone monuments that the Vikings would erect on the burial mounds of one of their leaders. Numerous large stones were set in the earth, with other stones on top bridging the open space between them. There were two circles of stones, the outer about a hundred feet in diameter. There appeared to be a road leading off between banks to the northeast, where the land dipped down slightly, indicating there was probably a river or stream.

"What is this place?" Tam Nok asked.

"The holiest of our places," Penarddun said, as they continued forward. "It is now called Stonehenge. No one knows how old it is. It was here long before the Romans came.

"Some say the Ancients built it when they first came here. That is what I believe. Who else could have moved the stones? Some come from the Preslie Mountains over two hundred and forty miles away. Some, I think, from over the sea, in the land of the Irish, from a place known as the Dance of the Giants in Killarus."

Ragnarok had landed in Eire Land several times, and they were as strange a people as the Britons. But he doubted either had the ability to move such large stones, especially across the water between the two islands. Even one of those stones would probably sink the stoutest longship. And why would anyone go to such trouble?

"There are some who say the stones did not even originate in Eire Land. That they came from a dark land far to the south of even Rome and Greece, a land where the people's skin was black and many strange creatures walked the Earth." Penarddun continued. "Who could have done such a marvelous thing? Even an army of the strongest men like your Viking friend could not move one of the larger stones.

"Others talk of high priests and priestesses. A man, one of the earliest of our order, named Myrddinn Wyllt in the old tongue, Merlin in the new, is said to have brought the inner ring of stones here by floating them in the air."

Ragnarok would have laughed, but he remembered the Valkyrie flying through the air and seizing Thorlak. Perhaps this Merlin was not human either, Ragnarok thought.

"Merlin was one of the first of our order that we know of," Penarddun continued. "Many now talk of him as a legend, a man of magic and spells, but he was more a seer, one who could see over the lines of time forward and back.

The Christians call him a demon, but he was no demon. He was one who had a link to the Ancients and the Ones Before."

The stone structure was now a quarter mile away. Ragnarok looked about, half-expecting to see Valkyries swooping out of the sky, but all was still except for the noise of the clothes through the grass and their feet on the ground.

"The stones do heal, I know that," Penarddun said, "because I have seen it."

The monument was very close now. The ground dipped slightly, a small trench circling the entire thing. Then they passed through a ring of holes dug into the ground. Ragnarok wanted to look in the nearest hole, but the women didn't pause.

The outer circle of standing stones was over four times Ragnarok's height. He felt dwarfed and insignificant as he walked under the lintel stone that went from one standing stone to the other.

Inside was another circle, five taller pairs of standing stones, also topped with lintels, that left an opening toward the northeast. Penarddun paused under a lintel stone, not going into the center, horseshoe-shaped clearing. Ragnarok felt cold, as if the air had gone chill. He did not want to go any farther. There was a strange power here, he had no doubt of that. He had raided several churches and had felt some of the power of the Christian god inside them, but that was nothing compared to the sense he was getting here.

In the very center was a small stone, about three feet high by two in circumference. Unlike the larger stones, which all had rough surfaces, this stone was carved smooth, a perfect pillar. From the open end of the horseshoe, a path went straight out toward the northeast, the road Ragnarok had spied earlier. The dirt in the path was worn down by generations of feet.

"What you seek should be under that," Penarddun said. "We call it the memory stone.

"No one has dared touch that stone for as long as it is remembered among the Druids." She waved her hand about. "We worship here, but go no farther than where I am standing. After purification in the River Avon, we come up the Processional Way—there is a stone in the midst of the pathway—the heelstone, which is a warning against coming that way for those who are not believers.

"When the midsummer sun comes up, it is on line with the memory stone, highlighting and then casting the longest shadow possible toward the sunset stones." She gestured at the pair of tall stones they were between.

"The legend is that the memory stone was placed here by the ancient ones when they first came here fleeing the Shadow, that the stone is not to be disturbed until it is time."

"Is the time now?" Tam Nok asked.

"You should know the answer to that," Penarddun said.

"The Shadow is growing," Tam Nok said. "I saw it over Angkor Kol Ker, my people's city that was destroyed by the Shadow. I saw it in other places as I traveled here. In the high mountains north of India was a place of the Shadow. In the vast emptiness of the land of the steppe riders, there was another. Along the shore of the Norsemen, there was a place of Shadow. It was the same in all four places. The Shadow is darker now than it has been in living memory. The words handed down among my people say that when the Shadow becomes black, the end is near. The same was the belief of those who lived near the other places of Shadow I passed. There were some differences in the legends and story, but the core was the same.

"The Earth is unquiet in places. It trembles and shakes. Mountains of fire are rumbling, in some places bringing forth burning rock. I have traveled far and across many lands and it is true everywhere. The only thing that can stop the Shadow from taking over the rest of the world is the Shield left us by the Ones Before. My search for that weapon has led me here, so I must believe it is time."

Ragnarok didn't think it was time to go forward. He thought a hasty retreat back to his ship was long overdue. He felt a trickle of sweat roll down his left temple, a strange thing, given the unnatural chill in the air.

Tam Nok walked into the very center of Stonehenge and up to the memory stone. She placed her hands on it. She knelt, hands wrapped around the stone, her head against it as if listening.

Ragnarok fidgeted, nervous with the ponderous weight of the lintel stone above his head. There was a dull glow on the horizon, in the direction the horseshoe opened to. Dawn was not far off.

Tam Nok stood and waved for them to come forward. Ragnarok would have preferred to go in any other direction, but he knew he could not show fear in front of the women. He walked forward, his feet dragging as if in deep sand.

"We must lift the stone," Tam Nok said.

Ragnarok noted there were strange, very faint carvings in the top of the stone. "What does that say?"

"I do not know," Tam Nok said.

"I thought you could read the writings of the ancients."

"I can, but this is something different."

"How are you sure then that we should disturb this?" Ragnarok asked.

"I paid you," Tam Nok said. "Lift the stone."

"You paid me to bring you here," Ragnarok said.

Tam Nok pulled her hood back and turned to stare at the Viking. Her almond eyes searched his. Ragnarok took a step back.

"Please help me lift this stone," Tam Nok said.

"We do not have time for all this!" Penarddun said. "Dawn will be here soon, and we must be away by then."

Ragnarok looked down. He had no idea how deep the stone went into the ground. He put his ax down and squatted, wrapping both arms around the rock. He lifted with his legs, straining.

The stone didn't move at all.

He tried once more, putting all his energy into moving up. His hands slid off the stone, and he fell backward onto the cold dirt. He started to get up, then paused, putting his head against the ground. He listened for several seconds, then stood.

"Someone is coming." Ragnarok pointed to the east. "From that direction. Mounted on horses."

Penarddun stepped back. "The king's men."

Tam Nok was looking in the direction he pointed, then she slowly pivoted, doing a complete circle. "Others are coming, also. More dangerous than men on horses. Valkyries. And something else," her voice trailed off as if she were listening. "Someone else is coming."

Ragnarok picked up his ax. He did not like their situation—in the middle of a large plain with horsemen and demonesses bearing down on them. "We must go."

"We have to get what is under the stone!" Tam Nok insisted.

"It will do us no good if we're dead," Ragnarok argued. "And I can not lift it right now by myself."

Penarddun was still moving, passing through the lintel of the inner circle, escaping to the west.

Ragnarok grabbed Tam Nok's arm. "We must leave now." He pulled her after Penarddun. The eastern sky was brighter, the sun ready to rise above the horizon.

Tam Nok shook his hand off her shoulder. "We have to get what is under the stone."

"Fine," Ragnarok agreed. "Tomorrow night. Now, can we get out of here?"

Tam Nok pulled her hood back up and followed through the inner circle then the outer. Ragnarok could hear the horses now, hooves thudding on hard-packed dirt, coming closer. He looked over his shoulder. A troop of men, about eight or nine, were a half mile away and heading directly for Stonehenge.

Tam Nok dashed forward and grabbed Penarddun. "That way!" She pointed to the north.

"We can make the barrows and hide," Penarddun protested.

"There is more danger from the barrows," Tam Nok said. "The Valkyries are coming from there." Without another word, she ran to the north. Penarddun glanced at Ragnarok, who shrugged, then sprinted after his charge. The Druid priestess followed.

Ragnarok felt a chill on his neck, even as he began releasing the battle lust inside of himself. They were clear of the outer circle of standing stones. The horsemen were still heading toward Stonehenge, not aware that there were interlopers in the area.

Ragnarok and his companions passed through the small ditch and were clear of Stonehenge. The nearest barrow was a half mile away. Ragnarok knew if they were spotted, the horsemen could run them down before they could reach that cover. And the sky to the east was growing brighter with each passing moment.

Ragnarok stopped and turned, not to the east, but facing south. He realized Tam Nok had also stopped and was looking in the same direction. Penarddun ran a few more yards, then also stopped.

Something was moving very fast in the southern sky, coming directly toward them, about a hundred feet up in the air.

Ragnarok released the battle rage. Three Valkyries were coming toward them, bloodred cloaks floating behind in the air.

Ragnarok heard yells to his left. The horsemen had spotted him and his partners. The Valkyries would be on them before the horsemen, and there was no doubt which was the greater threat. Out of the corner of his eye, he saw Tam

Nok pull the small shield she had used in the fjord out of her cloak and unsheath her long knife. The shield was a foot high by six inches thick—not very large, in Ragnarok's opinion.

"We will cross to Valhalla together," he said.

"You are in too much of a rush to die, warrior," Tam Nok said. "Think about living."

Penarddun was behind them. She had dropped to her knees upon spotting the Valkyries, and she was chanting in her Druid tongue.

The Valkyries spread out, twenty feet between each, and descended until they touched the ground less than ten feet in front of Ragnarok and Tam Nok.

"Hlokk, Goll, and Skogul," Tam Nok said, identifying the creatures from left to right.

Ragnarok knew the names from the legends his mother had told him: Hlokk the Shrieker, Goll the Screamer, and Skogul the Rager. The only way he could tell the difference between them was the pattern of red and black on their cloaks, and he didn't have the time right now to study that.

"I have never seen them out of the mist, in the open," Tam Nok said. "This is something new."

Ragnarok cared little for their names or if this was something new. So far, the creatures had been totally silent. They were dark shadows, seven feet tall, their shape hidden under their cloaks, their faces flat and featureless except for the burning red eyes. Ragnarok felt the malevolence of that stare like the fury of a pack of wolves closing on a wounded animal.

Ragnarok had never believed in giving away the initiative. Without another thought, he dashed forward, ax upraised, toward the Valkyrie on the right, Skogul.

He swung a mighty blow, and Skogul swept a long arm out and took the blade straight on. Ragnarok's arms almost went numb from the recoil of the ax bouncing off the Valkyrie's arm without leaving a dent. With the other arm,

Skogul hit the Viking a backhanded blow on the side and threw him ten feet in a tumble.

Ragnarok got to his knees, then his feet, shaking his head. The other two Valkyries were circling around Tam Nok and Penarddun. Skogul was flowing forward toward Ragnarok, claws now extended on both hands. The bottom of her cloak was a few inches clear of the ground with nothing apparently supporting her.

A thundering sound came from behind. A horse and rider flashed by Ragnarok on his right, the rider screaming a war cry, tip of the spear leading.

Skogul slid left, the spear just missing. The creature's left hand, claws first, slammed into the rider's chest, piercing the linked-iron armor shirt. The warrior screamed and writhed like a spitted fish as Skogul lifted him off the horse, which bolted away in terror.

Ragnarok growled and ran forward, swinging his ax at the arm that held the man. Skogul threw the dying warrior directly at the Viking, knocking him to the ground once more and covering him with the last spurts of blood out of the Saxon's chest.

The rest of the mounted warriors were thundering down on the Valkyries, screaming their war cries. A golden beam shot out from Goll toward Tam Nok, who reflected it with her small shield. Another beam from Hlokk flashed and was bounced away.

Then the seven remaining soldiers of the king were among the Valkyries in a flurry of swords, spears, and claws. Tam Nok grabbed Ragnarok as he started to charge toward Skogul once more.

"No! You can not defeat them here and now!"

Ragnarok heard the screams of the men being killed by the demon creatures. Penarddun was already fifty feet away and running furiously to the north, toward the river. Ragnarok felt caught between fighting the Valkyries, the king's men, and doing what his charge said.

Tam Nok pulled him once more, and Ragnarok followed. She moved surprisingly quickly, and he had to lengthen his stride to keep up. He risked a glance over his shoulder and saw that only two warriors still stood, unhorsed, fighting back to back as the three Valkyries closed in. And then they were down in a flurry of claws.

The first ray of the sun sliced across the plain and hit the memory stone, casting a long shadow toward the center Mega-Sarsen stones.

Ragnarok paused as the Valkyries screamed in unison, the sound echoing across the plain. He stopped and spun, ax at the ready, but the three were leaving the corpses, bloody claws reluctantly letting go of mangled bodies. They floated up almost a hundred feet and then, as if blown by a strong wind, rapidly disappeared to the west, chasing the darkness.

Thirteen

THE PRESENT

Foreman slapped his palm on the conference table in frustration. *Glomar* had just reported that someone had picked up the phone in *Deeplab*, but no message had been sent. And that the ship's radar indicated *Deepflight II* was at the habitat. Foreman wouldn't put it beyond Dane to not report in.

Foreman studied the data as it came up on the computer screen. Nagoya had oriented the Can too late to pick up anything other than faint traces of muons in the area deep below the habitat—right around the eight-mile-wide circle of lesser activity.

"Could our bogey be in there?" Foreman asked into the small boom mike in front of his lips that connected him with the Japanese scientist.

"Yes, it is possible." Nagoya's voice came through the earpiece in Foreman's left ear.

A light had been flashing on the console since he'd gotten hold of Nagoya, and Foreman finally gave in. "Hold on a minute," Foreman said as he switched to access the direct line from the NSA. "Yes?"

Conners jumped right into it. "We've got activity in the Atlantic SOSUS system. Electromagnetic feedback. Very faint, but it's there. Just like the way it started out of Angkor in our MILSTARS satellite network."

"Was it caused by the large bogey?"

"No. This is separate from that."

"An attack?" Foreman demanded.

"It's not even strong enough right now to be called much of anything," Conners said. "I'd say it's a recon. A probe using our own system."

The earpiece in Foreman's right ear suddenly came alive with Nagoya's excited voice. "We have more muonic activity!"

Foreman looked down at the computer screen. A line of muons was coming out of the triangle representing the Bermuda Triangle gate and heading directly toward the Milwaukee Depth.

"Give me a size," Foreman ordered.

"Width over a mile and a half wide, and it's moving fast," Nagoya reported. "I've never seen anything like it, not that large and that strong."

Foreman picked up a phone. "Captain Stanton, try the habitat again."

He clicked on his boom mike. "Conners, do you have a bogey?"

"Negative. We're not picking up anything solid on SOSUS, just water disturbance as if someone was drilling a tunnel through the water. And it's very strong!"

DeAngelo was hooking up cables from the submersible to connectors in Red 2 to recharge the batteries and oxygen. Dane, Sin Fen, and Ariana were currently in Blue 3, the communications pod.

The phone to the surface buzzed, cutting short their discussion on what might have happened to the crew. Dane picked the phone up, turning on the speaker box.

"Yes?"

"Where the hell have you been?" Foreman's voice echoed in the sphere. "What's going on?"

"Has the *Glomar* picked them up yet?" Dane asked.

"Picked who up?"

"Sautran and his crew. The escape pod is gone."

"The pod never came up," Foreman said.

Dane wasn't quite sure he heard right. "But it's gone."

"It's gone, but it didn't come up," Foreman said. "The pod has a transponder on it, and the *Glomar* would have picked it up. They've got nothing."

"How about telling me what's going on?" Dane demanded.

"Something came up to the habitat from below," Foreman said. "That's all we know."

"Whatever it was," Dane said, "it got the pod then. I checked the log, and they lost all systems just prior to the bogey arriving."

"There's something else headed your way," Foreman said.

"From below?" Dane asked.

"No. From the Bermuda Triangle gate. Turn on your computer data link."

Ariana flipped on the large computer in the bank of equipment. The screen glowed, then an image appeared.

"This is a link from an imager in Japan tracking muons," Foreman informed them.

Dane could see the thick line growing longer, coming toward their location. "What is it?"

"We don't know. Some sort of disturbance in the water."

"How long do we have?"

"Two minutes," Foreman said.

Dane looked at Sin Fen. He could feel a pounding in his left temple, a heavy thump with each heartbeat.

"How do you shut this thing down?" he asked Ariana.

"Why do—" Ariana paused, then nodded. "Shut down

the master computer and the backup. That turns everything off, but I'm not sure about rebooting. I didn't read that far in the manual."

"Shut the computers down," Dane ordered.

Ariana pulled the keyboard to her.

"What are you doing?" Foreman's voice bounced off the curved walls.

"We'll be back in touch," Dane said, then he cut the commo link.

Ariana was typing into the keyboard for the computer.

Dane checked his watch. "One minute and thirty seconds."

A mile-and-a-half-wide cone of black rammed through the ocean, propagating a shock wave outward in all directions. It reached the edge of the Puerto Rican Trench at the same depth as *Deeplab*.

There it split in two branches. One, a mile and a quarter in circumference, dove down into the depths; the other smaller one continued straight ahead.

"Thirty seconds," Dane said.

Ariana didn't bother responding. Sin Fen was seated to the side, hands pressed to the side of her head. "It's from the gate," she said.

"I know," Dane agreed.

"From the Shadow," Sin Fen amplified.

"I know that, too," Dane said. "Fifteen seconds."

"I think I've got it," Ariana said.

"You 'think'?" Dane repeated.

Ariana hit the Enter key.

The lights went out, leaving the three sitting in absolute darkness.

A second later, Dane felt a spike of pain rip through his brain, bisecting it from front to rear. He collapsed to his knees, bumping against Ariana in the process.

The pain rose until he couldn't stand it anymore, curling into a ball on the metal grating, mouth wide open, muscles tight.

Then the pain was gone.

A beam of light cut through the darkness, a flashlight in Ariana's hand. "Are you two all right?"

Dane got to his knees and looked at Sin Fen. "That was close."

The Cambodian woman just nodded.

Dane cocked his head. "Did you hear something?"

In the next second, the habitat shook violently, and all three were knocked to the floor, the flashlight smashing to the grating and darkness engulfing them once more.

Captain Stanton was on the gantry, watching the inertial dampener move up through the thirty-foot safety mark and continue.

"What the hell is going on?" he demanded.

Thirty-five feet and finally slowing. The dampener stopped at forty-two feet, a new record, and one that had to have come from below as the sea around the *Glomar* was almost completely flat.

"Something hit the habitat," the senior engineer in charge of the rig reported.

"Is it still there?"

The engineer looked down at his telemetry and blinked. "I've got nothing coming back! It's either not there or completely shut down."

Foreman had watched the line from the Triangle bifurcate. The top one ran right through the location of the habitat, continued for about a quarter mile, then slowly receded back.

The other one went deep, straight down, to the very bottom, intersected with the large area of muonic activity at the bottom of the Milwaukee Depth, then also receded.

A voice crackled in his ear. "We're picking up something solid inside the line of propagation," Conners reported. "The large sphere is going back to the Gate."

"Nagoya," Foreman spoke into the phone. "What do you have?"

"Both lines of muonic activity are pulling back," Nagoya reported. "But the Bermuda Triangle gate is now twice the size it had been. It extends farther to the south, within twenty miles of the *Glomar Explorer*."

"Is the target still in the Depth?" Foreman asked.

"Yes. We're still reading it at the same size."

"Oh, shit," Conners cursed. "We've got a problem! There's a wave moving southeast—a solid line being picked up by SOSUS."

"So?" Foreman was concerned about the gate, not waves.

"Low height, long wavelength, a lot of power," Conners said. "The computer says when it hits the shallow water near Puerto Rico, the wavelength will shorten, and the wave will become fifty feet high. A major tsunami is going to hit northwest Puerto Rico in fifteen minutes."

Fourteen

999 A.D.

Ragnarok groaned as he sat up. His chest rippled with pain. He opened his tunic and looked. A tattoo of black and blue in the shape of the Valkyrie's arm was imprinted on his chest. Almost lost in it was the red mark where he had been burned the previous week by the same creatures. So far, they had dealt all the injuries.

"Ah," Ragnarok leaned over and spat. It hurt to breathe so he took a dozen very deep breaths, feeling the fire in his chest until the burning was a steady blaze, then he ignored it.

He looked about and blinked. Tam Nok was in the river, water flowing up to her waist. She was naked, her upper body brown and slender. Ragnarok realized he was staring and looked away. Penarddun was a huddle under a red cloak a few feet away, still asleep.

"You should clean yourself," Tam Nok said.

Ragnarok picked up Bone Cutter and pointedly examined the edge, trying to see if it had been damaged when he hit the Valkyrie named Skogul. "Water is for drinking and sailing on," he replied. There was a dullness to the edge along the part that had hit the demoness. Ragnarok pulled out his sharpening stone and got to work.

He heard Tam Nok coming out of the water, and he kept his eyes on the ax. There was a rustle of cloth and Ragnarok gave it a few seconds before looking up. Tam Nok had her cloak on and she was seated on the bank of the river. Her short white hair was plastered against her skull, and for the moment she looked very young and vulnerable. Ragnarok realized that she was barely past her twentieth year, if that. Young for someone who knew so much and was on such a difficult mission.

This morning they had reached the river and turned to the west, running for a half hour before collapsing in this spot. The River Avon wasn't very wide or deep, but it was below the level of the Salisbury Plain and afforded them some protection from observation. Ragnarok knew that the king's men who were killed by the Valkyries during the dark hours would be missed sooner or later. Ragnarok looked up at the sun. It was after midday.

Tam Nok saw him staring at her and reached up to her head, feeling her hair. "It used to be black," she said.

"What happened to it?"

"One day I looked down in a stream I was crossing and I saw that it had changed color."

Ragnarok had known a man whose hair had changed like that. Who had gone out on the sea to fish for the day and not returned for three weeks. And when he came back, his hair was white, his eyes haunted, and he was mute. He never spoke again, dying less than six months later.

"What occurred just before your hair changed?" he asked.

"It happened when I started my journey. I had to go into the dark area near my home." Tam Nok shook her head. "There are some things it is best not to speak of."

"If we are to travel together, I think—" Ragnarok began, but he noted that Tam Nok wasn't looking at him but beyond, with a strange expression. Ragnarok sprang to his feet and turned, ax in hand.

An old man was standing on the edge of the plain where it began descending to the riverbank. He wore tattered rags, and his face was obscured by a large, bushy gray beard. The man was holding a staff of what appeared to be black wood, perfectly smooth and over six feet long. Something on the tip of the staff was reflecting light, almost blinding Ragnarok. He squinted. An intricately carved ornament—a seven-headed snake. The other end of the staff ended in a spear head, which also shone in the sunlight.

Ragnarok had never seen such a weapon, but it must have meant something to Tam Nok, because she pushed past the Viking, rattling off something in her native language.

"Now, slow down, woman," the man said in Ragnarok's tongue but with an accent the Viking had heard before— far to the north on this godforsaken island in the land where there were hills and bogs and deep lochs and the people dressed in clothes with patterns that told what family they belonged to. A strange people who the Vikings respected in battle because they were capable of being as insane as the Norsemen when it came to the blood lust.

The man walked down to their small camp. Penarddun, woken by the voices, opened her bleary eyes. She blearily stared at the man for a few seconds, then her eyes widened. "Lailoken!"

The old man went to the river and knelt, dipping his face into the water and drinking deeply. His head came up, the beard dripping water. "Some have called me that," he acknowledged. His gray eyes softened and grew distant. "It has been a long time, though, since anyone did so." The eyes sharpened, and he looked at Penarddun. "You are one of those who worship the stones and trees and stars."

Penarddun dipped her head. The man laughed, then twirled, holding the staff out from him, the spear end cutting the air. It was as if he had suddenly disconnected from reality for a few seconds, then, just as quickly, he stopped and became serious.

His gaze shifted to Ragnarok. "A ravager from the sea. I have seen your people fight along the shores to the north and east of here. I learned your language from one of your fellows stranded in my country. You are a long way from the ocean, sailor of the north." He stepped closer. "Tell me, do you enjoy the killing? Or is it the dying? If I remember correctly, your people seem to relish both."

He didn't wait for an answer as he turned his attention to Tam Nok. "I have not seen your like before. Nor do I know the tongue you spoke to me in. I assume since you travel with this large barbarian, you know his tongue." He reached out with a hand encrusted with dirt. Tam Nok didn't flinch as he ran a finger along the sides of her eyes. "Most strange. Most strange. Do you see differently?" He laughed, an insane edge to the sound. "Oh, I think you do. I think you do!"

"My name is Tam Nok. I am from the kingdom of the Khmer." She pointed at his staff. "The Naga on your—"

"The what?" Lailoken interrupted. "The what?"

"The seven-headed snake. We call it the Naga in our land. It is sacred."

Lailoken looked at his staff as if seeing it for the first time. "A sacred snake with seven heads? People are so strange, aren't they?" He laughed. "I thought it pretty, so I took it." He shook his head. "It is so hard to remember everything." He held the staff at arm's length and looked at it as if seeing it for the first time. "Yes, it is sacred. That I remember."

"Who are you?" Tam Nok asked.

The old man shook, as if a sudden chill had raced through his body, then he turned serious. "She called me Lailoken. That is what I was called long, long ago. When I counseled the king. The first king I counseled, that is.

Yes, I told him much. But he didn't listen. They never listen."

"We will listen," Tam Nok said.

"I warned them!" He stopped and smiled, transforming his entire face into that of an old, gentle man. "They called me Lailoken. They called me other names. Later. Myrddin. When I was with another king. Have you heard that name?"

"Myrddin?" Penarddun's voice quavered.

"Yes."

"Merlin in the new tongue," Penarddun said.

"I prefer Lailoken. It is the name my mother and father gave me. Sometimes the languages get confused in my mind. I know many languages and have been to many lands. But you—" He pointed at Tam Nok. "You are something new."

His voice changed once more and became manic. "I told the king. The first king. I told him about the dragons. One red. One white. Fighting, fighting, fighting. All the time. And that's why his walls collapsed. He could not build his castle."

"King Vortigen?" Penarddun asked.

The old man nodded.

"Vortigen ruled over five hundred years ago," Penarddun said in a lower voice to Tam Nok and Ragnarok.

"It was a long time ago," Lailoken acknowledged. "I told him of the dragons under Dinas Emrys. The red and white. And if he drained the pool, the dragons would come out and he could build his castle. Of course, I also told him that the white dragon would kill the red. And since his symbol was the red dragon, he did not take this news well. But he was not a believer. The white, ahh . . ." Lailoken trailed off.

"The white was the line of Artor—Arthur," Penarddun whispered.

"Yes. But there was more to the prophecy," Lailoken said. "All people remember is Artor and the table and the stories of the sword and the warriors in their armor. And even now, most don't think it was true. But those things were not important. What was important is I saw the future. I saw the Shadow coming once more. I wanted them to prepare. To stop fighting among themselves."

"The Shadow?" Tam Nok pressed.

His eyes closed, and he pressed his hands against the side of his head. "Darkness coming out of the earth. A wall of darkness. And out of the darkness, death and suffering for all. The earth itself will shatter, fire will come forth. There will be a deadly rain that will kill the beasts and all the plants. All life. The witches, three sisters, will come first, to clear the way."

That struck a chord with Ragnarok. "The Valkyries?"

"Valkyries?" said Lailoken. "In your land, they are called that. Witches. Demonesses. Succubesses. Handmaidens of the devil. Forerunners of the darkness. Whatever." Lailoken suddenly sat down, the staff across his knees. "I am tired. And hungry. I have traveled far to be here."

"Why?" Tam Nok asked as she pulled some dried meat and stale bread from her pack and handed it to the old man.

Lailoken's voice lightened once more. "Why am I tired? Because I traveled far. Why am I hungry? Because I ate little while I traveled. Why did I travel far? Because I needed to get here."

Tam Nok was very patient. "Why are you here?"

Lailoken stuffed his mouth with bread, and flecks came out of his mouth when he answered. "To meet you, of course. At least I think it is you I am supposed to meet. I am not so sure of things now as I used to be."

Ragnarok frowned. The old man looked like a beggar—except for the staff—and he spoke like a crazy man. He had seen such before, living on the edge of a village, begging for food, babbling about all sorts of nonsense. There were some who believed the crazy to be the mouthpieces of the gods, but Ragnarok thought they were just broken people.

Tam Nok shot him a dirty look, as if she knew what he was thinking, then she sat next to the old man. "Lailoken, please tell me why were you seeking us?"

"To help you." He shoved a piece of dried meat into his mouth.

"How?" Tam Nok asked.

Lailoken laughed, spewing pieces of half-chewed meat. "How? How should I know? You should know. What help do you need?"

Tam Nok's voice was patient. "We need to lift the memory stone at Stonehenge."

Ragnarok snorted. "We need to survive the attacks of the Valkyries first."

"It was not called Stonehenge when it was built. And it was not built for your people—" Lailoken pointed a finger at Penarddun—"to dance around and worship."

"Why was it built?" Tam Nok asked.

Lailoken shrugged. "I have forgotten. It was before even my time." Lailoken held up the staff. "This will help you do both things you desire." He tossed it toward Ragnarok, and the Viking, despite his surprise, caught it with one hand. It was deceptively light. The shaft was not wood but a material he had never felt before but he sensed was very strong. He held the spear in front of his face. The head was a foot long from the point and spread to a width of eight inches at the base. Ragnarok reached to test the edge with a finger, but halted as Lailoken hissed a warning.

"Don't do that. You'll slice your finger off and not know until it is on the ground in front of you."

Ragnarok pulled his other hand back. The edge did appear to be very sharp. He flipped the staff and looked at the carved figure. A seven-headed snake, the likes of which he had never seen before. He had heard of such from his mother. It was a creature called a hydra.

"That can open the memory stone?" Tam Nok asked.

"So I have been told, and so I tell," Lailoken said.

"Who told you?" Tam Nok asked. "The Ones Before?"

Lailoken's hand paused on the way to his mouth with a load of bread. "Ones Before?" He seemed to be deep in thought for several seconds. "They want to help, but they can't come here like the Valkyries can. Not anymore. Long ago, long ago, they could. Many changes. Things they don't even understand, so I do not pretend to understand." His voice changed tone, becoming singsong. "So they told me. Told others. Gave us signs. Sent messages. But many didn't listen. Don't listen."

"If we take you to the stone," Tam Nok said, "will you open it for us? We will listen, I promise."

Lailoken leaned over until he was lying on his side. "Yes. I will open the stone. But first I must sleep."

Fifteen

THE PRESENT

The first thing Dane was aware of was that there were others around him. Alive. He reached out with his mind—Sin Fen and Ariana were very close. Pushing further, he picked up DeAngelo's swirling dreams. They were all unconscious.

Dane sat up and opened his eyes. It was cold and pitch black. There was not even the slightest bit of light for his eyes to adjust to. He remembered the flashlight Ariana had had. He reached down and got on his hands and knees.

He touched a body and checked vital signs. Pulse was good, and as far as he could tell by feel, nothing was broken. From the mental impressions he was receiving, he knew the body was Ariana.

He continued with his search and, given the small size of the sphere, came across Sin Fen's unconscious form a few seconds later. Dane did a quick medical survey of her, also, as he had been taught three decades ago in special forces training and had reinforced with his years of search and rescue experience. Sin Fen also seemed to be battered but not broken. Dane paused before continuing to look for the flashlight. He reached up and placed his hands on either side of her head.

He focused his mind. The surrounding darkness and silence helped, reducing his sensory input to just the grating under his knees and the head between his hands.

Dane saw a massive, flat-topped pyramid. It was large, over five hundred feet high, made of black stone, reminding Dane of one he had seen in Mexico, but larger than that, even larger than the Great Pyramid in Egypt. The stone glistened in the sunlight.

A line of people in various colored cloaks were lined along the steep stairs on both sides. At the very top was a stone slab, surrounded by a ring of people in black robes. All were dark-skinned with black hair.

A body was lying on the slab. A woman. She was different than those around her: fair-skinned with very blond, almost white hair. Her blue eyes were wide open, staring straight up. She wore a red robe. She turned to one of those in the black robes who held a staff in his hand, and her mouth moved.

She was saying something, but Dane heard nothing. There were three men and a woman standing at one end of the platform, not wearing robes but rather shiny armor with leather underneath. Swords were at their waists, bows slung over their shoulders, and spears in their hands. Their faces were hard—a look Dane knew well. Warriors who had seen much death. He could tell they were anxious, wanting whatever was to happen to occur. He knew, simply by seeing them, that they had accompanied the woman on the slab to this place after a long and perilous journey. The female warrior cast a nervous glance to the north. In that direction Dane now saw a dark cloud—the Shadow filling the horizon. A gate was open and growing, coming toward the pyramid.

The woman on the slab finished speaking. She looked straight up into the perfectly blue sky above. The cloaked man she had been talking to placed his hand on her fore-head. She nodded very slightly. He removed his hand. He moved over and placed his staff in a small hole next to the slab she was on. It slid down a foot and then stopped.

The other priests and priestesses were chanting. A halo of blue light surrounded the woman's head. Her body arched upward, her mouth rigid with pain, but Dane could hear nothing. The man twisted the staff. The glow around the woman's head was growing larger. Something was happening to her head.

Dane squinted, trying to make out what exactly—

A lance of pain ripped through Dane's head above his left eye, knocking him backward. In the process of doing so, he let go of Sin Fen's head, but it didn't bounce back on the deck as she sat up in the darkness.

The pain was gone as quickly as it had come.

"What's the status?" Sin Fen asked.

Dane rubbed his forehead. "It's dark, we have no power, and I can't find a light."

"Ariana must have cut all power completely when she shut the computer down," Sin Fen said.

"Better than have that thing get into the computer like it did her airplane in Cambodia."

"We have no clue what happened. We don't know if what hit us was a probe from the gate."

Dane could hear Sin Fen moving in the dark.

"You know it was," Dane said. "You could sense it just as I could."

Dane shut his eyes as a beam of light cut through the darkness. Slowly, he opened them. Sin Fen had turned on an emergency light above the master computer. Ariana stirred, and Dane helped her sit up.

"How are you doing?" Dane asked her.

"I'm living," Ariana replied. She squinted into the light. "The habitat seems to be intact. What the hell hit us?"

"I don't know," Dane said.

Ariana shivered. "It's getting cold."

"Can you get us powered up?" Dane asked.

Ariana nodded. She sat down in front of the computer and pressed a button. The screen glowed. "At least this is working. It will take me a little while."

Captain Bateman had been left alone for hours. Submariners tended to stay out of areas they weren't supposed to be in, and the computer center led to no other area—a dead end—and because of that, and because the computers had run efficiently for that entire time period, no one had tried the door.

Bateman closed a panel and checked his watch. He was ready. Now it was just a matter of time. He leaned back and pressed both hands against the side of his head. Pain, like the ticking of a watch, was throbbing on the right side, just behind his ear. He slid his right hand across the skin and felt a bump underneath. It seemed to his fingers to be vibrating slightly to the same beat as the pain.

He closed his eyes, then opened them, confusion showing. For the briefest of moments, he didn't know where he was or what he was doing. But the moment passed, and a curtain came down over his thoughts. He slumped back once more.

"The habitat seems to be fine." Dane's voice was like ointment on a wound for Foreman, who had been convinced *Deeplab IV* and everyone in it was gone.

Foreman looked up at the status board. There were red lights flashing. An officer ran up. "Sir, we have confirmed the NSA's tsunami alert for the northwest coast of Puerto Rico. Whatever came out of the gate generated a lot of power, and it's headed for the coast."

Tsunami is Japanese for "harbor wave." The mile-and-a-half-diameter projection from the Bermuda Triangle gate toward the Milwaukee Deep had generated a force that disturbed the mass of water it passed through, much as a child moving his hand through his bathwater caused a disturbance, except this was billions of times more powerful.

In the deep water of the Puerto Rican Trench, the effect was negligible, even though it had almost destroyed *Deeplab IV*. But as the effect went southeast, the depth decreased dramatically, transforming the power of the tsunami. The generated wave, no more than twelve inches in height at the beginning and initially traveling at four hundred miles an hour, slowed as it got closer to land. The energy that had been in the velocity was reflected by the rising ocean bottom, forming an ever-higher wave. The distance between the wave crests also shortened, changing the power vectors in the wave.

There was no time for a warning. Those on the shore noticed that the water seemed to draw away, as if the tide had suddenly gone out. If it had been Hawaii, where people knew about tsunamis, this would have given those who saw it warning, but Puerto Rico had not been hit by a killer wave in over a generation. Some people even walked out onto the suddenly dry ocean bottom, picking up fish that had been left behind by the sudden disappearance of water.

The water returned with all the vengeance of a thousand runaway freight trains lined shoulder to shoulder, moving over two hundred miles an hour. Water is very heavy, a gallon weighing eight and a half pounds. A bathtub full of water weighs almost three quarters of a ton. There were millions and millions of bathtubs full of water lifted by the force of the wave that approached the northwest tip of Puerto Rico. Added to the weight, the force of moving water increases as the square of the velocity. Even though the wave slowed considerably as it grew in height, it still hit the shore at over sixty miles an hour.

The first tsunami hit the coast with a crest of sixty feet. The first to die were those who had walked out onto the beach. Thousands more died with the first wave, not so much from drowning but by being smashed by debris picked up and carried with the wave as it thundered inland. Coastal villages that had survived the numerous hurricanes and tidal surges associated with that weather event in the region were obliterated as the wave thundered ashore.

Fishing boats were carried a quarter mile inland. Houses, the majority built of wood, were shattered and smashed, the debris becoming part of the wave still moving inland. Cars and trucks were picked up and tossed about like toy models.

The survivors of the first wave barely had time to pick themselves up before the second, slightly smaller wave crashed ashore. Eight waves in all hit the island in the space of five minutes, battering the coast as if the very hand of God had come down and wreaked punishment upon the people.

The beach to a distance of a quarter mile inland was scoured clean of all buildings except those made of the stoutest reinforced concrete, which were few and far between. Trees were knocked over, power lines ripped out of the ground, sewage systems flooded, the water table contaminated—all in the space of those five minutes.

In that short period of time, over eight thousand people died and the wounded numbered in the tens of thousands, overwhelming the island's surviving medical capabilities. Local hospitals were destroyed, and because most of the roads had been washed away, help was slow to get to the region.

The seawater that had been dumped on the island slowly made its way back to the ocean, carrying with it a tide of corpses. Most of those who died were never found.

Sixteen

999 A.D.

Ragnarok put his ear to the ground and listened, but there was no sound of horses' hooves striking the Salisbury Plain. Then he stood and scanned the night sky. The stars glittered back at him from a perfectly clear heaven. No cloaked Valkyries riding the wind. Of course, at the speed they had arrived the previous evening, he knew they could appear in a few seconds and be on top of them. Then he would find out how Lailoken's staff would work against the demon women.

He felt the power of this place. The stones were very, very old, aged beyond any Viking grave markers he had ever seen. He could sense the generations of worshipers before Penarddun and her kind, stretching back to an unknown people gathered here, worshiping gods he had never heard of.

The bodies of the king's men lay fifty meters away, where the Valkyries had slaughtered them. The fact that the bodies had not been stripped of their armor or weapons told Ragnarok that no one had dared come near the strange stone structure during the day.

The condition of the bodies reinforced the legend of the Valkyries as the men had been maimed badly. Ragnarok had noted where armor had been sliced open as easily as a thin cloth shirt. There was no sign that any damage had been inflicted on the Valkyries. Ragnarok knew it would not be long before the patrol was missed and other soldiers of the king came searching.

"I need the help of your Norse warrior," Lailoken said to Tam Nok. They were standing around the memory stone, the towering formation of Stonehenge surrounding them.

Ragnarok stepped between Tam Nok and Penarddun and next to the old man. "What do you want me to do?"

"I will open the stone," Lailoken said, "but I am too weak to lift it."

Ragnarok simply wanted to be back on his ship, to feel the deck moving under his feet and the snap of the wind in the sail, to smell saltwater in his nostrils. Not to be standing in the middle of an English plain, the smell of cow dung in his nostrils, a chill wind blowing over hard stone the only sound. "Let us get this over with."

"Put your arms around the stone," Lailoken ordered.

Ragnarok grasped the cold stone to his chest, his knees bent. Penarddun had her hands raised to the sky, chanting in her native tongue. Ragnarok hoped she was appeasing whatever gods ruled the stones now.

Lailoken lifted his staff up and slid the spear end into the small slit on the top. It fit perfectly, sliding down two feet into the stone. The old man wrapped his gnarled hands around the Naga on the other end and twisted. The staff turned smoothly. Ragnarok heard a noise, metal on metal, and he could feel something move inside the stone. Penarddun's chanting grew more earnest.

"Lift!" Lailoken ordered.

Ragnarok strained, and the stone moved ever so slightly. He let the stone back down.

"Do you need help?" Tam Nok asked.

Ragnarok growled at her, got his feet under him better, and lifted once more. He grunted as the stone smoothly slid up out of the hole. Ragnarok staggered back, then bent his knees, dropping the stone on the ground, upright, next to the hole. He kept a hand on it to prevent it from falling over as he straightened up. The stone was five feet high, the bottom flat. The part that had been buried was darker and smoother, protected from the elements. Looking at it, Ragnarok realized the stone must have been in the ground for a very long time. He could see two dark holes on the side where the lock must have been.

The old man and two women were on their knees around the hole, looking down into it. Ragnarok could see little as they blocked his view into the dark pit. However, he could tell that the pit was lined with something.

Ragnarok jumped back and yelled in alarm as a blue, unearthly glow suffused the memory stone. A beam of blue touched him in the chest, slid up across his head, then flashed to Penarddun. It quickly raked across her in the same manner, then went to Tam Nok. There it paused, locked on to the amulet on her chest, then bounced from there up to her head. She stood, transfixed for ten seconds, then the blue light snapped out and they were left in darkness once more.

Lailoken was the first to move, reaching out to Tam Nok and placing his gnarled hands on her shoulders. He peered into her eyes. Ragnarok had his ax ready, and he was staring at the stone like he would a snake, ready to strike it if something else happened. Penarddun was on her knees, hands over her eyes, muttering a prayer over and over.

Tam Nok blinked and shook her head. She placed her hands on top of Lailoken's and nodded. "I see where I am to go."

Lailoken released the Khmer woman, and she turned back to the hole and got on her knees. Tam Nok reached down and pulled out a flat piece of metal from the very bottom. It was a foot wide by a foot long and so thin it bent slightly in her hand. Ragnarok had never seen such a metal. It looked almost like silver. Tam Nok tilted it so that the starlight reflected off the surface. Ragnarok could see lines etched on it.

Ragnarok shivered, and he looked about. His view was limited by the large stones surrounding them, but there was nothing moving on the plain that he could see. Still, that didn't mean there was nothing out there.

"Let's get out of here," Ragnarok recommended, his voice harsh and echoing slightly off the stones.

"Put the memory stone back," Lailoken said.

The last thing Ragnarok wanted to do was touch the stone. Lailoken saw that and laughed. He placed his hands on top of the stone. "There is nothing to be afraid of. It is done."

Ragnarok reluctantly put his ax down and wrapped his arms around the cold rock. He replaced it by the simpler method of scooting it over to the hole and dropping it down inside. It slid into the hole with a thud. Lailoken turned the staff, the lock clicked, and he pulled the spear head out of the hole.

"I am done here," the old man said "It has been a very long time."

Tam Nok had taken out her map and was comparing it to the metal plate. The etchings on the plate were a continuation of her scroll. Ragnarok knelt down and stared. There was a gigantic country to the west of Greenland. The coast stretched down and down to the south. Farther than around the tip of France to the coast of Hispanola, which he had talked to sailors about. Into the middle sea, the Mediterranean, where the Romans and Greeks had sailed. There was land below, stretching almost to the very bottom of the world. Ragnarok felt like a child, his expeditions to Iceland and Greenland, of which he had been so proud, now appeared to be a child's wandering from the village rather than a warrior's epic journey.

"What happened to you?" Ragnarok asked.

Tam Nok was focused on the map. "I was given directions. Where to find the Shield. And what to do when I get there."

Ragnarok looked up and noticed that Lailoken was walking out of the circle of stones. He tapped Tam Nok on the shoulder and pointed. She hurriedly put the map back in the bamboo, the metal sheet into her pack, and ran after him.

"Won't you come with us?" Tam Nok asked the old man.

Lailoken paused. "Another journey?" He shook his head. "I have been on many, but I am too old now. My mission is done. This is your responsibility. The stone chose you just as it chose me a long time ago. I am done."

"The staff?" Ragnarok prompted.

"Ah yes. The staff." Lailoken smiled. "I am forgetful in my old age." He held the staff out, and Ragnarok took it. The old man stretched both arms over his head slowly, then back to his side. "It is nice to be free." He laughed, then turned to Tam Nok. "Remember, the shortest distance between two points is not always a straight line. In fact—" He laughed once more, a manic edge to it. "The shortest distance is sometimes not a distance at all. There are shortcuts if you know what to look for. Trust the voice. I wish you well on your trip." He strode off into the darkness.

"I must go, also," Penarddun said. "I have done what you asked. My people can't know what has happened here. They would not understand. *I* don't understand. In all my years praying here, I have never seen such a thing."

"Thank you," Tam Nok said.

"I don't know if I've done a good thing," Penarddun said. "The king's men will be back here. And those demon witches. You should leave, too." Without another word the

Druid pulled her hood up over her head and slipped off into the night.

Tam Nok pulled the straps on her pack tight. "Back to the ship. I will show you where to go once we get there." She held out her hand, and Ragnarok reluctantly gave her the staff.

Seventeen

THE PRESENT

The sub pens in Groton are capable of holding the largest underwater craft the U.S. Navy deployed, the Ohio-class ballistic missile submarine, which is almost two football fields long. There were four main pens, not only long enough to hold the biggest sub but wide enough to put five side by side. Just north of Groton, technically called the New London sub base, the pens were on the Thames River in eastern Connecticut.

In pen number 2, nestled between an Ohio-class and a Los Angeles–class attack submarine, the *Scorpion* was easily dwarfed. Security around the pen was heavy. The crew was quartered in barracks hewn out of the rock right next to the pen holding their ship as the powers that be in Washington tried to figure out how to explain their sudden reappearance after being proclaimed dead thirty-one years ago and the even more perplexing fact that not a man in the crew had aged more than a day in all those years.

While the crew members underwent intensive debriefings—which so far failed to yield any more information about what had happened to the ship in the Bermuda Triangle—teams of technicians were going through the ship, searching for any physical clues to solve the mystery.

They had already gone through the entire ship, excluding the nuclear reactor, and now they were preparing to go into that last off-limits area. Donning protective garb, a team of four nuclear specialists opened the thick door blocking the plant control compartment from the reactor itself.

Clad in their bright yellow suits, they walked through the tunnel separating the livable part of the ship from the deadly rear. And they finally found something out of the ordinary. Sitting on the floor of the main reactor chamber was a silver cylinder, three feet high by two in diameter. Three beams of golden light came out of the cylinder and penetrated into the containment wall where the core resided.

The investigators were still staring at this in puzzlement when a beam of gold from the cylinder raked across their bodies, then continued to the rear of the ship and locked into the reactor's core.

A split second later, the *Scorpion*'s reactor went critical.

The *Scorpion*, the subs tied up inside the pen, and the entire crew of the *Scorpion* along with the other navy personnel inside, were vaporized in the nuclear explosion.

Designed to withstand a close hit by a nuclear weapon, the top of the sub pen buckled, broke, and collapsed, but it managed to contain most of the explosion. The walls between pens 2 and 1 and 3 shattered, causing massive damage to the submarines in those other two pens.

Foreman was the calm in the center of a storm. Alarms were screeching, phones were ringing, and orders shouted, the noise only partially absorbed by the sound panels on the sides and roof of the War Room.

The generals and admirals were reacting to the twin disasters in Puerto Rico and Groton, moving ships and planes and men to help minimize the aftereffects and help the survivors.

To Foreman, both of those events were already in the past. And both were threats of things to come in the future. The tsunami was just a taste of what might be coming out of the gates shortly. The nuclear explosion in Groton was more of a mystery to him.

The chairman of the Joint Chiefs of Staff, General Tilson, strode up to Foreman and slammed a fist down on the top of the conference table. "We just lost as many sailors as we did at Pearl Harbor! I'm recommending to the president that we nuke the Bermuda gate."

Foreman could see a vein bulging in Tilson's forehead. "Sir, that may be exactly what the Shadow wants us to do. We don't have enough data yet—"

"Yet?" Tilson leaned forward. "You've been studying these goddamn things for fifty years, and you don't have enough data yet? Do you have more now? Do you?"

"I don't think a nuke would do any good," Foreman said. "The gates have strong electromagnetic and radioactive properties. We believe the laws of physics inside the gates are different than ours."

"Then get me something I can use to fight this," Tilson said. "Because if you can't, I'm going to go to the president and recommend we shut these goddamn things with the strongest weapon we have available, and that's a goddamn nuke-tipped cruise missile right smack into the center of these things."

Tilson stalked off to rejoin the branch chiefs in the forward part of the War Room. Foreman leaned back in his chair and closed his eyes for a second, running recent events through his mind.

In all the excitement, the information he had been given by Conners about SOSUS had been shuffled to the bottom of his crisis reaction. Most of what was going on in the War Room was out of his hands now. He knew the most important thing was to be able to figure out not the what, but the why of recent events. He punched the direct line to the NSA.

The other end was answered immediately. "Conners."

"Any changes?" he asked.

"Other than the tsunami and the nuke blast in Groton? We're tracking fallout from the sub pen from our eyes in the sky. So far, it doesn't look too bad, and the current winds are seaward, which is lucky. The eastern tip of Long Island will get a little hot, but we think the dosage won't be fatal.

"We've downlinked to the relief agencies in Puerto Rico, giving them the latest sit-rep. It looks pretty bad there.

"As you can see from the data we've forwarded you, the Bermuda Triangle gate is now farther south, closer to the Milwaukee Depth. The other gates are beginning to show some activity, particularly those in the water."

"What about the SOSUS infiltration?" Foreman asked.

"No change."

"Can we shut SOSUS down?"

"Maybe that's what the Shadow wants," Conners said. "Maybe there's a plan, and they want you to react. We shut SOSUS down, we're effectively going to be blind under-water."

"We'll still have the Can," Foreman said.

"True, but what if they send the *Wyoming* back at us?"

"Christ," Foreman muttered. Conners had been right before. "The *Seawolf* can cover the Bermuda Triangle gate if we shut SOSUS down."

"Then I'd check to make sure everything's OK with the *Seawolf*," Conners said.

Foreman punched in a number on his SATPhone, accessing FLTSATCOM, the Navy's communication system. After a brief burst of static, Captain McCallum's voice answered the other end.

Foreman wasted no time on pleasantries. "Where is Bateman?"

"Down below," McCallum responded.

"Get him."

"Wait one."

Foreman tapped a finger on the conference table as the seconds dragged into a minute. Then two.

"Captain McCallum?" Foreman finally asked.

The voice on the other end sounded harried. "Yes?"

"What's going on?"

"Captain Bateman seems to have locked himself into our computer control center. We can't get in there nor can we raise the crewmen who were on duty in there."

"You need—" Foreman began but he was interrupted by a yell from McCallum.

"What the hell! XO, abort dive. Abort!"

There was a few seconds of static, then McCallum's voice shouting. "XO, what is going on?"

"Captain McCallum?" Foreman leaned forward. "Captain McCallum!"

The only reply was the hiss of static.

On board the *Seawolf*, McCallum was dealing with a unique situation, one that his training had not prepared him for. The nose was already under as the submarine began to submerge. Except the captain had not given the order, he had six crewmen still on the top of the sail with him, and the hatch below him was open.

He dropped the SATPhone as he yelled once more into the intercom. "XO, abort dive!"

Commander Barrington's voice echoed out of the speaker with an answer McCallum didn't want to hear. "We can't, sir! Controls won't respond!"

"Emergency override, blow all tanks," McCallum yelled.

"We've tried, sir. No response."

McCallum looked forward. The sea had covered the forward deck and was now around the base of the sail.

"Clear the bridge! Clear the bridge! Emergency dive!" McCallum yelled. The six-man bridge crew reacted well.

The captain stood aside as the crew members on the bridge dashed past him and slid down the ladder to the operations center. Water began breaking over the top of the bridge as the last man went by him. McCallum jumped into the hatch, grabbing the side of the ladder with both hands and sliding down until his head was clear.

"Bridge clear, close hatch!" he yelled.

"It won't close, sir!" A crewman was standing next to the ladder, slamming his palm against the large button that controlled the hydraulic arm that shut the four-hundred-pound hatch.

A wave of water splashed through the open hatch, in-undating McCallum. He shook his head, getting saltwater out of his eyes. He had less than five seconds before an unstoppable tunnel of water poured through the opening.

"Down! Close the bottom hatch!" McCallum ordered the two sailors just below him.

"Sir—" one of the men began to argue, but McCallum had no time.

"Move it!" he screamed as he pulled out the manual crank arm.

They disappeared through the bottom sail hatch, and the hatch swung shut, trapping him in the sail access tube. Another wave of water slammed McCallum against the ladder. He gasped in pain as three ribs broke from the impact.

The *Seawolf* was now almost completely underwater except for the very top of the sail. McCallum desperately turned the crank, and the top hatch slowly began to shut.

Another wave splashed through, blinding McCallum once more, but he had no time to clear his eyes. He blindly kept turning.

The top of the sail went underwater, and a torrent poured through the open hatch, battering Captain McCallum as he struggled with the crank. He felt water around his feet and knew that meant the sail access was already half-full of water.

Three more turns, and the hatch was three-quarters closed, but the water was around his chest and still rising. The *Seawolf* was completely submerged now, and Mc-Callum knew alarms were ringing in the operations center below him because of the open hatch. He also knew this was never supposed to happen. The emergency computer system would not allow the crew to submerge the ship with the top hatch open. Either the system had failed or someone had overridden it.

The water reached his neck, and McCallum pushed himself as high as he could in the compartment while still turning the handle. He took a deep breath as water lapped over his face. The handle stopped turning; the hatch was shut.

McCallum opened his eyes. With the boat angled down, there was a small air bubble, perhaps a foot deep by two feet wide, in the upper rear of the compartment, and he pushed against the ladder to reach it. His face pressed into the air, and he took a deep breath, savoring the oxygen.

Even with just the second breath from the air bubble, McCallum could tell the air was turning bad, and he had less than a couple of minutes of good oxygen. Breathable air was something every submariner was an expert on. He also knew that Barrington was in a bind; the optimal solution would be to blow air into the sail to clear it of water, but if the sub was in an uncontrolled dive, the XO had a hell of a lot more on his hands than clearing the sail. At least McCallum had shut the outside hatch, which gave the hull pressure integrity. The inner hatch was only designed for emergency use and was rated down to five hundred feet, while the outer was rated to the sub's maximum dive depth of three thousand feet.

McCallum took another breath, his hands gripping the ladder tightly. The air was laced with carbon dioxide. He figured he had another minute before he blacked out and slipped under the water. McCallum kept his mouth shut, trying to hold the air in his lungs as long as possible before letting it out. Slowly, he exhaled and took another slow, deep breath, feeling the pain of his broken ribs, then clamping his mouth shut.

His ears hurt. McCallum blinked. The sail was pressurizing. The water level began going down, and he quickly took several shallow breaths of the fresh oxygen being pumped into the sail.

Before the water was completely clear, the bottom hatch clanged open, letting a splash of water into the operations center. Barrington stuck his head in but was knocked out of the way as McCallum slid down the ladder, ignoring the sting of pain from his broken ribs.

"Status?" McCallum demanded, still trying to get his oxygen level back up.

"We have no steerage, no dive control." Barrington confirmed McCallum's worst fears. "We're in a steady dive at four hundred feet per minute. Current depth—" Barrington turned toward the chief petty officer who was in charge of diving.

"Eight hundred feet and still steady down at four-oh-oh feet per minute," the chief reported.

"All controls have been overridden from the combat systems mainframe," Barrington continued.

"Bateman's gotten control of the CSM," McCallum said.

Barrington nodded. "Appears so, sir. He's nowhere else on the ship, and we can not gain access to the CSM room. No contact with the duty crew in there, and the hatch is locked from the inside."

"You blew the sail," McCallum said. "You must have been able to override—"

Barrington was shaking his head, cutting the captain off. "We disconnected computer control and manually diverted emergency backup from the tanks next to us. But we won't

be able to do all the tanks quickly enough to stop our dive.
I've got men trying to manually get to all the tanks, but
they'll never do it in time."

"What about the bow plane?" McCallum asked.

"Still trying to disconnect computer control," Barrington
reported. "Chief says it'll take them another five minutes
to disconnect and then a minute or two to reorient the
planes manually. We don't have the time, sir."

"Sixteen hundred feet and still steady down at four-oh-
oh feet per minute," the dive chief announced.

McCallum knew that the Navy's unclassified dive rating
for the *Seawolf* was eight hundred feet, but every naval
expert knew that was a joke. *Jane's Fighting Ships*, the
standard handbook for ships, rated the boat as being able
to dive to two thousand. The Electric Boat Division at
Groton had assured the Navy that *Seawolf* could do three
thousand feet safely. Nobody knew exactly how far the ship
could go because no one dared test it beyond three thousand. McCallum had taken *Seawolf* down to two thousand
eight hundred during the shake-out cruise, the maximum
that safety regulations allowed him.

"Everything's set to keep us diving?" McCallum asked.

"Yes, sir."

McCallum ran options through his mind, one after the
other. "He couldn't have reprogrammed the entire system."

"We can't blow ballast, and we can't control the bow
planes," Barrington said. "That's enough to put us through
max depth in—" the XO checked the stopwatch that hung
around his neck—"just under four minutes."

"OK, we do what he won't have planned for and adjusted the computer for." McCallum stepped out of the puddle of water that had formed under his feet. "Is the combat
systems compartment secure?"

"We can't get in, sir," Barrington said. "All hatches are
secure. We could try to burn through, but that would take
a good half-hour."

McCallum nodded. "All right. Dive Chief, flood the CSM compartment."

A look of confusion, followed by comprehension crossed the chief's face. "Aye, aye, sir."

Bateman looked up blankly as a spray of water burst out of a pipe in the ceiling, followed by several others that increased in flow until a torrent of water poured into the compartment.

He stared at the rising water, then pulled his gun out, put it against the side of his head directly over the small bump behind his right ear, and pulled the trigger. Brains and blood splattered across the room to be immediately washed away by the surging water.

Sparks flew as the saltwater entered the mainframe computer and shorted out the workings.

Lights flashed in the operations center, then the emergency backup power came on, bathing the room in a red glow.

"All systems controlled by the computer are down," Barrington reported.

"Do we have manual control?"

"Yes, sir."

"Twenty-eight hundred feet and still steady down at four-oh-oh feet per minute," the dive chief announced.

McCallum barked out orders. "Chief dive planes full up. Blow all ballast manually. Engine room full reverse."

McCallum didn't need the dive chief's verbal report. He could clearly see the red digital display that showed the submarine's current depth. They clicked through 3,000 as the crew raced to do manually what they normally used their computer-assisted controls to do. In the forward part of the ship, the computer control on the dive planes had released, and men struggled to turn the large fins with a crankshaft.

"Gentlemen, we have a new dive record for the Seawolf-class submarine," McCallum announced.

"Thirty-one hundred feet, and dive rate slowing through three-oh-oh feet per minute," the dive chief reported.

McCallum looked over at his executive officer. "Let's hope the boys at the Electric Boat Company weren't sleeping on the job."

"Thirty-two hundred, and dive rate slowing through one-five-oh feet per minute."

Barrington nodded. "We're going to—"

The entire ship suddenly vibrated like a guitar string pulled too tight, cutting off whatever the XO was going to say.

McCallum's eyes were riveted on the dive meter. The numbers were moving less quickly, but the submarine was still going down. Thirty-three hundred feet, and the sound was getting louder. McCallum could feel the fear coming off everyone in the operations center like a wave of penetrating cold air that settled in the spine and wrapped around the stomach. It was a moment every submariner had had nightmares about and prayed they'd never face.

"Trim?" McCallum asked.

"Nose down six degrees and leveling," Barrington answered. "We're having to adjust for the flooded CSM."

Given that the *Seawolf* was 353 feet long, that meant the nose was a bit deeper than the rest of the ship. McCallum's eyes shifted forward to the hatch in the front of the operations center.

He knew if anything gave, it should come from that direction. And if anything gave, everything inside would give. The interior hatches would pop like paper against a compression jack all the way through the ship. It would all be over in a couple of seconds.

"Level," the dive chief announced to a hushed audience. "Dive rate zero."

McCallum looked at the gauge: 3,563.

"Take her up," McCallum ordered. "Slowly. Dive Chief, please note depth for the record."

Dane, Sin Fen, Ariana, and DeAngelo listened to the report from Foreman inside the communications sphere. A tsunami hitting Puerto Rico, the nuclear explosion at Groton, the near-sinking of the *Seawolf*, the infiltration of the SO-SUS system, and the increase in size of the gates: the litany was shocking.

Dane leaned back. The only noise in the sphere after Foreman's voice fell silent was the sound of the heater blowing hot air. He felt tired and confused. The images from Sin Fen's mind disturbed him as much as the news Foreman had relayed.

"The Shadow is paving the way for an all-out attack." Sin Fen broke the silence.

"That's what Conners at the NSA thinks, and it certainly appears that way," Foreman agreed. "Groton and the *Seawolf* were both attempts to cripple our underwater warfare capability. The tsunami was simply a side effect."

Dane stirred. "Side effect? Thousands dead, and you call it a side effect."

"Hundreds are dead at Groton," Foreman snapped. "Six nuclear submarines worth over two and a half billion dollars are destroyed. We're still trying to figure out how much radiation escaped the pen and how many people will be affected by the fallout. That's on top of the radiation from the nuke strikes in the Atlantic. I'm calling the tsunami a side effect because it was a result of the force that came out of the triangle and attempted to destroy *you*. Save your pontificating for someone else."

"I'm not pontificating," Dane shot back. "I'm just trying to keep some perspective on the stakes involved rather than the cost. There's a difference, you know!"

For a few seconds, only the sound of the heater blower filled the communications sphere.

"And SOSUS?" Ariana asked. "Is it just a ploy, or is the Shadow trying to do underwater what we stopped them from doing through the atmosphere?"

"There's no radioactivity detected yet," Foreman said. "Just some electromagnetic abnormalities. Hell, they might even be using SOSUS like we are—to keep track of what's going on underwater."

"What are you going to do?" Dane asked.

"The prudent thing would be to shut SOSUS down," Foreman said, "but I think Conners is right. We should hold off on that and keep an eye on the gates."

"Let me ask you something," Dane said. "You're talking about the possibility that you could be getting set up on the SOSUS network. We're at this spot because of the map etched on the *Scorpion*'s sail. Now it looks like the sub was booby-trapped by the Shadow. Maybe this was a trap? Like the Greeks putting a sign on the Trojan Horse? Not only did we take the horse in, we followed the directions on the side of it."

"I don't think so," Sin Fen said. "I do not believe the writing and map on the submarine were from the Shadow. Remember, there are two sides inside the Triangle. Both could have used the *Scorpion*."

Dane laughed at the absurdity as he had a moment of clarity. "The *Seawolf* was keeping tabs on *us*, too, wasn't it, Foreman? If this was some sort of trap or double-cross, you were ready to blow us out of the water." Dane didn't need an answer. He knew it was true. But he also knew that what Sin Fen said was true: The writing on the side of the *Scorpion* had not been a trap. A human hand, a free human hand, had written that.

"You said Captain Bateman from the *Scorpion* was the person who tried to sink the *Seawolf*," Dane said. "What about the rest of the crew of the *Scorpion*?"

"They all died in the explosion at Groton," Foreman said. "Bateman died on board the *Seawolf*."

"But that means the Shadow can manipulate people," Dane noted. "That's something new."

"Something new as far as we know," Foreman agreed.

"Why does it seem like every time we find out something new about the gates and the Shadow, we learn how little we actually know?" Dane asked.

"How did the Shadow get the *Scorpion*'s reactor to go critical?" Ariana asked.

"Before the explosion, the video feed from the team that went into the *Scorpion*'s reactor showed a cylindrical object with golden beams emanating out of it," Foreman said.

"Like the beam that went into the mainframe computer on board our plane in Cambodia?" Ariana asked.

"Right," Foreman said. "The military is calling what's just happened a reconnaissance in force. The Shadow is checking out the opposition before making its main strike. And because the Shadow focused on our underwater capability, particularly near the Bermuda Triangle, and because that gate is the only one that has increased in size, we have to assume that's where the attack is coming from."

"Or directed," Ariana said.

"There's no target of strategic significance in that area," Foreman said.

"I'm not talking about a target here," Ariana clarified. "I'm talking about the attack. Look what happened to Puerto Rico as the result of the tsunami. The Mid-Atlantic Ridge is not too far away from here. If the Shadow focuses energy into that rift between the tectonic plates, God knows what havoc they could wreak. It would make the wave that hit Puerto Rico look like a splash in a puddle. They could easily take out the eastern seaboard of the United States and a large part of Europe. And if they're coordinating this attack through other gates as appears to be—" Ariana paused, letting the others figure it out for themselves.

"The whiz kids here have done projections on the most advanced computers they have," Foreman said. "Wargaming what could happen if the Shadow fires all twenty-three of the Tridents left from the *Wyoming*. Given that the Trident's range is about four thousand miles, they can cover a large part of the Atlantic along the mid-ocean ridge.

"There's a lot of variables—ocean depth, crust depth over the magma between the tectonic plates—but with each warhead exploding at about a hundred and twenty kilotons, the computer says that at the very least the effect will be numerous volcanoes boiling up, along with earthquakes, on a magnitude we have never experienced in modern history. As you've noted, the resulting tsunamis will devastate the East Coast of the United States and most of Western Europe.

"That's at a minimum," Foreman continued. "There is also the possibility that there could be a crustal displacement of the tectonic plates. Since we're not even sure exactly how the tectonic plates are moved, we're not sure of the forces involved, but if those forces from inside the Earth are channeled by the explosions, God knows what could happen."

"And what if they use the other nuclear weapons they've accumulated over the years?" Ariana asked. "What if they also launch assaults along the Pacific Rim out of the Devil's Sea gate? The Mediterranean from a nearby gate? The Red Sea?"

"I'm having them war-game that worst-case scenario," Foreman said.

"We don't need a computer simulation," Sin Fen said. "If the Shadow launches such an assault, you can be assured they know what they are doing. It will be the end of mankind. The entire surface of the planet will change. Continents will be moved, much as Antarctica, which most likely was Atlantis, was moved from the middle of the Atlantic to the South Pole."

Dane broke the silence that followed that statement. "So we're back to where we were at the start of this. We need to find out what's below us. I think the gate coming this way lets us know it's important." He stood up. "We're wasting time sitting around talking about it. Let's get going."

Eighteen

999 A.D.

"Have you ever heard of a place called Thule?" Tam Nok asked. She had the metal plate out and was hunched over it, her finger tracing the lines, her lips moving as she read to herself.

Ragnarok lowered his hand, which he'd been using to block the sun so he could scan the surrounding terrain. They were hiding in a streambed, bushes surrounding them and large trees towering overhead. Stonehenge was many miles behind them, and Ragnarok knew they would reach the shore early this evening once they began walking again. He was tempted to continue during the daylight, but the alarm over the dead patrol must have been raised by now, and he knew they would not last long against a unit of the Saxon king's army.

Ragnarok could almost smell the sea over the horizon. He longed for the thunder of the waves on the shore and the sight of his high-prowed ship pulled up on the beach, waiting for them. Dusk was only about an hour away, and then they could move.

"I have heard of Thule," Ragnarok acknowledged, sitting back down on the dirt embankment, then leaning back, hands behind his head. "To the north, beyond the ice and snow and fire. Or so the old ones say."

"What fire?" Tam Nok asked.

"It is said fire comes out of the ocean as one approaches Thule," Ragnarok said. "I have seen such fire once when sailing along the coast of Iceland."

"There are strange writings here." She indicated the metal map. "Some of them revolve around Thule."

He closed his eyes, remembering his mother's words. "Fire and ice, the beginning of all things."

"Tell me the story of the beginning," Tam Nok asked.

"You knew of the Valkyries," Ragnarok opened his eyes and looked at her. "You called yourself a disir. If you know those things, you know of the creation and the stories of the gods."

Tam Nok shook her head. "I knew of those things because you knew of them."

Ragnarok frowned. "What do you mean by that?"

"I can not explain it right now. Please, tell me the Viking legends of the beginning."

Ragnarok remembered his mother, the family gathered around the fire in the end of their lodge, the wind howling outside. Her voice, low and soothing, as she told the stories of the gods and goddesses. He felt a pang for what he had lost and for the first time, he didn't smother that feeling with a surge of anger and desire for revenge. It was simply there, a heavy weight on his chest.

"The world was dark and there was no order. No rule. No goodness. In the center of the world was a chasm, so large one could not see the bottom. If you threw a stone off, you never heard it hit, so deep was this split in the earth called Ginnungagap.

"To the north of Ginnungagap is the kingdom of Niflheim, a dark world always covered in fog. This is where Thule is also located. To the south of Ginnungagap is the world of fire and constant light, called Muspellsheim. Here lived Surtr, the flame giant whose only duty was to protect his land from those from Thule.

"But Surtr became bored as he was alone in Muspellsheim. He swung his mighty flame sword to practice and produced much steam, which rose toward Ginnungagap and froze in strange shapes. From that ice came two other creatures: Ymir, the first of the giants, and Audhumbla, a large cow."

Ragnarok cracked open his eyes to see how Tam Nok was taking all this. It had always sounded so right, so normal, when told in a Viking lodge among his own people, but telling the creation story in the land of the Saxons, to a woman from a far land, he wondered for the first time. Tam Nok was watching him, her face betraying no emotion.

"Ymir became hungry, so he milked Audhumbla. Of course, the cow had nothing to forage on in the land of ice. Nevertheless, she licked the ice and in doing so, uncovered another creature, long buried. This was Buri the Producer. He was the grandfather of Odin, the god who rules now in Asgard.

"Full of milk, Ymir became tired and lay down to sleep. The heat from Surtr's sword made him sweat, and from this sweat came Thrudgelmir, the six-headed giant from whom all the frost giants are descended."

"A six-headed giant?" Tam Nok asked. "A man?"

Ragnarok nodded.

"We have a legend of a seven-headed snake, the Naga," Tam Nok said.

Ragnarok shrugged. "The only snakes I know of in the legends are Jormungand, one of the spawn of Loki and Angrboda and the hydra. Jormungand is a most terrible creature that was cast into the ocean by Odin. It grew so long there, it eventually encircled Midgard. The hydra is a beast that fights for the darkness—six heads, not seven—and it spits poison. I have never seen one, but I talked to a man who said he encountered one in Eire Land."

"I have never seen a real Naga, either," Tam Nok said. "It is strange how different stories can come out of perhaps the same thing, twisted over the years of telling to fit the land where they are told in."

"This is not a story," Ragnarok said. "This is the way the world began."

"But my people have a different way the world began," Tam Nok said. "I have traveled far, and in each land I have listened to their story of the beginning of man, and there are always things that are similar. The snake in the ocean is also in my culture. It is part of the story of the way the world began and the way the world ends. Please continue," Tam Nok urged.

Ragnarok thought for a second to remember where he had stopped his tale. "The god Buri had a son, named Bör, who married a giantess named Bestla, and they had three sons: Odin, Vili, and Ve.

"A war started between the children of Bor and the children of the monster Thrudgelmir. They fought for many, many years in the depths of Ginnungagap.

"Finally, Odin and his brothers were able to ambush and kill the first of the frost giants, Ymir. His boiling blood killed most of the rest of the giants. Only a few escaped on a ship, sailing on the ocean of blood, to establish a new land to the south, where they started a new race.

"Odin, flush with victory, decided to make a world. The only thing he could use was Ymir's body. They already had the oceans from his blood. From the flesh they created Midgard—" Ragnarok pointed down—"where we live. Ymir's flesh is the earth, his bones the hills, his teeth the cliffs of the fjords, his hair the trees and grass, his skull the sky above.

"One day while walking, Odin came upon two trees that had been knocked down. One was ash, one an elm. Odin breathed life back into these trees, giving them a spirit and a thirst for knowledge. They were the first man and woman." Ragnarok spread his hands. "Since then, man and the gods have had many adventures. Too many for me to tell in one day."

"How does it all end?" Tam Nok asked.

Ragnarok thumped his chest. "It ends in a great battle. A battle for which my mother named me: Ragnarok—the final conflict between the forces of light and darkness."

"Why did your mother give you the name of this battle that has yet to be fought?"

"I do not know," Ragnarok admitted.

"Was your mother a seer? A priestess?"

"My mother could see things—" Ragnarok paused— "but she could not see useful things. If she had, my father would still be alive."

"Seeing things does not mean you can change things," Tam Nok said. "Maybe she did see what would happen but knew there was nothing she could do about it."

The thought had never occurred to Ragnarok.

"Would your father have listened if your mother warned him about whatever it was that you thought she should have seen?" Tam Nok asked. "Would he have changed his actions?"

Ragnarok reluctantly shook his head. "No, he wouldn't have done anything different. He had too—"

"Too much pride?" Tam Nok finished the sentence.

"Maybe," Ragnarok said. He didn't add that he knew his mother had warned his father.

"And who wins the final battle?" Tam Nok asked, bringing him back to their present situation.

"Both sides lose," Ragnarok said. "The gods and monsters pair off and fight. Thor and the large snake Jormungand fight each other. Thor kills the snake with his mighty hammer but not before the snake bites him and fills him with venom."

"A mighty hammer?" Tam Nok repeated. "An interesting weapon."

"You think that is what we are searching for?" Ragnarok asked. "Thor's hammer?"

"I think we are looking for a Shield, but I have learned that Shields can take many forms," Tam Nok said.

"Didn't the stone tell you about the Shield?"

"Some," Tam Nok said evasively.

"Is our destination Thule?"

"No. Thule is mentioned, but where we must go is here."

Ragnarok leaned over and looked at where her finger was pointing. It was to the west and south of Greenland, along a far coast that stretched along the entire left edge of the metal plate. Ragnarok shifted his gaze across to the adjoining map sheet of Tam Nok's. The location was south of the Roman Ocean on that map sheet. Ragnarok was an experienced sailor, but the concept of such a long journey staggered him. Tam Nok's finger rested on a small island in the middle of the vast ocean.

"It will take a year to go there!"

"I don't have a year," Tam Nok said.

Ragnarok took a stick and measured the distance from Norway to Iceland. Than he measured along the coast of the strange western land down to the spot she indicated. "It depends on the winds and currents," he finally said. "Maybe we can make it in six months. Four, if all is favorable."

"We must be there before the year's end," Tam Nok said.

Ragnarok rubbed a hand through his beard. "Seven months. We should be able to if Odin smiles on us. And if the Skraelings let us pass."

"Skraelings?"

"A fierce people who live in this strange land across the ocean," Ragnarok said. "They are said to have red skin and be very fierce. I did not believe the stories overly much but—" he shrugged—"now I have seen you and you have brown skin and come from a land in the other direction I never heard of. So I think maybe there are these red people, and the stories I heard were real."

He tapped the map sheet. "It will be difficult to find an island like this, out of sight of land."

"I will find it," Tam Nok said. "We must get to the boat. Every journey begins with the first step. We will worry about red men when we see them." She rolled the map up and put it back in the bamboo case. She slid the metal plate inside her pack.

"There was a lot of writing on the metal," Ragnarok noted. "What did it say?"

"It will take me time to translate much of it. It is in a very old tongue, one I learned among many other languages. I've read what I need for now. I will try to translate the rest later. Then I will tell you what it says."

"You treat me like a child," Ragnarok said. "Your gold can only take you so far. My crew will not want to cross the large sea for any amount. I will have to convince them to do it. But I am not sure you are worth convincing them for."

"It is not about me," Tam Nok said. "We must find the weapon to fight the Valkyries and the Shadow."

Ragnarok shook his head. "The Valkyries are demons. We are not gods. Why must we fight them? Why not let them fight among themselves? Maybe we are interfering with something that should not be trifled with."

"It is my duty to—"

"*Your* duty," Ragnarok said. "Not mine. How did you know my name when we first met?"

Tam Nok pretended to concentrate on the straps for her pack, avoiding his gaze.

"How did you get me to run in the fjord and then again near the stones? I have never run from a battle, even when it appeared I would die. But I have run twice since I met you."

Tam Nok looked up, her almond eyes fixing him. "Now who is lying? You've run from a battle before. Once before. Did you not?"

Ragnarok was completely still, only the skin along the left side of his face moving ever so slightly as a muscle under it jumped.

"What do you know of my past?" he finally asked.

"What you have let me know," Tam Nok said. She reached out and placed her hand briefly on his forehead. "It is there, always there, even when you are thinking about something else. Like the bubbles on top of a kettle of boiling water."

"What is there?"

"Your anger. Your rage. It consumes you. You think it is about your father, but it is really about your mother."

"How do you know such things?" Ragnarok grabbed her by the shoulders and shook her. "You are a witch."

Tam Nok didn't react. "I am a priestess. We are taught to read people."

"How do you know what happened to my parents?"

"I don't," Tam Nok said. "I only know that whatever happened to them has shaped you, like the blacksmith shaped your new ax." She reached up and removed his hands from her shoulders. "Why don't you tell me what happened?"

Ragnarok turned from her and sat down, his elbows on his knees, his head in his hands. He felt the pounding in his temples, the rage of blood lust and revenge. His palms pressed tighter and tighter against his skull until he felt a soft pair of hands on top of his, pulling back.

"In my land, we say the past is done. There is nothing that can be done to change it. You have to live and move on."

"Never!" But he allowed her to pull his hands away from his face. She gently placed hers on his temples.

"I see betrayal."

Ragnarok nodded. "My father was betrayed."

"Tell me." Tam Nok moved back and sat across from him.

"He was a war leader. A man of honor. The man who all in our village turned to. The king—" Ragnarok spat— "the man who anointed himself king of the Vikings demanded that all the villages pay him tribute and provide warriors and ships when he called for them. My father owed allegiance to no one but his people. He saw no reason to do either.

"The king called a meeting to discuss this with those who did not readily submit. Under a flag of truce. My father went, even though my mother warned him not to."

Ragnarok paused and shook his head. "My father was a very brave man. He went with only two men, as the king said he also would come. They met on an island off the southern coast of Norway. There were a dozen other leaders like my father there. Each with only two of their most trusted men as had been agreed.

"The king came with ten ships full of warriors. He told them they could submit or die. My father fought, even though he knew there was no chance of victory. The king's men killed him, cut his head off, and sent it back to us."

"And you swore revenge," Tam Nok said.

"Of course."

"But you don't have the strength yet to attack the king," Tam Nok said.

"He will pay. One day—"

"And your mother?" Tam Nok asked. "She *did* warn him."

Ragnarok stood, throwing his pack over his shoulder and holding his ax in one hand, Lailoken's staff in the other. "It is time for us to go."

"Your mother told you to submit, didn't she?" Tam Nok

pressed. "To make peace and accept the future. Or else you would die futilely like your father."

Ragnarok walked away from the priestess. "It is time to go," he said over his shoulder.

Nineteen

THE PRESENT

"Confirming hatch sealed." DeAngelo reached up and put his hand on the red light indicating the top hatch in the forward sphere of *Deepflight* was sealed. Dane knew what he was doing by touching the light. Just like a jumpmaster in airborne school, the eyes followed the hand to double-check.

DeAngelo repeated the confirmation request into the small microphone on the headset he wore. "Sin Fen, please confirm rear sphere hatch sealed."

"Confirm hatch sealed," Sin Fen reported from her place five meters to the rear of where Dane and the submersible's commander were located.

DeAngelo triple-checked that on the status board in front of him. "Hatches sealed. *Deeplab*, we are prepared to release."

Ariana's voice came through clearly. "All secure here. I will disconnect umbilicals in ten seconds. Good luck. I'll keep the porch light on."

"Thanks," Dane said. He knew she wasn't happy about being left behind in *Deeplab*, particularly left alone, but someone had to maintain the habitat.

There was a click, and he knew the commo and power umbilical cords were pulled back into the habitat. They were on their own now, isolated from the rest of the world.

DeAngelo was prone next to Dane, his hands on the controls. There were dull metal-on-metal sounds.

"We're clear of the habitat," DeAngelo said. He pushed forward on the two levers. "Descending."

Dane had a slight feeling of disorientation as the submersible nosed over and headed for the depths. That feeling was on top of something deeper, more primeval.

"Aren't you afraid you'll hit something?" Dane asked. All the screens showing the outer view were black as DeAngelo had both the visible and IR external lights off.

"Like?" DeAngelo asked.

"A whale?"

"We're much deeper than whales can go," DeAngelo said. "Sperm whales can only dive down to about four thousand feet. Actually, some species of seals can dive deeper than whales—about another thousand feet deeper."

DeAngelo pointed at the depth meter, the red numbers clicking through 22,000 feet. "This deep, the ocean is almost a desert. There's very little life and certainly none large enough to cause us any damage if we hit it."

"Something's out there," Dane said.

DeAngelo looked over at him. "What—" He paused as Sin Fen's voice came through their headsets.

"He's right. Something is out there."

"And alive," Dane added. "To the north. Near the gate." He closed his eyes. "In the gate. It knows we're here. It's hungry for us."

"What are you talking about?" DeAngelo asked.

Dane opened his eyes. "You are going to have to trust us. This is why we are here. To feel things others can't feel."

DeAngelo flipped some switches. "I'm turning the IR lights and cameras on so we can see but not be seen."

Dane looked at the screens. Nothing but black with the cone of IR light shining through. He shook his head. "We're safe for now. It can't come out of the gate. But the gate is growing. Sin Fen," he said, "do you sense it?"

"It is growing," Sin Fen agreed. "Very slowly, but it's creeping in our direction. We do not have much time."

"We'll be at the bottom of the Puerto Rican Trench in an hour and a half," DeAngelo said. "Do you sense what is down there?"

Dane shook his head. "Not really." He looked up at the screen. "Sin Fen?"

"There is a blank spot below us I can not see into."

"I feel that emptiness, also," Dane said.

"Is it dangerous?" DeAngelo asked.

"Being in this submersible is dangerous," Dane said. "We'll see what is down there when we get there."

"Passing through twenty-four thousand feet," DeAngelo said. "We're in range to get sonar images, if you want. But remember, if we turn the sonar on, we're giving our position away to anyone who is listening."

"Turn it on," Dane ordered. "We're going to have to eventually see where we're going."

DeAngelo locked down the levers in the descending spiral position and flipped a switch. *Deepflight*'s sonar began painting a picture of the bottom.

Dane watched the sonar screen as an image of the Milwaukee Depth coalesced. A bowl-shaped depression with steep sides formed. The north side of the Milwaukee Depth was almost vertical, an underwater cliff of vast dimensions.

"Do you have the location of the circle that Foreman's people discovered?" Dane asked.

"The computer is orienting the stored image right now," DeAngelo said, "comparing it to what we're picking up on sonar."

A green circle appeared on the screen. One edge of it touched the very bottom of the Milwaukee Depth, but the majority was off to the north, outside the edge of the depression on that side, beyond the mile-high cliff.

"That's strange," DeAngelo said. "If the reading is true, then this thing, whatever it is, must be under the ocean floor."

"Take us to the part that touches the Depth," Dane tapped the screen.

"Roger that."

Dane glanced up at the video feed to the rear sphere. Sin Fen was looking at her sonar display. Dane reached out to her mentally, but the only image he picked up was her interest in what she was seeing. They were now in the hole in the ocean floor that constituted the Milwaukee Depth.

"Twenty-six thousand feet," DeAngelo announced. "We're three quarters of a mile above the bottom. I'm slowing our descent. Things are getting tighter. I'm going to find the north wall and use it to guide us down."

On the sonar display, the north wall grew closer and closer as DeAngelo steered them toward it.

"There!" DeAngelo said.

Dane looked at the display that showed the outside view lit by the IR searchlights. A gray vertical wall appeared on the screen. Alternating between the sonar display and the outer view, DeAngelo took them down along the flat north wall of the Milwaukee Depth.

The depth gauge clicked through 27,000 feet, and DeAngelo slowed them further.

"That wall's not natural," Sin Fen said.

"Hold up," Dane ordered DeAngelo. *Deepflight* came to a halt, floating at 27,600 feet.

A horizontal line had appeared on the rock wall, a black mark against the gray wall, almost a foot thick. It extended left and right as far as the camera could see. Dane leaned forward, getting closer to the screen. The wall below the line seemed to be the same rock as that above, but the rock was totally smooth on the lower portion. The upper portion also appeared to overhang the rock below by a couple of feet. Dane checked the sonar. The wall was completely smooth below.

"The line curves very slightly," he said. "Follow it to the right," he told DeAngelo.

The twin propellers churned, and the submersible moved along the rock wall, tracing the line.

"It is curved," DeAngelo confirmed. "We're descending very slowly."

Soon Dane could see that the line was on a sloped forty-five-degree angle, heading down. "It's a big circle," he said.

"Semicircle," DeAngelo corrected. "As wide as that curve is, we're going to be at the bottom halfway down."

Dane checked the sonar. The bottom was less than three hundred feet below them, and the curve had yet to go through the vertical.

"Two hundred from bottom," DeAngelo announced a minute later.

"This thing is big." Dane was calculating in his head. "Almost a half mile in radius."

"The question is," Sin Fen said, "what is it?"

"One hundred feet and slowing." DeAngelo's eyes were glued to the sonar. The line slid by. "Fifty feet."

Dane could feel the submersible slow, his body pressed slightly against the pad beneath.

DeAngelo switched on the camera in the belly of the sub. Inky blackness met the IR searchlight.

"Twenty-five feet."

The bottom appeared on the screen. It consisted of striated black rock that met the gray wall. The line was exactly vertical where it disappeared into the black rock. Dane reached out with his mind but felt nothing.

"This sure as hell ain't natural," DeAngelo muttered as he brought *Deepflight* to a hover. "What now?"

Dane looked at the projection of the muon circle against the sonar pattern and their own location.

"Go west," Dane said, "along the wall. Take us to the center."

"Roger that." DeAngelo turned the submersible, and they scooted along, keeping the bottom twenty feet below and the wall fifteen feet off their starboard side. The gray rock was perfectly smooth, and Dane wondered if it was rock at all.

"Is the bottom view normal?" Dane asked DeAngelo.

"The only time I've seen anything like this is when I was in the Pacific off Hawaii—molten rock that hits seawater and cools quickly. But that was near the surface— magma that flows on land and then goes into the water. Magma that comes out directly into the ocean from a vent doesn't look like this."

"So how do we have this type of rock at twenty-eight thousand feet?" Dane asked.

"Hell, how do you have this smooth stuff to our right?" DeAngelo asked in turn. "I've never seen anything like that, either."

"It's a door," Sin Fen's voice came over the intercom.

That's what Dane had been thinking, but the sheer magnitude of the door itself and the depth they were operating at made it hard to accept the concept.

"Damn big door," DeAngelo said. He glanced at the sonar. "It's over a mile wide."

"It doesn't appear to have been opened in a while," Dane said. "The bottom half looks like it's blocked in."

"Besides the constant low-level field surrounding whatever is behind the door," Sin Fen said, "Nagoya picked up spikes of muonic activity in this area several times."

"We've got something ahead on the wall," DeAngelo said.

Dane looked at the video screen. The IR searchlights lit up a black circle in the center of the gray. The black was forty feet in diameter. The infrared light didn't reflect off it but rather seemed to be absorbed.

"Can we see it in normal light?" Dane asked as De-Angelo brought them to a hover.

"It won't look any different," DeAngelo said, but he turned on the outer lights anyway. The computer automatically switched to the normal light video cameras.

DeAngelo was right; it looked the same. A black circle that seemed to grab the light and suck it in. Dane had seen something like it before.

"It's a gateway," he told the other two. "Flaherty came to me in Angkor Kol Ker through something like that, and we went through the same thing to go from Angkor to the *Scorpion.*"

"A gateway in the middle of what looks like a door?" DeAngelo said.

"I've got a smaller gate in my door at home," Dane said. "My dog uses it."

"I don't think I like that analogy." DeAngelo had turned them straight on, facing the black circle.

"The question is," Sin Fen said, "what is on the other side? Where does it lead? If it's like the small gate you went through at Angkor, it could transport us anywhere."

"There's only one way to find out," Dane said.

"I don't know if that's a good idea," DeAngelo said.

"We're here," Dane said.

"But maybe that's solid," DeAngelo protested.

"Then I'd suggest you go into it very slowly," Dane said.

"I don't—" DeAngelo began, but Sin Fen cut him off.

"Go ahead. There is something on the other side."

"Great," DeAngelo muttered. He edged the two drive levers forward, and they approached the black circle at a crawl.

Dane tried to push his mind forward, through the door, but he was picking up nothing. He wondered what had made Sin Fen say there was something on the other side.

The nose of the submersible was less than five feet from

the black circle. Four. DeAngelo slowed them even more. Three. Two. One.

Dane felt the air around him change, press in as if taking on a thicker consistency. Pain rippled across his brain, and he was dimly aware that alarms were going off and DeAngelo was throwing switches and pushing buttons in a flurry of activity next to him.

Dane looked up at the screen. Water all around, but the black circle was behind them now. And there was light suffusing the water from above.

"What happened?" Dane asked.

"Extreme pressure change outside." DeAngelo pushed another button and the wail of the alarm stopped. The sudden silence accompanied the end of the pain in Dane's head.

"Change to what?" Dane asked.

DeAngelo simply pointed at the depth gauge. It read thirty feet.

"How can that be?" Dane asked. "Where are we?"

"I don't know," DeAngelo said.

"Why don't we surface and take a look?" Sin Fen suggested from the rear sphere.

DeAngelo edged back, and the submersible headed for the surface. They popped up, and Dane blinked as the topside cameras recorded the scene around them.

They were floating in the center of circular body of still, dark water, about three miles in diameter. A smooth black beach, two miles in width, encircled the water, slowly rising and ending at a rock wall that curved up and in, meeting a half-mile over their heads. A large glowing orb, so bright the camera had to click in place two filters to prevent overload, lit the entire cavern.

Dane had no doubt that this was the muon space that Nagoya's instruments had recorded. But what hadn't been recorded were the hundreds of ships and planes that littered the black beach all around them, slowly revealed as the

cameras rotated. It was an overwhelming vista; Dane saw
ships ranging from Roman galleys through modern war-
ships. Planes from old propeller biplanes through an SR-71
reconnaissance jet, all tumbled on the metal floor like a
madman's model toy collection. There was even a massive
dirigible, the metal skin half-collapsed, lying on its side.

Some of the ships and planes were partially destroyed
or disassembled. On the far shore, a huge oil tanker had
been stripped of its hull, only the steel girders remaining,
like a beached whale that had decomposed to its skeleton.
A large warship of what appeared to be World War I vin-
tage was missing its bow up to the first gun turret, the metal
cut cleanly.

There was no sign of the crews, just the relics.

"It's a graveyard," Dane whispered, trying to take in the
large numbers and immense variety of craft he was view-
ing. He reached out with his mind but picked up no signs
of life.

"Let's hope it's not our graveyard, too," DeAngelo muttered.

"Look to the right," Dane said. "Between that yacht and
the B-24 bomber."

The escape pod from *Deeplab* lay on the black beach,
the latest addition to the macabre scene.

Ariana Michelet saw the small dot representing *Deepflight*
disappear off her sonar screen. She waited for it to reappear,
hoping that it had simply gone behind something, but the
minutes passed, and nothing happened.

She picked up the phone linking her to the *Glomar* and
reported this new development. Captain Stanton told her
she had a call that he was relaying.

She waited, then with a belch of static, Foreman's voice
echoed through the operations sphere.

"Do you have any idea where *Deepflight* is?" Foreman
asked.

"It went into the circle of muonic activity," Ariana reported. "That's what you wanted from the very beginning, isn't it?"

Foreman ignored her question and asked one of his own. "You're aware the Bermuda Triangle gate is growing? Along with the other gates?"

"We heard that it grew when the line of activity came out, but not that it's still growing."

"Latest imagery indicates a growth rate that will put it over your location in eight hours," Foreman said. "You'll be inside the gate then."

"And?" Ariana said. "What do you expect me to do about it? Abandon *Deepflight*? It'll take the *Glomar* six hours to pull *Deeplab* up, anyway."

"I'm just keeping you informed," Foreman said. "The electromagnetic activity through the SOSUS system is continuing and increasing. The president has ordered all available ships and subs to sea in preparation."

"In preparation for what?" Ariana asked.

"That's what the president asked me, and that's what I'm hoping Dane and Sin Fen can tell us when they get back."

"I'll let you know as soon as they reestablish contact." Ariana cut the transmission and sat back in the command chair.

Twenty

999 A.D.

"No."

Ragnarok almost smiled at Bjarni's curt assessment of the course he had just indicated on the map. The wind was blowing steadily out of the southeast, and the sail was tacked to allow them to take full advantage. The islands that lay off the southwest tip of England had passed by off their starboard side an hour ago, and they were now south of Eire Land.

He had Tam Nok's two maps—paper and metal—laid out on the rearmost rowing seat. He tapped the metal one at the spot Tam Nok had said they had to get to. "We have to get there."

"The currents will be against us." Bjarni amplified his answer. "We can not go to the southwest directly. You know that." The old man leaned over. "The sea comes this way—" his gnarled finger traced a path in the opposite direction from that Ragnarok had indicated. "Even if the wind is with us—which it won't be—we could not fight the sea. We would, at best, sit still in the same place, at worst, be pushed back. Even now—" he gestured at the sea around them—"we are being pushed to the north even though our dragon head faces due west."

"There has to be a way," Ragnarok argued. Tam Nok was still sleeping in the forward part of the boat, and Ragnarok saw no reason to waste any time. He wanted to head in the right direction immediately.

Bjarni sighed and knelt down next to the maps, Ragnarok joining him. He was simply glad to be back on his ship. Hrolf and the ship had been waiting as promised at the same point on the beach the previous evening. Ragnarok and Tam Nok had boarded without incident, and they'd immediately set sail and continued through the night, putting distance between themselves and the land of the Saxons.

With the light of day, it was time to make a decision, and Ragnarok knew that was not going to be as easy as Tam Nok would like.

"The only way we could get there—" Bjarni stabbed the map with his finger—"is to travel in a large circle this way." He traced a route to the south of Iceland, beneath Greenland, and along the coast of the large land that lay to the west. "Then we can catch the current and ride into the center of the ocean to the place you wish to go," Bjarni concluded.

"How long would that take?"

"A year. Maybe less, if all goes well," the helmsman said. "But we would be traveling where no one has ever gone. Strange waters are dangerous waters. And we would have to winter somewhere along this coast." He indicated the large continent. "And stop often for resupply. No one I know has ever made a journey that far."

"Remember what Lailoken said." Tam Nok was standing over the two of them. "He said the shortest distance would not be a straight line."

"But going all the way around in almost a circle is certainly not the shortest distance either," Ragnarok said.

Bjarni had picked up the metal plate and was studying it.

"He also said something about a shortcut," Tam Nok said.

"How can there be a shortcut?" Ragnarok argued. "We know where we are, and we know where we wish to go. We can not go in a straight line, and any other route would take too much time."

"There is a tunnel," Tam Nok said. She took the map from Bjarni and pointed to a spot off the northern coast of Iceland.

"A what?" Ragnarok looked where she was pointing.

"It says here in these runes that there is a tunnel," Tam Nok said.

"You can read the markings?" Ragnarok asked.

"It is a language from the Greeks," the priestess replied. "I learned some in my travels. I do not understand much, but this word here, it is the word for tunnel. And this thin line goes from there to here, which is where I wish to go. I believe the line is the tunnel."

"This place," Ragnarok said, "off the coast of Iceland, is where Ginnungagap, the great chasm of ice and fire that separates the gods, is reported to be. I have heard stories of the sea opening up, of monsters climbing out of the depths. A tunnel in the great chasm would not be strange. The legends say the gods can travel through the underworld."

Hrolf had been hovering in the background, and now he added his opinion. "I do not wish to travel through the underworld."

"We do not even know for sure if there is a tunnel there," Ragnarok said.

"Monsters and demonesses who fly—" Hrolf spat. "We are intruding in things beyond us."

"It may be beyond us," Tam Nok agreed, "but it affects us."

"How?" Hrolf demanded. "All we have heard are your stories. You talk of a threat to the world, but I see no threat except when we stick our noses where they should not be."

"My people were—" Tam Nok began, but Hrolf interrupted.

"*Your* people. Not my people."

"All people have been affected by the Shadow," Tam Nok said. "Where do you think you come from?"

"Not from the same place as you," Hrolf said. He held out his arm and placed it next to hers. "We are very different."

Tam Nok shook her head. "That is just skin color. I live in a hot, sunny place. My people have been there for many generations just as yours have lived in a cold, dark place for many generations. We adapt to where we live. In my journey here, I have seen many different types of people. The ones who built the Great Wall that I passed through. With eyes like mine but their skin was more yellow. The riders of the steppes. All different but all the same. Not here—" she rubbed her hand along her arm—"but here." Tam Nok pressed her hand against her chest over her heart. "And here." She pointed at her head.

"The stories, the legends, are different in detail but the same in meaning and depth. All speak of a great flood long ago. They give different reasons for it, but all knew of it. Even those who live in the very high mountains far from the ocean, who would not have even seen the flood. How do they know of it? Because their ancestors came on the flood. All our ancestors did.

"The battles between gods—all have different names for their gods, but there is much that is the same in the way the gods act, the way they fight. Even this tunnel under the Earth. Every culture I have passed through speaks of an underworld."

Tam Nok reached out and placed her hands on Hrolf's chest. "This Shadow destroyed our ancestors and scattered them so far around the world that you stand here now and don't believe we are kin. But we are. And it will happen again, except this time, there will be no one left. Unless we stop it."

All activity had ceased on the ship. Other than Tam Nok speaking, there was only the sound of the sail snapping in the wind and the water passing by the hull. Every Viking was staring at the small, brown woman, listening to her words.

Hrolf looked down at her hands on his chest, then reached up and placed his old, worn ones over hers. "I do not know of these things you speak. I would like to believe we are all one people. Then maybe we would stop killing each other and hating so much." The old man's eyes lifted to Ragnarok's. "I will go where my captain commands."

"We have to go northwest anyway," Ragnarok said.

Tam Nok nodded. "We will go that way. I know it is the right way."

Bjarni stood and relieved the man on the rudder. He pushed on the tiller, and the dragon's head swung around to the northwest.

Twenty-one

THE PRESENT

"This can't be right," DeAngelo said. "I'm reading normal atmospheric pressure out there."

"Why can't that be right?" Dane asked.

"Because the muonic circle of activity was at twenty-eight thousand feet depth," DeAngelo said. "Which means we're still that deep."

Dane was still staring at the video monitors, taking in the variety of craft lying on the metal shore. "The large door must be a pressure lock. This whole thing is pressurized."

"But—" DeAngelo was at a loss for words. "Do you know what it would take to build such a—something this big? Something that strong?"

"Technology we don't possess," Sin Fen said from the rear sphere. She was on her feet, reaching toward the hatch.

"What are you doing?" DeAngelo was startled.

"Going outside."

"That's a good idea." Dane stood and reached up, grabbing the hatch handle. "Unlock the hatches," he told DeAngelo.

"I—" DeAngelo gave up and turned to his controls.

The light flashed red, and the automatic warning sounded as DeAngelo released the locks. Dane turned the handle, and with a slight hiss, the hatch swung open. He climbed up the ladder and stood on the small metal grating on the top of the forward sphere. Sin Fen was on top of the rear sphere, fifteen feet behind him.

"There's no one here," Dane said.

"I know," Sin Fen concurred.

The air was thick, almost oily, just like the air inside the Angkor gate. But Dane didn't feel the sense of danger he had felt the two times he'd gone inside that gate.

"Where do you think all the crews went?" Dane asked.

"Into the gate," Sin Fen said. "This is a holding area for the ships and planes."

"Some of them look like they've been held here for thousands of years," Dane noted. He yelled down into the sphere to DeAngelo. "Can you take us close to the beach?"

In reply, *Deepflight* began moving through the water, producing the only disturbance in the mirrorlike surface.

When they were ten meters from the shore, DeAngelo yelled up to them that they were as close as he could get without grounding the submersible.

"Ready to take a dip?" Dane asked.

In reply, Sin Fen climbed down off the sphere and slid into the water. She began swimming for the shore. "The water is not cold," she yelled over her shoulder. "That's strange."

Given that the water on the other side of the door was thirty-six degrees, that was indeed strange Dane thought, but no stranger than the cavern itself and the craft that surrounded them.

Dane jumped into the water and swam after Sin Fen. The water was not only reasonably warm, it felt different, as the air did. Thicker and slimy. Dane was glad when his feet hit something solid beneath them. He stood and walked onto the beach, water slowly dripping off him. The first thing he noted was that the beach wasn't of sand but rather was a strange material, almost a metal, but with a slight yield to it. It also was almost warm to the touch and seamless, extending to the smooth rock wall a half mile away. "Hell of an engineering job," Dane said.

They walked up to the pod, not surprised to see the hatch was open. Dane stuck his head in briefly.

"Empty?" Sin Fen asked.

"You know it is," Dane said.

Sin Fen was looking about at the craft closest to them. "Where do you want to start?"

"I don't even know what we're looking for," Dane said.

"There should be captain's logs in most of these ships," Sin Fen said. "That's a maritime tradition almost as long as there has been writing."

"Let's go clockwise," Dane suggested.

They walked around the pleasure yacht. There was a group of a dozen large rafts, long logs tied together with vines. A long rudder made of a single log, carefully carved, extended back. There was a pole in the center of each that held a drooping sail.

"Who do you think was on the ocean using those?" Dane asked as the went past them.

Sin Fen picked up a piece of cloth off one of the rafts. It was stained red, with sticklike figures drawn on it. "Looks Central American. But very old."

Beyond the rafts was a freighter. Something about it struck Dane. He angled toward it so he could see the faded name painted on the bow. "The USS *Cyclops.*" He looked up at the ship. "A manganese ore freighter. Disappeared in March of 1918 with all hands while sailing near the Bermuda Triangle. The best guess of the naval investigative board is that she turned turtle in heavy seas, trapping all hands, before eventually sinking. The *Poseidon Adventure* was based on that finding."

"Well, now we know they were wrong," Sin Fen said as they walked around the bow of the ship.

A row of five Spanish galleons lay in front of them, evenly spaced from the edge of the water to the rock wall to their left. "A historian would give his right arm to be here," Dane said as they walked between two of the ships.

"A treasure convoy from the New World that never made it back to Spain," Sin Fen said. "There's probably billions of dollars worth of treasure here."

"Probably," Dane agreed. He paused. "Look at that."

A small, single-masted ship was in front of them. It was less than fifty feet long by ten wide. There were holes in the upper sides where oars poked through. Dane walked up and placed his hand on the wood.

"This is very old."

There were some markings carved into the prow that Sin Fen was studying. "Phoenician," she finally said. "I don't know what it says, but I recognize the writing."

"And how do you know that?" Dane asked. "Seems strange that a woman from the slums of Phnom Phen would recognize Phoenician writing."

"I spent many years in school after meeting Mr. Foreman," Sin Fen said. "Because we knew the gates were very old, one of my areas of study was ancient cultures."

"How would a Phoenician ship get caught in the Bermuda Triangle?" Dane asked. "I thought they didn't navigate outside of the Mediterranean."

"Actually, it's speculated the Phoenicians sailed out of the Mediterranean and all the way around Africa. Remember, we've determined that something came out of the gate. We have no idea how far that thing might have gone to grab these craft."

Dane was already looking past the Phoenician ship. "Flight 19."

Five TBM Avengers were lined up wingtip to wingtip. Dane climbed up the wing of one and looked in the cockpit.

The windshield was pulled back. The name Lt. Presson was stenciled on the side, just below the cockpit.

"Foreman saw these planes disappear on radar in 1945." Sin Fen joined him, standing on the wing.

"You can tell him where they went," Dane said. He reached into the cockpit and pulled out a map. It was folded open, showing southern Florida. Radio frequencies were written in pencil on it. He looked at the compass. It pointed north. Reaching farther in, he flipped a switch on the control panel. There was a crackle of static.

"The radio works," he said. "That means the batteries still have juice. Normally, that would mean either someone's recharging the battery, or this plane has been flown recently. Neither of which I think has happened."

He straightened and looked about. He still sensed no danger. The absolute silence, the size of the cavern, and all the abandoned planes and ships filled him with a sense of awe, not fear. He looked out onto the water. *Deepflight* was sitting still, DeAngelo on the top of the forward sphere, a pair of binoculars in hand, taking in all the ships.

"We've solved the mystery of all the disappearances around the Bermuda Triangle," Sin Fen said as they climbed down off the wing of the Avenger.

"We solved one mystery by uncovering another," Dane said. Two freighters, probably from the early age of steam, were side by side in front of them. They walked around.

"These look like craft that were lost in the Atlantic," Dane said. "What about the ships and planes lost in the Devil's Triangle gate? And in the other gates?"

"Perhaps there is a place like this near all the gates," Sin Fen said.

"Then the Shadow has been studying us for a long time," Dane said.

"We already knew that," Sin Fen said.

"We didn't know they were doing this much studying." Dane waved his hand, taking in the cavern.

"What makes you so sure it's the Shadow that's behind all this?" Sin Fen said. "I don't sense any danger here, do you?"

"Not immediate danger. But there was fear on these ships and planes when they were taken and brought here." He turned toward the center and scanned. "I see several submarines but no Ohio-class. You couldn't miss one of those if it was here. That means the *Wyoming* is still missing."

"Let's keep looking," Sin Fen said. "Maybe a more modern ship will have a recording or even video of what happened to it."

"I wouldn't count on it, given the electromagnetic interference around the gates," Dane said. "That looks pretty modern," he added, indicating a black-hulled catamaran whose decks were completely encased in flat, planed sections, joined at angles. It looked like a stealth fighter attached to twin hulls, about eighty feet long by thirty wide.

"The *Nightfarer*," Sin Fen said.

"You know that ship?"

"A prototype for a stealth ship the Navy was considering."

"Let me guess," Dane said. "Foreman sent it into the Bermuda Triangle gate on a recon mission."

"*Sent* is too strong a word. That is what Foreman would say," Sin Fen said. "Let's say he gave it a nudge in the direction of the gate when the Navy was doing some testing."

"How long ago was that?" Dane asked.

"Two years."

"And it went into the gate and just disappeared?"

"Yes."

"So he learned the same thing he learned with the *Scorpion* three decades earlier," Dane said. "Great logic."

"I believe Mr. Foreman was hoping the stealth capability of the ship might help it evade detection."

"Wrong guess," Dane said, "and the crew paid for it."

They were at the side of the *Nightfarer*. The skin of the ship was not metal but rather some sort of hard rubber.

"Special radar-absorbing material." Sin Fen saw him feeling the hull. "Even when at full speed, this ship only gave off the radar signature of a seagull."

"It didn't help them." As Dane climbed up the side of the ship, he halted and looked down at Sin Fen. "Anything else you've forgotten to mention to me? Any other craft Foreman sent in here we might come across?"

"Not that I know of." Sin Fen said.

"How much of what Foreman knows do you know?" Dane asked.

"Whatever he has let me know," Sin Fen answered evasively.

"Does Foreman know all that *you* know?"

Sin Fen paused. "What do you mean?"

Instead of answering, Dane opened a hatch on the side of the ship. Sin Fen followed him. They made their way to the bridge. It was a small, high-tech operations center. A red emergency light activated as he opened the hatch, giving off a muted glow. Dane sat in what must have been the captain's seat, while Sin Fen took a seat just in front of him and to the right. There were no windows to the outside world. Like the *Deepflight*, a number of video screens lined the front wall.

"If that Avenger still had power," Dane said, "let's see what we have here. The light says there's a good chance we can power some of this stuff up." He swung an arm that had a laptop computer attached to it in front of him. He hit the power button. The screen glowed.

"So why are the batteries still fresh?" Dane asked as the computer booted.

"Maybe they're held in the same statis the ships and planes seem to be in," Sin Fen said. "If you'll note, there's no rust—at least no more than they had when they came here—on any of the metal hulls."

"Does that mean we're not growing any older, being in here?" Dane asked as he slid his finger across the touchpad.

Sin Fen looked startled. "I hadn't thought of that."

Dane shifted his attention from the computer screen to his female partner. "I think you're lying."

"Why would I lie?"

"That's something I'm going to have to figure out." Dane typed into the keyboard. "I've got the captain's log." He scrolled down. "Just like *Deeplab*, it goes off-line before we get any useful information about what happened to the ship."

Dane leaned back in the captain's chair and looked about the control room. He turned the chair to the right and dialed in a frequency on the FM radio transmitter.

"What are you doing?" Sin Fen asked.

"Worked once before," Dane said. He keyed the mike. "Big Red, this is Dane. Big Red, this is Dane. Over."

"Last time you did that, you almost got blasted to bits," Sin Fen said.

"I'm not set up for Morse," Dane said, "and we're not next to a gate." He waited, then resent the message. There was nothing but static coming out of the speakers. Dane tried several more times, but after five minutes, he realized that his former teammate, Flaherty, who had gone over to the other side with the Ones Before, wasn't listening.

Dane turned off the radio. "Let's keep looking."

They left the bridge of the *Nightfarer*, the light turning off behind them automatically. Dane surveyed the beach they had yet to traverse.

He pointed. "How about something we don't recognize?"

Sin Fen looked. A long, slim ship, about a hundred meters long by five wide, was a quarter mile away from them. It had a hull made of black metal, much like the floor beneath them, but was open to the sky on top. A single, very thin mast of the same black metal extended up twenty meters. On the rear was a raised platform on which rested a black box, about two meters cubed.

"Ever see anything like that in the history books?" Dane asked.

"No."

"Then let's check it out."

They crossed the black beach and arrived at the strange ship. Dane grabbed the gunwale and pulled himself up and into the boat. The floor was level, with rows of seats extending the length of the ship to the raised platform in the rear, which had steps leading up to it. Everything was made of the same black material. Dane ran his hand along the side. It was similar to the material the shore was crafted from.

He helped Sin Fen clamber on board, then they walked to the rear. Behind the black cube was a semicircular panel, with levers and buttons amid what looked like computer displays.

"Pretty modern for an old-looking ship style," Dane noted.

"No propellers though," Sin Fen said.

"So what is this for, then?" Dane indicated the panel. Under each lever and button there was writing, a form Dane had never seen.

Sin Fen ran her fingers across the lettering. "Runes."

"Viking?" Dane asked.

Sin Fen shook her head. "Similar, but not the same. More of a root language, because I see some similarities to Sanskrit. Similar to what was on the wall of the watchtower you found near Angkor Kol Ker."

"Can you read it?"

"Some."

Dane waited. A large, four-masted schooner was to the right of the ship he was on. The name on the bow was

Atalanta. Dane recognized the name from the book he had
read on the Bermuda Triangle. The *Atalanta* had been a
training ship for English midshipmen. It, like the rest of
these ships and planes, had disappeared with no survivors,
no bodies recovered, no sign of wreckage.

Farther around the cavern he saw a B-29 bomber in vin-
tage condition parked a half mile away. Next to it was a
cigarette boat, the type used by drug smugglers throughout
the Caribbean.

"This boat has a propulsion system," Sin Fen finally
said.

"Yeah, a sail," Dane pointed.

"No, a propulsion system other than the sail," she said.
She nodded toward the black box in front of them. "It's in
there. I don't know how it works, but the controls for it are
here." She indicated several levers and a small wheel.

"And this—" her right hand was over a flat black piece
of what appeared to be glass. "This is some sort of—well,
as best I can make out, some sort of active display that
helped the pilot of the ship."

"I don't get it," Dane said. "Is this another kind of secret
government ship we've never heard of?"

"No," Sin Fen said. "This is old, very old. This may be
the oldest ship in here."

"How can that be?"

"Because this is an Atlantean ship," Sin Fen said.

Twenty-two

999 A.D.

"Sail!" The voice came from the lookout perched on the platform attached to the mast.

Ragnarok looked up. The man was pointing forward. Ragnarok climbed up until he was next to the man. It was a fine, clear day, with a stiff wind pushing them to the north. They were well west of the Faroes by Bjarni's calculations. Their last sight of land had been three days ago, the Hebrides off the coast of Scotland. It would be another day before they saw the white coastline of Iceland.

Ragnarok shielded his eyes and squinted. A small ship was on the horizon, tacking across their projected path, heading east. Hrolf climbed up and joined him.

"What do we have?" the old warrior asked. His eyes were bad, and Ragnarok knew he probably couldn't even see the ship.

"A small boat," Ragnarok answered. "I'm surprised to see it this far at sea." He noted the sail. "Three black lines on the sail."

"Straight up and down?" Hrolf asked.

"Yes."

Hrolf spat. "Lika-Loddin."

Ragnarok had heard of the man but never met him. *Lika* was the Norse word for "corpse," and Loddin had received that name for his bizarre way of making a living.

"Close on his ship," Ragnarok ordered Bjarni.

As the distance between the two Viking ships closed, Ragnarok looked for Tam Nok. She was huddled under her cloak, just behind the first oar seat, studying the metal map. She had other documents from her bamboo tube spread out around her. Ragnarok climbed down from the mast and walked forward.

"Have you learned anything more?"

Tam Nok looked up. "I am beginning to understand this old writing."

Ragnarok pointed at Loddin's ship. "There is a man on that boat who might be able to give us more information."

Tam Nok gathered the documents and put them back in the tube. She stood next to Ragnarok. "He sails alone?"

"Yes. His ship is small, and one man can handle the sail. If he is becalmed, he sits and waits. He is a strange man but a very good sailor. He knows these seas better than anyone, particularly the icy waters to the north where we are heading."

Loddin's ship was less than two hundred meters away now. It was less than ten meters long by four in width. A man was in the rear, arms wrapped around the tiller. He was a tall man, not quite to Ragnarok's height, but close. He wore leather pants and a long-sleeved leather shirt that was stained black. On the sides of the ship, above the waterline, were several long bundles wrapped in heavy canvas, tied with thick rope.

"What is that?" Tam Nok asked.

"Bodies. He is called Lika-Loddin, Corpse-Loddin, because he travels the seas searching for the bodies of those who were trapped in the ice the previous winter. He finds them, then boils the flesh off the corpses. He is now on his way back to Norway and then Denmark, where he will sell the bodies back to their families so they can receive a proper, if belated, burial. If he is here, he has already been to all the settlements along the coast of Iceland."

Ragnarok raised his right hand and bellowed a greeting to Loddin, as Hrolf supervised the lowering of the sail. Loddin didn't yell anything in reply, but he did leave the tiller and lower his sail.

The two ships glided up to each other, and Ragnarok's crew quickly tied them together.

"Ragnarok Bloodhand." Loddin's voice was low and hoarse, his face weathered and tanned.

"Lika-Loddin." Ragnarok extended his hand over the gunwale of his ship to the other.

Loddin looked at the hand for several seconds, then grasped the forearm in the traditional greeting, his own forearm in Ragnarok's grip.

"Are there any supplies you need?" Ragnarok asked.

Loddin released the grip. "What do you want from me?"

"I am offering you the hospitality of the high seas," Ragnarok said.

Loddin's face twisted in what might have been a grin. "No one offers Lika-Loddin hospitality without wanting something in return. Are you looking for someone?" He waved his hand at the canvas bags tied to the side of his ship. "I have had a good spring harvesting the ice."

"We are traveling far to the north," Ragnarok said. "Beyond the north tip of Iceland."

"Beyond Ginnungagap?"

"You have seen Ginnungagap?" Ragnarok asked.

"I have seen many strange things—although she is new." Loddin pointed at Tam Nok, who had pulled her hood down. "Who are you?"

"She is a disir," Ragnarok said. "Her name is Tam Nok."

"A disir?" Loddin gave her a crooked smile. "Do you want to bless the bodies I carry, priestess? Insure they move

on to a better life? Or have they already moved on? I have
often wondered about that, and now that I am face-to-face
with a priestess of the gods, I must know. I sell these bodies
back to their families so that they can receive a proper
burial, but isn't it already too late?"

Tam Nok was just staring at the man in the other boat.
"I think you know more about that than I do," she finally
said.

Loddin laughed. "I think I do."

"You have seen the Shadow," Tam Nok said, catching
Ragnarok and Loddin by surprise.

"The Shadow?" Loddin stepped up closer to Ragnarok's
boat. "The darkness on the ocean?"

Tam Nok nodded.

"I have seen it. Beyond Ginnungagap. I find many bodies nearby. On the ice. Frozen. Their ship gone. Very
strange, but good for business."

"How can you sail there, when they can't?" Ragnarok
asked.

"He can sense when it is dangerous," Tam Nok said.
"The others—they get off their ships because they are being
drawn into the Shadow. And they fear it more than they
fear being abandoned on the ice."

"That is the way it seems to be," Loddin acknowledged.

"Vikings afraid?" Ragnarok could sense the unease from
his men. Running into Lika-Loddin wasn't the best thing
for morale, even on a normal journey, and this one had
been anything but normal since they met Tam Nok in the
fjord.

"You have never seen the Shadow," Loddin simply said.
"If my ship was being drawn in . . ." He shrugged. "It depends. It might be interesting to see what is in the darkness.
Some of the things I have seen around it are strange
enough."

"Like?" Tam Nok prompted.

"You're going there," Loddin said. "Perhaps you will

see for yourself." He turned to Ragnarok. "I need water and salt."

Ragnarok ordered Hrolf to get the supplies. Tam Nok started to say something, but Ragnarok hushed her. "Show him the map."

That perked Loddin's interest. After the supplies were passed over, Loddin climbed into Ragnarok's boat and knelt down next to the map Tam Nok laid out on the deck.

Loddin tapped the metal portion of the map. "Where did you get this?"

"She brought the paper map with her," Ragnarok said. "We uncovered the metal part at the place of the large stones in England."

"Interesting." Loddin seemed to be a different man now. "I have seen something like it."

"Where?" Tam Nok asked.

"A monk from Eire Land. Have you ever seen the boats they go to sea in? It's amazing that they can even float. A wood frame with sealskin stretched over it. Fine for a calm day on the lake, but to dare the ocean in such—they are crazier than I.

"I was in the southwest part of Eire Land last year. Going back by a different route, since I had three bodies of monks from a monastery. I delivered the bodies. The monks did not pay enough for them to make the trip worthwhile. But I did meet an interesting man, the leader of the monastery. He knew I had traveled these oceans many times, and he brought me to his chamber. He had a map like that."

"Where did he get it?" Tam Nok asked.

"There is a large stone slab, set on top of several other large stones at an angle—" Loddin used his hands to indicate what he was speaking of. "The locals call it the Druid's Altar, although the monk told me it would not be beneficial to me to use that name around the monastery. He was an interesting man. Went by the name of Brendan."

"He found the map he had under the monument?" Tam Nok pressed.

"Somewhere among the stones." Loddin shrugged. "He wasn't specific about that. But he asked me the same thing you are asking. About the way north of Iceland. And beyond." He reached down and tapped the metal. "He was very interested in getting across the sea to this large land. I told him I had never been that way.

"Then he asked about going to the north. Near the Shadow."

"What did he know of the Shadow?" Tam Nok asked.

"Not much," Loddin said. "He had a map like yours. He wanted to know about there." The corpse-carrier touched the map at the site of the runes indicating the tunnel.

"Did he say why?"

"He is a priest of the Christian faith," Loddin said. "Maybe he was looking for the hell they preach about. Or the heaven. Who knows?"

"Who are these Christians?" Ragnarok asked. He knew that the so-called Viking king in Denmark had advisers of that faith urging him to convert. From his recent experience in England, it was obvious that those who worshiped in this new faith had little tolerance for the older beliefs.

"They believe there is only one god and one demon," Loddin said.

"Then how do they explain the Valkyrie demonesses, who I have seen with my own eyes?" Ragnarok demanded. "How can there only be one god? Is this one god the god for war and love at the same time?"

"According to Brendan, his god is a god only of love," Loddin said.

"Who protects warriors in battle then?" Ragnarok asked.

"The Christians pray to their one god for everything."

Ragnarok snorted. "That makes no sense."

Tam Nok spoke up. "Why is this monk interested in the Shadow then?"

"Because he believes it is something else," Loddin said.

"What?" the Khmer priestess demanded.

"He doesn't know. That is why he wants to learn more."

"Why?" Tam Nok asked. "If he does not believe in the demons and the gods?"

Loddin ran a hand through his dirty hair. "I asked him that. He said it was important we learn what this Shadow really is. If we think it is the work of gods, then we might not fight it. We might think it beyond our powers. But if we learn it is something else, then we will fight."

"Vikings fight the gods," Ragnarok said.

"Yes, we do," Loddin acknowledged, "but most others don't." He shrugged. "Really, I think this Brendan is just very curious."

"He is traveling there?" Tam Nok asked.

"Yes."

"When?" Tam Nok asked.

"I passed him two weeks ago. He was heading north." Loddin pointed at the map. "Going to the same place you want to go."

"How many people did he have with him?" Ragnarok asked.

"A crew of four. His boat is smaller than mine."

"Is there a tunnel there?" Tam Nok asked.

"There is something," Loddin answered. "If you pass through the fire and ice, you will see a fog bank that does not move. You will feel the evil inside."

"But you've gone inside," Tam Nok said.

"You are a strange woman," Loddin said. "My supplies are loaded." He stuck his hand out. Ragnarok took it but didn't let go of the other man's forearm.

"What is in the fog?"

"Monsters. The monsters old women tell of late at night to scare children." His arm was still in Ragnarok's grip, but he looked to Tam Nok. "I do not know if there is a tunnel in there. I barely got out with my life. I wish you the same luck."

Twenty-three

THE PRESENT

Captain McCallum stared at the bodies, noting the gunshot wounds that had killed all three. "Get them out of here," he ordered.

Seawater dripped out of computer hardware cases, and there was still an inch on the floor of the computer systems room.

"I don't assume we could get any of this on-line?" McCallum asked Commander Barrington.

"No, sir. It will all have to be replaced. I think the assumption was that if this chamber ever filled with water, the sub was sunk, anyway."

"Damn near was," McCallum said. *Seawolf* was still on station, in the narrowing band of sea between the Bermuda Triangle gate and the Milwaukee Depth. Normally, submariners liked having deep water below them, but the Puerto Rican Trench was a little too deep for McCallum's peace of mind after their near sinking at the hands of Bateman.

He watched as two sailors wrapped Captain Bateman's body in a sheet and strapped it to a stretcher. "I wonder if he was trying to warn us," McCallum said.

"Warn us?" Barrington repeated.

"Remember when he first came on board? He told us to be ready to fight without our sophisticated instruments." McCallum waved his hand around, taking in the now-worthless hunks of top-of-the line computer gear. "We've lost pretty much every piece of gear in the ship when the computers went down. But there's one thing we haven't lost," the captain of the *Seawolf* continued. "We still have the best damn crew in the Navy. It's time we break out the stopwatches and hand-held calculators. I want us to be ready to fight if anything comes out of that gate. Got that, XO?"

"Yes, sir."

While the Navy's most sophisticated weapons system was being forced to go back to the tools that submariners in World War II had used to fight, one of the U.S. Air Force's most advanced airplanes was almost directly overhead, flying a tight racetrack.

The Boeing 767 Airborne Warning and Control System was a more advanced version of the venerable E-3 AWACS that had flown hundreds of thousands of surveillance missions for NATO during the Cold War. The most distinctive feature of the plane was the thirty-foot-wide radome bolted onto the top of the fuselage. Inside was the Northrop Grumman AN/APY-2 radar, which rotated six times every minute. Able to read targets over 200 miles in any direction, the AWACS was able to paint a picture of the entire Bermuda Triangle gate.

Inside the AWACS, the crew watched their screens, alert for anything coming out of the gate, while at the same time coordinating the military forces that were converging on the perimeter.

Scores of fighters and bombers flew air cover around the gate. The aircraft carrier *George Washington* was on station and had the unique distinction of being the first naval vessel to field an army antimissile unit on its large deck. Several Patriot missile batteries along with their radar system were chained down on the large expanse of deck, their warning system tied in to the AWACS.

It was ingenious and also a sign of desperation. The Patriot was one of the biggest failures of the Gulf War while being labeled one of the greatest successes. While American commanders were crowing about thirty-three launches equaling thirty-three SCUD kills, the Israelis sent a high ranking diplomat to Washington to claim that at best, the Patriot had a 20 percent success rate. The reality, the Israelis claimed, was that in modifying their SCUD missiles to extend their range, the Iraqis had simply welded in new section of missile to hold the extra fuel. The result was that the vast majority of SCUDs broke up in flight due to poor structural integrity. Many of these breakups were errone-ously claimed by optimistic American commanders as suc-cessful Patriot intercepts.

Not only was the Patriot suspect, it had originally been designed as an antiaircraft system, not an antimissile sys-tem. Even with extensive modifications over the years, the manufacturer only claimed it was an antimissile system working against tactical systems, such as the SCUD.

The Trident was no SCUD, and the crews of the Patriot batteries and the crew of the AWACS knew that. The Pa-triot had a maximum speed of slightly over Mach 3, or about 2,200 miles an hour. The Trident at maximum speed was moving at over 16,000 miles an hour—a classic tor-toise and hare situation.

The hope was that if the *Wyoming* launched a second missile, that two fortuitous things could happen. One was that the launch would be close to the *Washington*. Second was that the launch would be caught early enough for the Patriots to be fired and catch the Trident while it was still accelerating upward.

It was a plan that fell back on the age-old military theory

of throwing everything possible at the enemy. Not only were the Patriot batteries on board the *Washington*, but the guns and ship-to-air missiles of every warship around the gate were oriented inward. Every plane was ready to turn over the gate and engage targets. There was no one among all the military personnel deployed in this operation old enough to have been there, but it was very much the same approach the American Navy had used in the latter days of World War II against Japanese kamikaze attacks.

On the other side of the world, Professor Nagoya was caught between loyalties. Foreman wanted the Can oriented full-time toward the Bermuda Triangle gate. Japanese government officials—those in the know at least—were well aware of the Trident launch that had come out of the Atlantic, and they were also aware of the fact that other submarines, two of which carried nuclear missiles or torpedoes, had been lost in their own Devil's Sea gate.

They were more concerned with the Pacific Rim than the Mid-Atlantic Ridge. There were many places where a well-placed nuclear explosion would trigger massive earthquakes with subsequent volcanoes and deadly tsunamis, a threat that Japan was particularly vulnerable to. These officials wanted the Can, which after all was built on Japanese soil with a large dose of Japanese money, to exclusively monitor the Devil's Sea.

Nagoya understood both parties' concerns, but he also thought both concerns were misdirected. The importance of the Can was not to be an early warning system against a threat they could do little about but rather to study the gates, to try to unlock the secret of what they were and possibly what was on the other side.

Still, Nagoya had spent enough years working for the government that he knew it was best to placate the powers that be. He had the Can switching between the two as quickly as possible, forwarding data to his own military's headquarters and the Pentagon War Room.

Meanwhile, he focused on studying the mound of data they had accumulated in the last twenty-four hours.

At least until the Can picked up a spike of muonic activity on the north edge of the Bermuda Triangle gate.

"We've got activity!" Colonel Croner, the supervising officer in the AWACS announced over the intercom. "Coordinates, four-seven-three-six-eight-one. Lock in all weapons' systems, prepare Patriots for launch on confirmation of Trident."

Croner only hoped one missile came out. What everyone was keeping their fingers crossed against was a multiple launch, with the *Wyoming* clearing all twenty-three remaining missiles in less than two minutes.

"We have a target coming out of the gate," a radar operator announced. "Vertical at grid. Signature—a Trident!"

"All systems engage," Croner ordered. "Keep your eyes open for a second launch."

The Trident ICBM was already shedding its first-stage rocket as four Patriot missiles roared off the deck of the USS *Washington* twenty miles to the north on an interception vector.

At the highest altitude they were capable of maintaining, Navy and Air Force jets were vectored in over the Bermuda Triangle gate toward the path of the upcoming missile.

It was already too late for any of the surface ships to engage with either their guns or their antiaircraft missiles, and those crews could only watch helplessly the battle on the screens in their operations centers.

One F-18 Hornet fighter pilot spotted the bright flame from the second stage of the Trident. He turned toward it, firing his air-to-air missiles on straight trajectory, as his radar couldn't lock on the fast-moving target, and then pressing his thumb down on the trigger of the 20mm Gatling gun, hoping that by some miracle something would hit the Trident.

It roared past him a half-mile away so fast he never saw the missile itself, just the flame and smoke from the burning rocket fuel. Then his warning lights went on as one of the Patriots locked onto his aircraft as the most convenient target.

He barely had time to scream a curse as the Patriot hit and the jet blossomed into a fireball.

The other three Patriots were already being outpaced by the Trident and, after expending their fuel, began to come back down to earth.

Unimpeded, the Trident's second stage fell off and the third ignited.

In the War Room, Foreman watched the explosion of anger and curses from the military men that surrounded him. Once more they'd thrown the best defense they had against the Shadow and failed. This time, though, the frustration was doubled by the fact that the Shadow's weapon was one of their own.

They'd known there was almost no chance of stopping an ICBM once it was launched, and that knowledge had just been confirmed.

Foreman was linked to the AWACS, and he had one major concern. "Colonel Croner, do we have multiple launches?"

"We show no second launch yet, sir. We're past due for a second missile if they're firing in salvo."

Foreman relaxed slightly. This wasn't the end.

He looked up at the master screen at the front of the War Room. The Trident was now being tracked by Space Command as it moved north-northeast across the Atlantic.

"Projected impact?" he asked of no one in particular.

"Spread pattern, along the Mid-Atlantic Ridge," an Air

Force officer answered. "This time, much farther north, at
max range, four thousand nautical miles." The officer used
a laser pointer. "In the vicinity of Iceland. We won't know
exact touchdown points until the warheads actually land."

Iceland is a geological anomaly, almost unique on the face
of the Earth. It was one of the few remaining landmasses
still above sea level, produced by the Mid-Atlantic Ridge.
It is a very young island, in terms of geographic age, still
in the throes of change.

The landscape was so twisted by the forces of nature
that ravaged it that it had been chosen by NASA to send
the crew of *Apollo* in 1968 to train on, as it was the one
place on earth they felt most closely resembled the lunar
surface.

In 1973, the island of Heimaey off the southern coast
had to be evacuated after a large eruption by the volcano
Helgafell. Earthquakes are common, and the island is dotted
with hot springs. The center of the island is a high plateau
surrounded by mountains leading down to the coast, where
most human habitation was clustered between the rocky
slopes and the sea. A tenth of the island's mass was covered
by glaciers, the largest being Vatrnajokull, which alone en-
compassed over 3,200 square miles.

The island had no armed forces, the only military present
being that of the Americans serving at the air base at Ke-
flavik. Thus the only ones who had a warning of the in-
coming Trident missile were those from the country that
had built the missile.

There was nothing for anyone to do except pray that
these warheads also struck the ocean, as the first missiles
had.

That hope disappeared in the flash of the first MK5 nuclear warhead detonating on the southern shoreline where
the Pjorsa River reached the ocean. Ten seconds later, thirty
miles to the north-northeast, the second warhead impacted.

In slightly over a minute, all eight warheads, each one many times the power of the one that was dropped on Hiroshima, impacted and detonated in a line bisecting Iceland, directly along the center of the Mid-Atlantic Ridge.

Only five thousand people died in those initial explosions, due to the sparse population in the interior and on the two spots of the coast directly affected.

In Reykjavik, the earth shook and the sky to the east glowed red. Electromagnetic pulse washed over the city, shutting down almost everything run by electricity. One hundred thousand of the quarter million people who inhabited Iceland lived in the capital city, and most rushed out to the streets, fearing an earthquake, then noting the glow in the sky.

The nukes had hit every thirty miles, close enough that the force of their blasts reached each other. In essence, the bombs split Iceland in half, letting lose the pent-up energy of the unquiet earth below.

Magma flowed into the cracked earth, pushing upward toward the surface. One of the bombs had been aimed directly into the crater of a long-dormant volcano. The nuclear explosion took off the top five hundred meters of the mountain. Within minutes, a secondary explosion blew the rest of the top of the mountain off as gases powered their way up.

In *Deeplab*, Ariana Michelet was getting live satellite imagery forwarded to her from Foreman through the *Glomar Explorer*. The center of Iceland glowed red in the thermal imaging, and already one volcano was spewing a large cloud of deadly gas into the sky, the trade winds pushing it safely to the north and east for the moment.

"What do you make of it?" Foreman asked.

Ariana knew the CIA man had access to hundreds of experts through the War Room, but she sensed he wanted the truth, up front and as quickly as possible. She knew what she was seeing. Ever since the previous Trident firing, she had been thinking about possible scenarios, and this fit.

"Iceland is going to be gone," she said.

"Gone?"

"It's already split," Ariana said. "Right over the rift between the tectonic plates that it sits on. There's going to be two dozen volcanoes active within twenty-four hours. While they fill the air with deadly ash, the landmass will begin to collapse in on itself, filling the void where the magma isn't coming up. Some of the island may remain above water, but I wouldn't want to be anywhere on it."

"How long?"

"Thirty-six hours."

"There's a quarter million people living there," Foreman said.

"There won't be in a day and a half."

Twenty-four

999 A.D.

Ragnarok had never been this far north. The main Viking community on Iceland was on the southwest coast where the warmer water made the weather at least livable. The coast that they had traveled around for the past day and a half was rocky, with numerous glaciers flowing into the ocean.

It was a bleak land, devoid of human contact. Early the previous evening, they had spotted a smudge of smoke. At first, Ragnarok had hoped it was a settlement, but as they got closer to land, they could see the smoke was coming out of the top of a mountain. As darkness fell, the smoke was lit from within by a red glow, something the crew took as an ominous sign. They pressed on, nonetheless, skirting the rocky shore.

"There!" Hrolf was standing next to him, near the tiller. He was pointing shoreward.

Ragnarok eyes followed the old man's finger. Steam was rushing up into the air from the craggy rocks onshore in a loud hissing they could hear a mile offshore. It went on for a minute, then subsided.

"This is not a good land," Hrolf said. "Odin is angry."

As far as Ragnarok was concerned, the god could express his anger all he wanted on Iceland. It was the ocean ahead that worried the Viking leader.

"We must leave the shore behind now," Bjarni said. The helmsman inclined his head slightly to the right. "The place we seek is that way."

"How far?" Ragnarok asked.

"Not far, if the witch's map is correct. Just over the horizon."

"Are you certain we are in the right place?" Tam Nok had come down the boat to join them.

"I've gotten us this far," Bjarni said. "I think I can get us a little farther without getting lost." He pushed the tiller over, and the dragon turned from shore to the open sea. The geyser erupted once more, spewing steam into the air as if warning them not to go farther.

Ragnarok crossed his arms over his chest, feeling the ship take the waves at a different angle. The shore slowly faded away, the sound of the geyser lasting even after it was out of sight.

But soon there was only the wind in the sail and the sea against the boat. The sun was going down in the west, with another two hours of daylight left, by Ragnarok's experienced eye.

"Will we make it before nightfall?" Ragnarok asked.

"We've made it," was Bjarni's simple answer. "Look."

A dark wall was ahead, growing closer. It was even thicker than the fog they'd been in off the coast of Norway where they had met Tam Nok. Ragnarok did not like the look of it at all. The wind was not moving the cloud. It sat like a festering scab on the surface of the ocean, hiding some terrible wound in the water itself.

"The Shadow is in there," Tam Nok said. "I have seen this before."

"What do you want to do, Captain?" Bjarni asked. "It will be dark soon."

Ragnarok was startled by the formality of the question, and he recognized the double meaning behind his helmsman's statement.

"We're here," Ragnarok said. "We will go in and see what is there."

As the dark wall got closer, Ragnarok issued orders preparing his men for battle. Shields were hung, bows notched, and swords drawn. Ragnarok moved to the front of the ship, Hrolf and Tam Nok at his side.

He felt the hair on the back of his neck rise as the dragon head entered the fog. As he crossed from light to dark, the air itself changed, becoming colder, thicker, with a sick taste to it. Ragnarok looked over the side. Even the water appeared different: darker, more malevolent. It did not smell of salt but danker, like an animal that had been killed and left too long in the open.

The ship slipped into the darkness, visibility dropping to less than twenty feet. Even sounds were different, the water against the hull now duller. The wind was gone completely, and Ragnarok let the ship coast for a minute before ordering half the crew to the oars, the other half to stand fast with their weapons.

"To the left," Tam Nok pointed.

Ragnarok could see nothing, but he had the order relayed to Bjarni at the rear of the ship instead of yelling it out. He had a feeling there was something out there listening, waiting, and he had no desire to provoke it.

"Look," Bjarni nodded to the right. A small boat made of sealskins stretched over a frame listed in the water. The skins were torn in places, and it was barely afloat.

"The Irish monk must have found what he was looking for," Ragnarok said.

"I hope we don't find whatever found him," Bjarni muttered.

"How far?" Ragnarok asked.

"I don't know." Tam Nok was staring into the fog as if she could see through it. "But not far."

Suddenly she turned to the right. "Faster," she hissed.

Ragnarok chopped his hand and the rowers picked up the pace.

"They're coming." Tam Nok had Lailoken's staff in her hand, the spear tip pointing to starboard.

"The Valkyries?" Ragnarok squeezed the wood handle of his ax.

"Yes. And more."

There was a startled yell from amidships. Ragnarok turned. A long red tentacle had reached out of the sea and was wrapped around one of the rowers. The man was lifted out of the boat before anyone could react, and he disappeared under the black waters.

"Kraken!" Hrolf hissed.

The other rowers nearby abandoned their oars and grabbed their weapons, staring fearfully over the side of the ship. Seconds later, a half-dozen tentacles came out of the water, waving about blindly, while a trio of screams came echoing over the water, one right after the other.

The arms came forward, onto the boat, searching for victims. Warriors hacked at them with sword and ax. Ragnarok was about to join the battle when he spotted a Valkyrie floating through the fog, coming toward the bow.

"I will deal with this." Tam Nok had the staff ready. "You get rid of the beast."

Ragnarok reluctantly ran to the middle of the ship, Hrolf at his side. With one swing of Bone Cutter, he severed an arm that had wrapped around one of his men. Two more dashed forward at him. Ragnarok recoiled as he realized there were six-inch-wide mouths on the tip of each arm, snapping open and shut, revealing rows of razor-sharp teeth. One of the arms hit a man next to him and bored into his body, eliciting an agonized scream.

Mouth still in the man's innards, the arm lifted him into

the air and tossed him overboard. Ragnarok ducked under the other arm and looked into the water. The body of the kraken was just under the surface, forty feet long, ten wide, two large saucer eyes over two feet wide staring up at him. A large mouth below the eyes had the body of the man just thrown overboard half ingested.

A tentacle slapped Ragnarok in his back, then slid along to bring the mouth to bear. He spun, ax leading, and cut a long, deep slice along the length of the tentacle. There were screams all around now and the curses and cries of men in mortal combat. Out of the corner of his eye, Ragnarok saw another man plucked from the ship. More arms were coming out of the water, as if the kraken had an inexhaustible supply.

Ragnarok struck once more with his ax, severing the arm he had just cut. Then he made his way to the mast. He grabbed a length of rope and began tying it around his waist.

In the bow, Tam Nok thrust at Skogul, as the Valkyrie descended on the ship. The Valkyrie knocked aside the haft of the spear with an armored hand and with the other reached for the amulet on Tam Nok's chest. Tam Nok rolled forward under the grasping arm, spinning the haft of the staff in her hand. The spear head impacted sideways on Skogul's back and sliced through the armor.

The Valkyrie's scream caused everyone on the boat, even those in the midst of battle with the kraken, to pause for a fraction of a second before going back to fighting. Tam Nok got to her feet. Instead of blood, black steam was hissing out of the cut in Skogul's armor.

Tam Nok swung again, as she had been taught by the master, and the tip of the blade cut along Skogul's chest, slicing cloak, armor, and the chain that held the amulet in one smooth stroke.

Tam Nok stepped back, staff raised, as Hlokk and Goll came down out of the fog, but the two Valkyries grabbed Skogul in their claws and lifted her out of the boat, disappearing into the fog. Tam Nok knelt and picked up the heavy amulet, cradling it in her hand as she read the runes that covered the outer circle.

A tentacle wrapped around Ragnarok's leg, knocking him down to the wood floor of the longship. He struggled to complete the knot on the rope around his waist as the tentacle tightened its grip. He looked up to see the tip of the tentacle raise up just like a snake preparing to strike. A flash of steel and the severed tip dropped to the floor. Hrolf the Slayer struck again with his sword at the tentacle where it led overboard. He cut through with two mighty blows, freeing Ragnarok.

The Viking leader got to his feet, rope tight around his waist. He caught Hrolf's eye. "Keep the ship moving!"

Ragnarok dodged another tentacle, then jumped up onto the side of the ship, ax raised high. He leaped into the air with a battle cry, swinging the ax down as he descended.

Ragnarok hit the water, and the edge of his ax hit the kraken dead between the eyes with a massive blow, parting skin and bone, burying completely inside the monster's head.

The kraken dove, taking Ragnarok with it as he refused to release his ax. He felt the pressure in his ears as they went down, then suddenly he was jerked to a halt as the rope reached its length. The handle was almost ripped out of his hands, but he gripped it with all his strength. Tentacles battered him on the head and shoulders as the kraken tried to find its tormentor in the dark water now filling with a thick green ooze from the creature's wound.

Ragnarok felt pain as teeth gnawed into his left side. He swung his feet under him, against the body of the kraken, then pulled with all his might. The ax popped free. Ragnarok took one more blind swing, caught up in the battle rage, ignoring the wound on his side, the lack of oxygen. The edge of Bone Cutter caught the kraken in the left eye, popping it like an overripe egg.

With all the power of its many tentacles, the kraken dove once more, disappearing into the depths.

Ragnarok kicked, still holding his ax, the weight almost enough by itself to defeat his efforts to surface. He broke into the dank fog, the rope pulling him along through the water. He could hear the splash of oars and Hrolf yelling. Ragnarok shook his head like a large, shaggy dog, getting hair and water out of his eyes. He was being towed thirty feet behind the longship, and the reason no one was paying attention to his predicament was the large black circle that had appeared in front of the longship. The dragon's head disappeared into the black. There were cries of fear, but Hrolf kept yelling the commands to row, and harsh training held the crew in place, doing their duty.

Foot by foot, the longship disappeared into the black hole, dragging Ragnarok with it, until there was only the rope coming out of the black hole. Ragnarok said a brief prayer as he got closer to the darkness, then he was in.

He felt a moment of disorientation, as if his body was being stretched, then a snap, and he was in bright sunlight, warm water. Ragnarok pulled himself on the rope toward the longship, climbing on board. None of the crew noticed their captain's arrival as they were all staring at their surroundings.

The ship was in a moat, over a half-mile width of water, that completely surrounded a massive temple. All around was a wall containing the moat. Beyond was the ocean, but his attention was drawn back to the temple. A stepped pyramid, it rose over 500 feet up, larger than anything manmade Ragnarok had ever seen in his travels. A broad set of stairs went up the sides facing them to the very top. The stones used were black and smooth, reflecting the sunlight in dark ripples.

There was no one about: no priests, no worshipers, not a human being other than the cluster of souls on board the Viking longship. Just the mighty temple, glistening in the sunlight.

Twenty-five

THE PRESENT

"I can read parts of this," Sin Fen said. "Enough to make some sense."

Dane could only see a pattern of runes that Sin Fen had been slowly scrolling through for the past thirty minutes. *Deepflight* was offshore, DeAngelo slowly driving the submersible around the edge of the beach, reveling in the diversity of the craft stranded in this cavern.

"Does it tell where the Shield is?" Dane asked.

"I'm getting to that," Sin Fen said. "It speaks of Atlantis and the war with the Shadow." She looked up from the screen. "But it also tells who the Atlanteans were. How they were able to develop such a magnificent civilization while the rest of mankind was still roaming the earth in small packs of hunter-gatherers."

Sin Fen reached up and tapped the side of her head. "Their brains were different. The Atlanteans developed differently than other humans. Perhaps there was something in their environment that required it. We've just discovered there's a thing called the doomsday gene. An ability to adapt rapidly—within a few generations—when extreme conditions call for it. Or perhaps Atlanteans were the original humans and the rest of the species developed differently.

"Scientists have often wondered why the mind has two distinctively separate hemispheres. Some say it's for redundancy, but that seems a bit of a stretch for me. If the head is injured enough to cause brain injury, then it's doubtful a person could survive back in the days before brain surgery.

"The bicameral mind existed for a different reason," Sin Fen continued. "Remember, the speech center is present in both hemispheres but active in the vast majority of people only on the left side."

"And ours is active on both," Dane said. "Which is why we can touch each other's minds—when the other person allows it," he added.

Sin Fen ignored the comment. "There is a connection between Wernicke's areas on each side of the brain. It's called the anterior commissure. Since Wernicke's area in the left hemisphere is the part of the speech process that brings meaning to our language, what is it on the right? And what happens when the two work in unison?"

She tapped Dane on the chest. "That is our problem, you and I. We have both Wernicke's areas functioning but little connection between them through the anterior commissure. But the Atlanteans—" She looked down at the display she had been reading. "This tells me the Atlanteans were more evolved than us.

"That's how Atlantis developed—keeping the telepathic mind and developing a written and verbal language. They were genetic freaks—a different branch from the development of the rest of the species. Think of it, Dane, what they could accomplish then. They had the best of both worlds. They could use their telepathy to get concepts across without the limitation of the spoken or written word, but then they could use the latter to work on the details of what they were doing, the specifics. And the two worked hand in hand, so to speak.

"Because of that difference, they developed in a fundamentally different way than we did. It's not a question of what they did, it's more a question of how they thought differently at the most basic level.

"There is a precedent for this," she said. "All the ancient civilizations, which we now know were founded by survivors of Atlantis merging with the locals, were different in some fundamental ways than our current civilization. It is thought that it was only when mankind became basically monotheistic that we changed.

"When man believed in numerous gods, the messages received from Wernicke's area in the right hemisphere— what I have told you is the voice of the gods—they were accepted. Man made decisions based more on those messages than clearly linear thinking.

"Ancient Egypt spanned over three thousand years at the height of its power, yet in those three thousand years how much did they develop in terms of technology?" Sin Fen didn't wait for an answer. "When archaeologists uncover a relic of old Egypt, they often have trouble dating it unless there are some sort of writings attached. But what if you lived three thousand years in the future from now? And you were excavating New York City? Hasn't New York constantly evolved, changed? New York a hundred years ago is very different from New York now and will be very different in a hundred years. Yet none of these ancient civilizations show this development."

Sin Fen was focused on the screen now, reading the runes. "They developed differently than our civilization. They started by harnessing forces at a level we're only starting to approach. That's the biggest difference. They worked on the inner self first, before the outside world. We don't have a clue how the brain truly works. They knew exactly and were able to exploit that knowledge to build a unique civilization

"Look at this boat," Sin Fen said. "It's an example of their technology. When we first saw it, we thought it was primitive, but it's more advanced than anything we've developed. Its power system is right there—" She pointed at the black cube. "No propeller, no jet—it works using the Earth's magnetic field to move the ship. They worked within the harmony of nature, not against it like we do."

"The Shield?" Dane prompted.

"We have to understand what happened," Sin Fen said. "The Shield is worthless without the knowledge behind it."

"Then how about the quick version," Dane suggested.

"The Atlanteans developed on their island continent in the middle of the Atlantic," Sin Fen said. "They explored the world around them but did not settle elsewhere. It appears they realized the differences between themselves and the humans on the other continents and desired to keep their bloodlines distinct.

"Of course, they weren't totally successful. They . . ." Sin Fen's voice trailed off as she scrolled through.

"The Shield," Dane reminded her. "The Shadow?"

"The Shadow came out of the west in the place we now call the Bermuda Triangle gate. The Atlanteans didn't know what it was. They sent ships—like this one—to investigate. And nothing came back. The Shadow began growing. And they learned of other gates on the face of the planet. They realized the threat—probably faster than we did."

"When was all this?" Dane asked.

"Around ten thousand B.C." Sin Fen watched the screen. "On the other hand, since they had never really experienced war, they weren't exactly prepared. They had to use what they had for defense, and they knew little more about the gates than we do.

"But they did develop something—the Shield." Sin Fen frowned. "It is hard for me to tell exactly what is meant.

How it worked. It used the power of the firestone. From what I read before, the firestone sounds a lot like nuclear power."

"Foreman hasn't nuked a gate yet, has he?"

"No. That would be a rather extreme step," Sin Fen said, "and based on what we do know, atomic weapons probably won't work. The firestone was like nuclear power, but not the same. It didn't need to be shielded. It was able to be harnessed quite easily. The Atlanteans used firestone to power some sort of weapon—the Shield—that they used."

"But they didn't win," Dane noted. "This ship is here. Atlantis is gone."

"They didn't win, but they didn't lose," Sin Fen argued.

"Where's the Shield?"

"According to this, the Atlanteans used the Shield from an outpost near the gate. Within visual sight of it. They stopped the expansion of the gate, but they acted too late. The seeds of their own destruction were already sown."

"How?"

"It seems the Shadow appropriated their use of the firestone just as it's taken our nuclear weapons. Sowed firestone around the base of the continent and used it to destroy Atlantis just as the Atlanteans were using their Shield against the gate. A pyrrhic victory."

"The Shield," Dane repeated.

"It was here," Sin Fen said. "This ship carried it to their defensive base."

"And?"

Sin Fen reached down and slid a lever forward. The side of the black cube slid down, revealing a six-inch-deep open space, backed with gray material. There was nothing in it.

"That's where the final parts of the shield were carried," Sin Fen said. She was looking back down at the display. "This ship carried the hardware, but not the power source."

"So we don't have anything," Dane said.

"Not yet."

"The message on the sail of the *Scorpion* was in Norse runes," Dane said. "It directed us here. There must have been a reason." He turned to the center of the vast chamber where *Deepflight* was cruising.

"DeAngelo!" Dane yelled. With the lack of any other sound, his voice carried clearly across the water.

"Yes?"

"Have you seen a Viking longship in here?"

"Over there." DeAngelo was pointing to their right.

"Let's go." Dane was already climbing over the side of the black ship.

"Run that again," Nagoya ordered Ahana.

In slow motion, the various readings that had been picked up by the Can and other surveilling instruments were displayed on an array of screens, all running at the same time.

"It's all about time," Nagoya whispered.

"Excuse me, sir?"

Nagoya felt the stir of excitement that came from sudden insight. "We never consider time a manipulative variable—always a constant. But it's been there, staring us in the face all the time. We wondered why the *Scorpion* crew didn't experience any time lag. Why Dane's teammate Flaherty hadn't aged. We assume that it was because they were in some sort of stasis, but what if there was no stasis? What if no time had passed for them?"

Ahana kept silent, recognizing the mood her professor was in, letting him think out loud, crystallizing a new theory.

"We really don't know what time is," Nagoya said. "We don't even know when the universe started. The Cosmic Background Explorer Satellite has given evidence that the universe was formed by an explosion fifteen billion years ago—the big bang. If that is indecd so, then t equals zero—then we have a start point to start our universal clock.

"That simplifies things, perhaps too much. There are still those who postulate theories other than the big bang. Those who say the beginning was the result of a quantum fluctuation. That's where we are now, with several different hypotheses about the very nature of our universe and time. We have Hawking's and his timeless quantum cosmology; Adrei Linde who talks of chaotic inflation; Roger Penrose and time-asymmetric cosmology. Then, like a large wall at the end, is Dyson's thermodynamic death of the universe theory.

"Take Linde and his bubbles of space-time foam." Nagoya didn't even seem to be aware Ahana was listening. "He says we are in one of those bubbles. That each bubble has its own physical laws, randomly selected from an infinite set. So perhaps these gates are where another bubble touches ours? And the quantum physics in that bubble is ruled by very different laws. So different that even time is different?

"Hawking, on the other hand, says there is only one set of physical laws. That time is an arrow, the direction of which coincides with thermodynamic law. But it is a theory that is incomplete, that does not explain data we have in our hands, data we have picked up in this very chamber.

"Then throw into this mixture the development of intelligent life. Not just us, but now we know there is other intelligent life, on the other side of the gates. Tipler postulated intelligence developing to de Chardin's omega point. Where all life that existed will be contained in intelligent information processing. That would require different pockets of intelligent life to interact, even if in a destructive way, because ultimately it would not be destructive at the omega point."

Nagoya shook his head. "But that is far beyond us right now and a case for the philosopher. What concerns us is the makeup of the gates. And if the gates have their own physical laws, different from our own, that means we must abandon our own rationality. We must abandon the linear thinking we hold so dear." Nagoya raised his voice so everyone in the operations center could hear him. "Iceland has been destroyed. A quarter million people dead. Please remember that our own country lies next to a fault even more fragile than the fault that just consumed Iceland. We will be next.

"I want you to reexamine all the data we have. I want you to make time a variable, not a constant. Throw all the rules out. Turns things backward, sideways, upside down. Any way you can imagine, no matter how strange. We need answers about what the gates are, and then we have to figure out how to shut those gates. Let's get to work!"

"Range one thousand meters and closing," Captain Stanton's voice was tight. "It's dark. Not fog—the edge approaching is too straight, moving too methodically."

Ariana could see the same thing underwater: a straight line on the sonar coming steadily toward *Deeplab*, the edge of the Bermuda Triangle gate.

"Five hundred meters."

"Recommend we shut down all systems now," Ariana said.

"We're going to drift." Stanton repeated his protest to that plan of action. "If *Deepflight* can't use its equipment, it won't be able to find us."

"There'll be nothing to find if we don't shut down," Ariana said.

"I back her plan." Foreman's voice was filled with static, the gate already affecting satellite communications with the *Glomar*.

"Three hundred meters," Stanton said. "I'm going to keep this line open to *Deeplab*. It's a passive system."

"All right," Ariana said, "but let's shut down. Now!"

"Roger that," Stanton said. "Shutting down."

Ariana began turning off the habitat's systems for the

second time, this time with a little more care. She left the emergency battery-powered lights on and the link to the surface.

Soon she was sitting in a dim red glow. "One hundred meters," Stanton's voice broke the silence.

"Fifty. I don't like this at all," Stanton said. "I can sense something. This is not good."

Ariana could feel the same thing: an overwhelming sense of dread, like a heavy wool blanket draped over her body and mind. She had the feeling of being trapped, exacerbated by being inside the small sphere of *Deeplab*'s communication center.

"Can't see more than twenty meters," Stanton said. "I can't see the top of the derrick. We've got no communications with the outside world anymore. You're going to get some oscillation as we've shut down the dampener. The sea's mild though—almost dead. So that's—" There was a crackle of static, then in the background, Ariana could hear a scream of sheer terror. Then several more as the first one was abruptly cut off.

"It's coming from the pool," Stanton said. He barked out orders to other men on the bridge, then came back on the intercom. "We can't see a damn thing."

A new scream, one that Ariana knew couldn't have come from a human mouth, echoed out of the intercom.

"Sweet Jesus," Stanton was leaving the mike open. "What the hell is that? It's in the air, port side. I can't see it, but that's where the noise is coming from."

The scream came again.

"It's closer." There were more human yells of fear and pain in the background. "I'm getting reports from the pool. Something's coming out of the water. Giant squid. Something like that. But—" There was a statacco noise, then the inhuman scream.

"Oh, God. I can see it. Hovering in the air. White face.

Red eyes. Long hair. Robes. It's some kind of demon. Just watching."

There was a burst of an automatic weapon firing.

"I can see one now. It's climbing out of the pool, just forward of the derrick. God, it's awful. Red body. A dozen arms at least. It's big. Sixty feet long. There's another. Another. There're dozens of them. They're coming over the side of the ship.

"And that thing. It's just watching. It's—" The sound of glass shattering blanked out whatever Stanton was saying. "They're here! They're here!"

The intercom went dead.

Ariana sat perfectly still, as if by moving she could bring down whatever had taken over the *Glomar* three miles above. Only her eyes moved, shifting around to the walls that surrounded her, that suddenly didn't feel very thick or secure at all.

Twenty-six

Eleven men were gone. Some of them warriors whom Ragnarok had known since they were boys playing at war with wooden swords. He felt Hrolf's eyes upon him as he made his mental roll call. The old warrior was slumped against the tiller, as Askell the Healer sewed up a jagged cut on the side of his face where one of the tentacle mouths had slashed home. Ragnarok coiled the rope that had connected him to the ship and put it back in place at the base of the mast.

Tam Nok was in the bow, mesmerized by the temple that dominated the view in that direction. Ragnarok found the temple impressive but not enough to distract him from the state of his crew and ship. Half the remaining men were wounded, and Ragnarok could sense the shock brought on by the dual assault from the Valkyries and kraken, followed by the transit through the black circle to their present strange location.

"The sun is wrong." Bjarni had his hands on the tiller, even though they weren't moving. He had not moved through it all, standing fast at his duty place.

Ragnarok squinted at the sky. He realized what the helmsman meant: the sun was higher in the sky than he had ever seen, even at the summer solstice.

"We are far south," Bjarni said. "I have never been this far south."

"Where are we?" Ragnarok asked Tam Nok.

The Khmer priestess was startled, broken out of her semitrance. "This is—this is here. The place we have been searching for."

"Where is the weapon?" Ragnarok demanded.

Tam Nok nodded toward shore. "We must land."

"The weapon," Ragnarok repeated.

Tam Nok held up the staff with one hand, the amulet around her neck with the other. "These—and the map— they are the pieces of the weapon." She pointed with the staff toward the top of the pyramid. "They go there." The staff moved, pointing now to the north. "See? The Shadow comes closer."

Ragnarok looked in the direction she pointed. A black smudge was on the horizon. He was certain it had not been there before.

"Rowers! To the shore!"

Twenty-seven

THE PRESENT

The wood was finely crafted, the dragon's head in the prow so expertly carved, Dane felt as if the eyes were watching him as he climbed into the longship. Sin Fen came up behind him. Shields still hung in place at some of the oar stations.

Dane knelt and touched the seat nearest him. There was a deep red stain in the worn wood. "Blood." He could feel something about the ship. He had to search his memory, then he realized it was the strange sensation in the pit of his stomach he'd had thirty years ago, riding in a Huey helicopter, across the Vietnamese border into Laos or Cambodia on one of the classified missions he'd conducted for MACV-SOG. Surrounded by the members of his team, trusting in their abilities, trusting in his own abilities, while at the same time having the fear of pending battle always lurking.

Dane closed his eyes, allowing the feeling to sweep through him. For a moment he was on the ship as it approached a beach, Viking warriors straining at the oars as bowmen fired volleys at defenders on the shore. There were screams and yelling, a tall warrior stood next to Dane, a massive ax in his hand, his eyes alive with rage. He was shouting something at Dane, the words in a strange language Dane had never heard before, but he felt there was some sense to it, something that—

"What are you seeing?" Sin Fen's words jolted Dane out of his vision.

"Nothing." He looked down the boat at the mast. Something glittered in the artificial light. Dane walked down to it, stepping over the rowers' seats. A dagger had been thrust through the center of a metal plate, about a foot square. Dangling over the dagger was an amulet in the form of a black circle on a silver chain. There were marks etched onto the metal plate and marks on the amulet's surface. Dane had to use both hands to pull the dagger out.

He handed the amulet and piece of metal to Sin Fen. "You're the expert. What does it say?"

"It's Norse. It says to take the amulet and the ship and go to the center of the water."

"That's it?"

"It's the same hand that wrote on the side of the *Scorpion*'s sail," Sin Fen said.

Dane thought of the warrior he had seen in his vision. "Let's go."

"How do we get the ship off the beach?" Sin Fen asked.

Dane grabbed a length of rope that was coiled underneath the mast. "DeAngelo can pull us out into the water."

Foreman looked through the stack of satellite imagery forwarded to him by Conners at the NSA. Iceland no longer existed. There were some peaks still above water, particularly the active volcanoes, but the majority of the island had disappeared into the cold North Atlantic.

Less than ten thousand people had escaped by ship or plane. It was a disaster unprecedented in the modern world

since the end of World War II. And it was only the beginning.

The next series of photos showed the Bermuda Triangle
gate. It had overtaken the *Glomar* and was less than fifty
miles from Puerto Rico, which was still trying to recover
from the tsunami.

Looking up from the imagery, Foreman could see the
status board at the front of the War Room. The *Seawolf*
and other forces were moving back as the gate grew larger.
The mood inside the room was somber, as everyone was
waiting for the other twenty-two missiles carried by the
Wyoming to come out of the gate. Given what had happened to Iceland, there was no doubt that it would be the
end of civilization if those missiles hit their targets. The
best guess was that the entire Mid-Atlantic Ridge would
collapse, giving birth to tsunamis that would devastate the
East Coast of the United States and most of Europe.

Foreman had been in contact with both Nagoya in Japan
and Kolkov in Russia, and both of them were convinced
some of the other missing nuclear weapons would come
out of the other gates, raising havoc in other parts of the
world. Computer simulations indicated that Japan would go
the way of Iceland, along with the Hawaiian Islands, the
Philippines, and Micronesia. Splits along the Red Sea and
Persian Gulf would lead to the end of the Middle East. The
gate near Chernobyl would complete the devastation started
years ago at that location.

His—and the world's—only hope lay in Dane and Sin
Fen. But at this point, even if they discovered the Shield,
would they be able to use it?

Deepflight pulled the Viking ship off the black beach with
surprisingly little trouble, the solid, one-piece keel helping
greatly in the process. From his perch atop the forward
sphere, Dane relayed steering commands to DeAngelo, who

was lying on his stomach below, hands on the steering levers.

Sin Fen was next to Dane, seated on the edge of the hatch, her almond eyes following the longship as it was towed behind them. Dane turned to her as they slowly made their way toward the center of the large body of water.

"Tell me what you've been keeping secret from Foreman all these years."

Sin Fen shifted her gaze from the Viking ship to Dane. "Secret?"

"You know too much while claiming you know nothing," Dane said. "If we're the same, why do you know so much more than I do?"

"I have been with Foreman for many years and—"

Dane cut her off. "I think Foreman is working for you more than you are working for him." They were close to the center of the water.

Sin Fen laughed. "I should have known better than to try to fool you. I can block you from my thoughts, but there is more to a person than simply what they think.

"I've been wrong," said Sin Fen. "When I told you in Cambodia about the brain and the hemispheres. Yes, that is the basis for the telepathic ability, but reading that information on the Atlantean ship, I realized I was putting the cart before the horse as you Americans say."

Dane could feel the edges of Sin Fen's emotions, and he picked up excitement and fear, twisted together around a core of enlightenment. "What have you learned?"

"The fact that I can learn," Sin Fen laughed, a manic edge to it. "Don't you understand, Dane? I pontificated in Cambodia to you about what made us different from the animals, and now I really know.

"It's our consciousness. Our ability to understand the *how*, more than the *what*. The what is genetic instinct. It's what all animals have. But we can figure out *how* things work. We're getting back to it, to the beginning, to the way the Atlanteans were. That is why the world has changed so much in the last several hundred years. More *how!*"

Dane had little idea what she was talking about. They were a quarter mile from the center of the chamber.

"Remember I said that ancient Egypt didn't change, didn't develop over the course of thousands of years? Why? Because the Atlanteans founded it, but humans lived in it. They *couldn't* develop, couldn't change. They could live there, but they didn't understand the how behind much of what they had been given. It was only very slowly, over time, that humans began to try to understand the world around them, to change it."

Sin Fen grabbed Dane's arm. "Tell Foreman about this. He has to know. This is important. There's a scientist—I can't remember his name right now—who has been doing research on this. On the development of consciousness in humans. If we can use what we know now about the Atlanteans, we can fight this Shadow."

Deepflight shook. Dane saw that the water was beginning to move, a whirlpool forming in the center of the chamber. "Why don't you tell him?"

"You'll find out very soon," Sin Fen said. "You'll see more than I could possibly explain if things work out the way I hope they do."

A black circle had appeared in the center of the whirlpool. The Viking ship pulled past them and was being drawn in.

DeAngelo's head popped out of the hatch. He saw the black circle, the whirlpool, and the rope tying them to the Viking ship. "Should we cut free or am I disturbing you two?"

"That's where we want to go," Sin Fen said.

"Leave the rope," Dane ordered.

The longship was sucked into the black circle, disappearing in a flash. The rope extended out, pulling *Deepflight* in. Dane gripped the railing around the top of the sphere.

The black circle drew closer, then they were in.

Dane felt disoriented, then blinked. The light was now coming from the sun, the air clean and fresh, with the tang of saltiness from the open ocean filling his nostrils. *Deep-flight* was bobbing in a gentle swell, open ocean all around, except to the north and west, where a dark cloud lay on the water. The longship was still tied to them, twenty meters away.

"What now?" Dane asked Sin Fen.

"We're in the right place," she said. She poked her head into the hatch. "DeAngelo, can you give me a sonar reading of the bottom?"

"Give me a sec," the pilot replied.

Sin Fen dropped into the sphere, followed by Dane, which made for a tight fit inside the small enclosure.

"There." DeAngelo pointed at one of the screens. "That's strange," he added.

"A hill?" Dane could see what the pilot was referring to: from a relatively level bottom, something was jutting up, the trace clearly outlined on the screen.

"With very straight sides," DeAngelo said. "That's not a natural formation."

"How deep?" Sin Fen asked.

"The bottom is real shallow, under a thousand feet." DeAngelo checked another screen. "Hell, it's under seven hundred feet right here, and the top of that thing is only a hundred and eighty feet below us."

"That's it," Sin Fen said. "We need to go there. It's a pyramid built by the Atlanteans—their outpost for the Shield. Can·you rig me a breathing tube?" she asked DeAngelo.

"For what?"

"I need to be on the outside," Sin Fen said.

"Why?" Dane asked. "We can get the Shield using the submersible's arms."

"It doesn't work like that," Sin Fen said. "The entire

pyramid is part of the Shield. Consciousness, Dane—" She placed her hands on the side of his head. "The mind can be a powerful weapon when focused correctly."

Dane felt a surge of emotion from Sin Fen's mind, an avalanche that he couldn't sort out. "I don't understand."

"We don't have time to discuss this," she said. "You'll figure it out later." She let go of him and turned to De-Angelo. "Can you do it?"

DeAngelo nodded.

"Rig it, then take me down to the top of the pyramid."

Twenty-eight

999 A.D.

Ragnarok saw the darkness clearly now. It was over the ocean, approaching the wall that surrounded the moat. Tam Nok stood next to him, at the very top of the pyramid, also watching the Shadow.

"It is time," she said.

"I see no weapon," Ragnarok said. There was only a large slab with the contour of a person etched into its surface.

Tam Nok ignored him, pulling her pack off. She pulled out a long piece of cloth, which she draped around her neck over her shoulders. It was dark red, with faint black writing on it.

She knelt down and bowed her head. Ragnarok felt foolish towering over her, ax in hand. He stepped back, glanced at the horizon. The darkness was growing closer.

The survivors of his ship were loosely gathered around the top of the pyramid, awed by their surroundings, still stunned by recent events. Hrolf walked up to Ragnarok and spoke to him in a low, hushed voice.

"It is the same as we saw off the coast of Iceland." He nodded toward the fog.

Ragnarok nodded.

"We will never go home," Hrolf continued.

"We will defeat the darkness," Ragnarok said.

Hrolf's old face cracked into a weary smile. "My friend, I have sailed with you on many a journey. This was the strangest and the last."

"My mother—" Ragnarok began, but the old warrior placed a hand on his shoulder.

"She is where she is. She let you go. Let her go."

A muscle on the side of Ragnarok's face quivered, but he realized the truth in the old man's words.

Tam Nok suddenly stood. "Let us finish it." She handed the staff to Ragnarok. "Here is what you must do."

Twenty-nine

THE PRESENT

Dane stared at the video screen, which showed Sin Fen
holding on to the top railing, a tube from one of the oxygen
tanks in her mouth. Her eyes were open as they descended.
He shook his head, trying to clear it. He felt drunk, at the
golden moment when the alcohol gave clarity before descending into the physical depression that was the by-
product of drinking. He felt like he was watching Sin Fen
float outside the submersible in a dream, slowly descending
into the water together. It didn't take long to reach the top
of the pyramid.

Diffuse sunlight reflected off the smooth black stone,
untouched by the sea or its creatures all these years. Sin
Fen turned and looked directly at the camera. She cut
through the fog in Dane's mind.

"Land on top, next to that slab," Dane ordered, picking
up the thought she directed at him.

Carefully manipulating the controls, DeAngelo brought
them to a landing on the top, ten feet from a large slab. A
pole with something on the top stuck up next to the slab.
Dane focused the camera, recognizing the Naga carving on

the tip, a representation of the real thing that he had fought in Angkor Kol Ker. He felt the power of this place, even though the Shield wasn't active.

Sin Fen was walking across the top of the pyramid to the slab, the air hose trailing behind her. She climbed onto the slab and sat on the edge, looking back at *Deepflight*.

Dane picked up the message she sent to him.

"We need to be closer," he ordered DeAngelo. "Close enough so that the remote arm can reach that pole."

"Why can't she reach it?" DeAngelo asked, even as he gave the engines a tweak and slid the submersible closer.

Dane saw it then as Sin Fen finally allowed him to. Why she wouldn't be able to turn the pole. What she planned on doing. This was the place the vision he had stolen from her mind had shown him. Where the woman in the vision had lain.

He moved over and slid his hand into the glove box that controlled the arm. He extended it until the mechanical fingers were stretched around the shaft of the pole. Then he slowly contracted his hand until the metal hand gripped the pole firmly. Even through the metal and plastic of the remote, he felt a jolt of power.

Only then did he look at the screen that showed Sin Fen.

999 A.D.

Tam Nok was calm, her voice steady. "You must leave the staff here," she told Ragnarok.

"Why?" The Viking had slid the spear end into a slit next to the slab. His large right hand rested on the snake heads carved on the other end, as Tam Nok had instructed him.

"This weapon only stops the darkness," she said. "It does not destroy it. There will be others who will need to use it in the future when the Shadow returns. We must make their journey less difficult than ours was. It is our duty to help those who come after us."

Ragnarok nodded. "I will leave it."

"I am ready," Tam Nok said. She lay down on the slab, in the form that fit her body almost perfectly.

THE PRESENT

Sin Fen lay down on the slab, half her body disappearing into the depression carved in the surface.

"What is she doing?" DeAngelo asked.

Dane ignored the pilot. He reached out to her, the mental bond stronger than he had ever felt. The air hose slipped out of her mouth and floated away.

I am ready, Sin Fen told Dane.

You should have told me the truth, he sent back to her.

I have tried, but even I don't understand all. That is up to you. There is no more time for that now. This is my task, that is your task. Do it.

Dane twisted his hand, the pole turning.

999 A.D.

Ragnarok twisted the pole as she had told him. It turned smoothly halfway around, then stopped. He felt the pyramid begin to vibrate under his feet and through the pole. He let go and stepped back. The darkness was very close now, less than a half-mile away.

A blue glow appeared around Tam Nok's body, coming up out of the slab. It was darkest around her head. Her eyes were still wide open, her mouth moving in prayer.

"It is time to leave." Hrolf was tugging at Ragnarok's arm.

"I must see." Ragnarok shook off his hand.

"She said to leave immediately," Hrolf reminded him. "We have a duty to fulfill also."

Something was happening to Tam Nok's face, her head. The skin was moving as if something were alive underneath.

"We must go *now!*" Hrolf insisted. "Look!" he pointed toward the darkness where three small dots had suddenly appeared, racing toward them.

Ragnarok looked longingly at the spear, the battle rage coursing through his veins. He wanted to fight the Valkyries, but he knew he had to do as Tam Nok had ordered.

Reluctantly, Ragnarok allowed the old warrior to lead him to the temple stairs, where the rest of his crew was already running down, taking three stairs at a time in their haste to get back to the longship and away from the temple and the approaching demonesses.

Halfway down, Ragnarok looked over his shoulder. The entire top of the pyramid was now enclosed in the blue glow. The Valkyries were less than fifty feet from the top, when like lightning, a streak of blue bolted out of the glow toward them. The lead Valkyrie disappeared in a flash. The other two kept coming, but two more bolts of blue destroyed them. A larger bolt then fired, straight toward the darkness. Where it hit there was a tremendous explosion in the air.

"Hurry!" Hrolf urged, his short, fat legs making quick work of the stairs. Ragnarok sprinted after him.

THE PRESENT

The blue glow had completely surrounded Sin Fen's body. Dane let go of the remote glove, releasing the pole. "Lift us up a little," he ordered DeAngelo.

As the submersible floated up ten feet, Dane suddenly felt pain, like an ice-cold spear slammed into the top of his head. He cried out. Even as he did, he realized he was experiencing only a fraction of what Sin Fen was, an echo of her mind still reaching out to him.

"My God!" DeAngelo exclaimed.

Dane opened his eyes, seeing what had caused the pilot's outburst. The skin on Sin Fen's head was peeling away, as if melting off the skull. Her eyes changed from something solid into two dark blue orbs of light. Her hair was all gone, and in a few seconds the skin beneath followed suit. White bone, suffused with blue lines, the two blue orbs for eyes, were all that were left.

Then the bone itself changed, becoming clear, until it was pure crystal, totally suffused with the blue light. Suddenly, a streak of blue shot out from the crystal skull toward the darkness of the approaching gate.

The submersible rocked from the shock wave.

"Get us out of here," Dane whispered.

DeAngelo didn't need to be told a second time. He throttled up and sped away.

Dane adjusted the camera, keeping it on Sin Fen—what had been Sin Fen—as more bolts of blue came out of the crystal skull, firing toward the gate.

As the image faded, Dane reached out and placed his hand on the screen, the last connection he had with her.

Thirty

999 A.D.

Ragnarok staggered, almost falling. He gathered himself and jumped, clearing the side of his ship and tumbling into the bottom. He got to his feet. "Row!" He pointed at the black circle they had come out of. "There!"

More bolts of blue were shooting off the top of the pyramid toward the darkness, hitting with massive explosions, the sound hitting Ragnarok and his crew, causing ear-splitting pain.

Ragnarok grabbed the nearest oar and began pulling as Bjarni pushed the tiller over and pointed them at the black circle. They touched the edge and were drawn in.

The sudden silence was blessed relief, but they were not off the shore of Iceland. Ragnarok knew that immediately from the warmth of the air. He stood, staring about in amazement. They were in a giant cave, a bright light like the sun shining over their heads, rock walls on all sides, a black beach circling the water they floated in.

There were ships, more ships than Ragnarok had ever seen, pulled up on the beach.

"What is this?" Hrolf slowly stopped pulling on his oar.

Tam Nok had given Ragnarok the vision of his future. He knew what his duty was.

"This is where I must stay, old friend." Ragnarok grabbed the grizzled warrior's forearm.

"We will stay—" Hrolf began, but Ragnarok cut him off with a shake of his head.

"No. You must go back. Go through the dark circle once more. It will take you back to Iceland. Then go back to Norway. To our village. Make peace with the king."

Hrolf nodded. "And your mother?"

"Tell her all is well with me and give her my wishes for her happiness. Now go. Take whatever ship you want. I will stay with mine." Ragnarok watched as Hrolf and the survivors claimed another Viking ship, one even larger than his, and pushed it off the strange shore. They passed him, oars hitting the water.

Ragnarok climbed up onto the gunwale of the longship. "Good sailing," he yelled, ax in hand. Hrolf gave the order to row to the few surviving crew members. Slowly, the other longship headed for the black circle; then, as the dragon head touched the black, it was sucked in and disappeared, leaving Ragnarok alone in the graveyard of the ships aboard his own ship.

THE PRESENT

"Back through the black circle," Dane ordered.

DeAngelo already had them headed in that direction. The inside of *Deepflight* was vibrating from the shockwaves racing through the water. They reached the black circle, and suddenly all was still.

Dane stared at the screens showing the graveyard. He

sensed a presence, not of someone alive and here, but of someone who had been here. A warrior who had painstakingly etched an important message into the metal of the *Scorpion*.

"Again through the black," Dane ordered. "It will take us outside."

Thirty-one

THE PRESENT

"Sir, look!" Ahana had lost her usual reserved manner and was literally jumping up and down in front of her workstation.

Nagoya immediately saw what was causing her excitement. The level of muonic activity around the Bermuda Triangle gate had pegged out the monitor.

"It just started," Ahana said. She turned to another monitor. "There. Just east of the edge of the gate—that's the source."

"Of what?" Nagoya asked, not expecting an answer, as he knew they didn't have that yet. "The muons are a by-product of something." He slammed his hand down on the desktop. "We have to find the key!"

"Sir—" Ahana was back at the first monitor. "Look at the gate!"

"The gates are shrinking!"

"Are you sure?" Foreman held the earpiece tighter against his head to hear over the commotion in the War Room.

"The gates are shrinking," Conners repeated. "I've got the latest imagery. Definitely growing smaller. There was some activity near the western edge of the Bermuda Triangle gate—what, I'm not sure—but the damn thing is retreating. Fast."

"They did it." Foreman didn't quite believe it. "They did it," he repeated, as if by saying the words out loud, it made it true.

"The *Glomar* has been uncovered," Conners said.

Foreman reached forward and picked up the SATPhone that linked him to the ship.

"*Glomar,* this is Foreman." He waited a few seconds, then repeated the call. There was a brief burst of static, then Ariana's voice, very faint, came back over the link.

"I think they're all dead on the ship."

"What's your status?" Foreman asked.

"I'm fine," Ariana answered, "but the *Glomar* is drifting, so I'm drifting with it."

"I'll get someone to it ASAP. And *Deepflight?*"

"It's just reappeared on my sonar, coming up out of the Milwaukee Depth. I'm going to try to ping it with sonar to bring it to me. What the hell is going on?"

"They did it," Foreman said. "The gates are shrinking! They must have found the Shield and used it."

"Oh shit," Conners's voice in his earpiece immediately doused his growing optimism.

"What?"

"We've got a bogey on SOSUS. Just uncovered by the Bermuda Triangle gate shrinking. It's the *Wyoming!*"

"Location?" Foreman demanded.

"South side of the gate. It's moving west."

Foreman looked up at the status board. The closest warship to that location was the *Seawolf.* He spun his seat toward his naval liaison. "Get me the *Seawolf* ASAP!"

•   •   •

"We've picked it up on the hydrophone," Captain McCallum told Foreman. "It's the only sensor we've got that's working right now. Wait one—" His XO, Commander Barrington, was signaling to him. "What is it?"

"*Wyoming* is going to launch depth. She's flooding her missile tubes."

"Jesus," McCallum whispered. "Mr. Foreman, *Wyoming* is preparing to launch. We are heading to engage." He put the SATPhone down.

"Flank speed straight at the target," McCallum ordered. "Range to target?"

Barrington shrugged. "Best guess is about two miles."

With all their computers down, every active device the billion-dollar submarine had to find and acquire targets was also down. Not only that, but they couldn't program the necessary information into their torpedoes or cruise missiles. Not only was *Seawolf* sailing blind, she was unable to target her weapons. McCallum had already considered what to do if this situation arose, and he immediately picked up a different microphone.

"AWACS Eagle, this is *Seawolf*."

"This is Eagle."

"Do you have the *Wyoming*'s location?"

"I'm linking you to the NSA," Eagle said. "Hold one."

A new voice, a woman's, came over the radio. "*Seawolf*, this is Conners, NSA. According to SOSUS, the *Wyoming* is one point six miles north of your location. Moving west at fifteen knots. I'm giving the coordinates to surface vessels to your west to target with cruise missiles."

Barrington held a hand up, getting McCallum's attention. "No more flooding noise. All launch tubes must be flooded."

"You don't have time for that!" McCallum yelled. "Her tubes are flooded. She'll launch in less than a minute."

He dropped the mike. McCallum stepped next to the firing platform. He pulled a key from around his neck. He flipped open a red cover and inserted it. "XO?"

Barrington's face was white. He pulled a key from around his neck and inserted it in another hole.

"On three," McCallum said. "One, two, three." The two men turned their keys. Lights on the panel went from yellow to flashing red.

"We have weapons armed status," Barrington announced.

McCallum let go of the key. "Weapons officer, fire tubes one through four! Spread pattern, range four thousand meters. Now!"

"Yes, sir. Firing one. Firing two. Firing three. Firing four."

The *Seawolf* shuddered slightly as the four MK-48 torpedoes left the ship. A spool of wire trailed out from each, normally allowing the torpedoes to be directed to their target by the submarine's sophisticated targeting systems. Right now, they simply churned through the water on a straight course, spreading apart from each other the farther they got from the *Seawolf*.

"One thousand meters," the weapons officer announced, checking his stopwatch.

"Sir—" Barrington began to speak then stopped.

"Two thousand meters."

"We're doing what we have to," McCallum said.

"Yes, sir," Barrington acknowledged. Every eye in the control room was on the weapons officer and the ticking stopwatch in his hand.

"I can hear missile doors opening on the *Wyoming*," the hydrophone man announced. "She's going to launch."

"Three thousand meters."

"No, she isn't," McCallum said. He reached down and hit the firing command button linked to the four torpedoes.

Four nuclear warheads exploded, a thousand meters from each other, three thousand meters from the *Seawolf*. Everything, including the *Wyoming* and the *Seawolf*, within five miles was destroyed.

Epilogue

Dane stood on the platform that ringed the top of the derrick, looking out past the *Glomar* to the open sea. There was a slight breeze, and the water was calm. The sun was coming up in the east, a glowing orange ball on the horizon, foretelling good weather for the day.

He heard someone coming up the metal stairs, but he didn't turn. He had sensed Ariana's presence coming up the stairs long before he heard her arrival. A new crew had been flown in by the Navy the previous day and pulled up *Deeplab* and the docked *Deepflight*. There was no sign of the original crew of the *Glomar* except for numerous blood trails, mainly centered around the well pool. More casualties to add to a list that was approaching a half million, Dane thought. Iceland was now only a dozen or so active volcanoes poking above the surface of the North Atlantic. Puerto Rico was still trying to clean up the damage from the tsunamis. The sub pens at Groton were hot, and a large evacuation had taken place for miles all around. The *Seawolf* was gone, with no trace of the wreckage, although the

Navy was still looking for both it and the remains of the *Wyoming*.

"Foreman wants us back in Washington," Ariana said. "He says Nagoya has some interesting hypotheses about the nature of the gates he wants us to look at."

"Can he keep them closed forever?" Dane asked.

"I don't know. From what Foreman said—and he was being very guarded—Nagoya has an idea how the gates work."

Dane didn't turn. "Where are all the people?"

"What people?"

"From the ships and planes we saw in the graveyard? From *Deeplab*?"

"On the other side," Ariana said.

"And what does that mean?" Dane asked.

"We'll have to go to Washington to see what Nagoya and Foreman have come up with," Ariana said.

Dane shook his head. "The answer isn't in Washington. And this isn't over. All we did was repeat history. We shut the gates, but they'll open up again. Next time, maybe we need to open the gates and take the war to the other side."

Ariana placed a hand on Dane's shoulder. They stayed like that for a minute before she turned to go. "I'll meet you at the helipad with Chelsea."

Dane heard her go down the stairs. He stared out over the ocean, but what he was really seeing was the tall Viking warrior standing in the prow of his ship, a large ax in his hand. He remembered the message etched into the side of the *Scorpion*.

"You will be revenged," Dane whispered before following Ariana.

Prelude

1628 B.C.

The pale blue Mediterranean sky was cut by a thick finger of smoke drifting skyward from the tall volcano in the center of the island. It was just one of the portents of doom for those who called Thera their home. Closer to the sea, on the western horizon, a low Shadow covered the blue water, a dark wall a mile high and over ten miles wide. Yesterday a ship had been sent out to investigate the strange cloud. It sailed into the black and never returned. Scouts had been sent up the volcano to look into the caldera to judge conditions and they had been overcome with toxic gases, their bodies still visible on the lip of high mountain.

The priestess who stood on the shoreline, staring at her daughter playing in the warm surf, had told the warriors what the cloud was and what would happen with the volcano, but being men and fighters, they had sent the ship and scouts anyway. A priestess's word had lost much power over the years.

There were dozens of priestesses on Thera who maintained the pyramid in the center of the capital city of Akrotiri but Pri Lo was the Defender, the dark red trimming

on her white robe and the crystal amulet she wore around
her neck signifying that unique position. She knew her time
was coming. Her people had lived in peace here for many
generations, the previous Defenders never being called
upon to play their role. Why her time coincided with the
appearance of the Shadow she didn't know, but she didn't
feel sorry for herself. She had been raised for the moment
that would come soon. She was completely focused on the
seven-year-old girl in the water. Her daughter, Pri Kala,
would be the Defender of her generation if she grew to
adulthood.

A rumble that she could feel through the sand under her
feet caused Pri Lo's gaze to shift from the sea to the large
volcano. It had begun emitting fumes two days ago, just
before the Shadow appeared to the west.

Why her ancestors escaping Atlantis had chosen this
dangerous island for their new home had been lost over the
millennia since the destruction of their mid-Atlantic island,
but Pri Lo accepted that there must have been a valid reason. They were centrally located among the burgeoning civilizations of the Mediterranean. Greece was to the
northwest, Persia to the northeast, Crete to the south, and
Egypt farther to the southeast. They were a sea away from
where their home had been.

Still, the Shadow had found them. It took the dark force
over eight thousand years, but the tale of terror that had
been handed down through the lineage of priestesses was
now a reality.

Another rumble caused her to shift her bare feet ner-
vously in the sand. She turned back to the ocean, staring
at the headland that guarded the south edge of the sheltered
cove. The boat was late. Pri Lo should be at the pyramid,
ready to fulfill her destiny, but there was something she
needed to do first.

She didn't want to, but she looked farther out to sea.
The Shadow was closer, there was no doubt of that. It was

creeping across the water, approaching the island. The blackness was absolute, drawing in the bright sunlight and extinguishing it. If it reached the land, Pri Lo knew the tales that were more horrible than the worst nightmares would come true.

Time was short. The other priestesses would be scouring Akrotiri, searching for her to take her place. Still Pri Lo waited. For she knew the Shadow could be stopped, but the volcano was another issue, one that she could not defend against. It was how Atlantis had been destroyed and there were many who didn't want to remember when the Earth itself raged.

Her daughter, a slight wisp, with blue eyes, fair skin, and red hair cut short, had a shell in her hands and was staring at it intently, as if reading something in the swirls on the surface.

"Kala," she called out as the prow of a sailing ship finally appeared around the headland, entering the cove.

"I do not want to leave you." Shell in hand, the young girl walked out of the water to her mother.

Pri Lo had known she could not keep her thoughts from her daughter. The connection was too close.

"You must go on this ship. It is your duty just as I must do mine."

Kala understood duty. Pri Lo had taught her the absolute of that. The ship was closing on shore, a man in the prow waving for them to wade out to it. There was a loud explosion inland. Pri Lo spun about in time to see the left side of the volcano crumble inward.

"Here." Pri Lo took the Defender crystal off her neck and slipped it over Kala's head. "This is yours now."

Her daughter met her gaze and Pri Lo saw wisdom beyond her age in those young eyes. There no point in pretending, in telling Kala they would meet again. What Pri Lo thought, her daughter knew. What she felt, her daughter sensed. They hugged briefly, intensely, then Pri Lo took

Kala's hand and led her into the water. They waded out until Pri Lo had to hold her daughter's head above water. She passed her to the captain along with a small purse filled with gold coins. He was from Knossos, to the south, and she had arranged this the previous night in a tavern near the wharves of Akrotiri. She knew he was trustworthy when she had met him and picked up the aura about him.

"You should come, too," the captain said as he lifted Pri Kala into the boat. The purse disappeared somewhere inside his shirt.

"I will stay," Pri Lo said.

The captain wasted no more time, yelling orders to his crew. They strained at the oars, pulling the ship out to sea. Pri Lo stood in the water, feeling the slight swell lap at her neck. Kala was next to the railing staring back.

There was not time to watch the ship until it cleared the headland.

I love you, Pri Lo projected toward the ship. She felt the emotion from her daughter come back, a wave of sadness and love. Then she turned and headed inland. When she reached the stairs that were carved into the rock wall of the cove she sprinted up them. At the top she paused to look over her shoulder. The ship's sails were set and it was racing to the south. It would make it before the Shadow arrived.

Pri Lo stumbled as the ground spasmed beneath her, cracks forming in the rock. She could see the white towers of Akrotiri a quarter mile ahead and, above them, the top of the pyramid where the priestesses awaited her. She ran, the calluses on the bottom of her bare feet striking the closely set rocks of the path.

The gates were open, the guards staring at the volcano. Several cried out to her as she passed. Now they believed, she thought as she sprinted along the main thoroughfare of the city; over ten meters wide it led to the base of the huge pyramid, the first thing their ancestors had worked on when they arrived here from Atlantis thousands of years ago. Three hundred feet high, made of stone blocks, it had a level top about twenty feet wide.

A broad set of stairs ran up the face of the pyramid and Pri Lo took them two at a time. A dozen priestesses waited, along with two warriors, one of whom held a staff, one end of which was a spear head and the other a seven-headed snake. Other than the people there was a large slab with the contour of a person etched into its surface.

"Where have you been?" Pri Tak, the head of the order, was an old woman, her face pale with fear. "I sent warriors looking for you."

Pri Lo ignored her. She took a dark red cloth from one of the other women, draping it over her shoulders. There was writing on it, runic symbols from long ago. Pri Lo looked to the sea. The Shadow was less than a mile from shore and closing.

Pri Lo climbed onto the slab and settled into the stone, her body fitting perfectly into the depression. "I am ready," she announced.

"There are prayers and—" Pri Tak began, but Pri Lo cut her off.

"There is no time for that. And there is no time for you to leave." She laughed. "Don't you see what's coming? You could not run far enough anyway. Best to have it over with here." She turned her head to the warrior, a man named Kra Tek, a brave fighter who had been entrusted with the spear. He was also Kala's father. She gave the slightest of nods and saw relief briefly race across his face. She knew she had chosen wisely in picking him—it was obvious in Kala. "Do it."

He slid the spear head into a slit next to the slab. His scarred hand rested on the snake heads. Without hesitation, he turned it.

The pyramid began to vibrate. A blue glow suffused the slab and Pri Lo's body. The priestesses were chanting prayers. The glow centered on Pri Lo's head, the skin rippling as if the bone of the skull was alive.

The skin began peeling off, the eyes turning into two glowing blue orbs. The bone appeared, bleached white, changing, metamorphosing from the inside out. The white became clear, crystallized, suffused with the blue glow. Her mouth was wide open, but no scream issued forth even though she was still alive, the channel for the power that was rising through the structure.

A bolt of blue shot out of Pri Lo's head toward the approaching black wall. When it touched the darkness there was an explosion.

Again and again, blue lightning seared off the top of the pyramid toward the Shadow until the black wall stopped moving forward, stopping less than a hundred yards from shore. The consistency of the darkness began to change, swirls of blue mixing with the black.

After a minute, the pyramid stopped vibrating, the blue bolts ceased firing and all was still for a moment. The priestesses and warriors who had fallen to the stone and covered their heads during the assault, slowly lifted their heads. The Shadow was fading, breaking apart, rays of sunlight piercing it. They stood, watching the shadow disappear, jubilation filling their hearts. Except for Kra Tek who was staring down at Pri Lo's remains. The body was gone, leaving just a pure crystal skull lying in the slab. He reached for the skull.

Then the volcano blew.

The explosion took off the top third of the mountain, sending hundreds of thousands of tons of ash, gas, dirt and rocks into the air. Toxic gas rode the shock wave downslope, killing every living thing it washed over.

Kra Tek cradled the crystal skull in his arms, turning his broad back to the coming death. The gas killed him instantly, then the blast of heat that followed scorched the flesh from his bones, but the hands still gripped Pri Lo's skull as his body slammed into the slab.

Several miles to the south, Pri Kala had watched the Shadow dispersed by the blue bolts. She had sensed her mother's power projected out from the island, then felt it fade to nothing other than the faint essence of her father's sorrow.

Then the large volcano in the center of the island exploded. Every member of the crew paused as the sound of the blast reached them. They could see the spreading cloud of debris. Rocks, trees, and other matter splashed into the water all around.

"Row you fools!" the captain yelled as he pushed the till, putting the stern of the ship square on toward the island. The tidal wave from the blast was over fifty feet high, bearing down on them at eighty miles an hour.

"Hold on!" the captain cried out. He held onto the till with one hand and with the other grabbed Pri Kala. Tears were running down her smooth cheeks but she gripped his hand. The wave hit and the ship rode it, the stern going up almost straight, several men sliding overboard, everything that wasn't tied down smashing forward. Then the ship leveled on the top of the wave, slipped down the less steep backslope and settled in the water.

Pri Kala looked back. Less than a third of the island was still above water. The Earth had not known such violence since the destruction of Atlantis over eight thousand years previously. People as far as a thousand miles away would hear the sound the volcano had made and the ash and dirt would circle the globe and drop the world temperature a couple of degrees for years. Once more the Shadow had been stopped but the price had been high.

Pri Kala's small hand reached up and felt the Defender crystal. She knew the Shadow would come again and she knew her duty.